Queen of Stars

Book Two of The Starfolk

Also by Dave Duncan

Stand-alone novels	*Against the Light*
	West of January
	The Cursed
	A Rose-Red City
	Ill Met in the Arena
	Shadow
	Wildcatter
	Pock's World
	Shadow
	Hero!
	Strings
The Starfolk	*King of Swords*
	Queen of Stars
The Seventh Sword	*The Reluctant Swordsman*
	The Coming of Wisdom
	The Destiny of the Sword
	The Death of Nnanji
The Brothers Magnus	*Speak to the Devil*
	When the Saints
Tales of the King's Blades	*The Gilded Chain*
	Lord of Fire Lands
	Sky of Swords
	The Monster War
Chronicles of the King's Blades	*Paragon Lost*
	Impossible Odds
	The Jaguar Knights

A Man of His Word	*Magic Casement* *Faerie Land Forlorn* *Perilous Seas* *Emperor and Clown*
A Handful of Men	*The Cutting Edge* *Upland Outlaws* *The Stricken Field* *The Living God*
The Great Game	*Past Imperative* *Present Tense* *Future Indefinite*
"The Venice Books"	*The Alchemist's Apprentice* *The Alchemist's Code* *The Alchemist's Pursuit*
"The Omar Books"	*The Reaver Road* *The Hunters' Haunt*
"The Dodec Books"	*Children of Chaos* *Mother of Lies*
Writing as Sarah B. Franklin	*Daughter of Troy*
Writing as Ken Hood	*Demon Sword* *Demon Rider* *Demon Knight*

Queen of Stars

Book Two of The Starfolk

by Dave Duncan

The characters and events portrayed in this book are fictitious. Any similarity to real persons, living or dead, is coincidental and not intended by the author.

Published by 47North, Seattle

www.apub.com

ISBN-13: 9781477849170
ISBN-10: 1477849173

Cover design by becker&mayer! Book Producers
Illustrated by Chase Stone

Library of Congress Control Number: 2013944240

Printed in the United States of America

Chapter 1

Very few people had ever heard of the Star Fire Gallery before the dragon came. Why should they? Star Fire was merely an obscure art store on the ground floor of a dingy office block in a city whose inhabitants were much more interested in oil and money than art.

On a hot and dusty evening in midsummer, Star Fire hosted a preview of *Mortality*, "An exciting, dynamic exhibition of the work of Avior, brilliant emerging Canadian sculptor." The showing did not go well. Most of the guests gulped down the wine, refused the cheese, and left in haste.

On Sunday the *Herald* art critic denounced the exhibit in words rarely found in a family newspaper; "obscene," "revolting," and "perverted" were among the mildest of the adjectives. When the gallery opened at noon, TV crews were on hand to film the line of curious patrons waiting to get in, and collect their reactions when they came out.

By Monday religious leaders were pontificating and the national press had picked up the story, slanting it to poke fun at the lack of artistic sensibility in an overgrown western cow town. One prestigious paper pointed out that a similar showing by the same artist in Toronto had gone without comment, not mentioning that the paper itself had ignored the event completely.

One journalist "revealed" that Avior's real name was Mabel Bonalde; she had been born in Venezuela and now lived in Saskatchewan. Ms. Avior, reached by phone, retorted that Avior was her true name, "Mabel" had been her mother's mistake, but a showing in a backwoods redneck desert like Calgary had been entirely her own stupidity. She then hung up.

By Tuesday picketers were parading outside the gallery, and local politicians were leaping on bandwagons, demanding action in the name of public decency. The mayor, while decrying any hint of censorship, floated a trial balloon about a court injunction. Even members of the faculty of the College of Art, who normally proclaimed their collective willingness to die for the cause of freedom of artistic expression, had trouble defending *Mortality*, although most of them did. The public shuddered in disgust and showed up in droves. At times the line stretched three blocks.

On Wednesday a passing motorcyclist threw a hammer through one of the plate-glass windows. Four people sustained minor cuts and the police closed the gallery in the name of public safety. At 6:10 that afternoon the building was sprayed with gunfire and—according to the later inquest—hit with an incendiary device. The gallery itself burst into flames, which spread to neighboring buildings before fire trucks arrived. Most workers had already gone home and the rest escaped unharmed, but one body was recovered from the gallery and two more from the street outside.

Details of the attack should never have been in doubt, because two TV crews happened to be on location and caught it all. Unfortunately, what they filmed was too fantastical to be credible, although it was dramatic enough to make every news broadcast in the world. Both cameras showed an assault by masked, armed men being repulsed by a dragon, a bright green, flame-blowing dragon of enormous size. Where it came from or went to, nobody could explain.

By Thursday the Star Fire dragon was an international sensation, with the world's most respected newspapers running headlines normally seen only on supermarket tabloids.

On Friday it was learned that the three bodies recovered had been "humanoid" but not *Homo sapiens.* The authorities also announced that all three corpses had disappeared from a locked morgue before they could be properly examined. Thus was a new conspiracy theory born and the "Star Fire Aliens" joined their dragon in the pantheon of the inexplicable, right up there with the Bermuda Triangle and Roswell, New Mexico.

Fade back to Wednesday, at about six o'clock . . .

Chapter 2

"Look at this one, dear," said the socialite with the blue rinse, pointing to a piece labeled "*Screaming Head.* Mixed media, $3,750." "You really ought to buy this to use as a centerpiece at your dinner parties."

"It would certainly cut down on the food bills," agreed the fat one with the botulin face. "I think this one would look quite splendid in your hallway, right next to that gorgeous plump Renoir of yours: '*Famine 17.* Mixed media, $3,900.' What sort of media is she mixing, do you know? They all look so gruesomely lifelike."

"No, dear. They all look so dead-like. That's the trouble."

Laughing, they advanced to *Child's Arm with Doll,* which they inspected with righteous revulsion.

The two overfed, overdressed women were the only visitors in the gallery, the door to which was still locked and police-taped after the incident with the motorcyclist and hammer. Long-time clients of Enid's, they had demanded a special viewing to see what all the fuss was about, but were obviously not in a buying mood. Since they had to know that Enid was in the office and could overhear what they were saying, they obviously did not care who knew their opinion of Avior's work.

Avior herself was clearly visible in a corner, repairing minor vandalism to *Fire Walker*, from which someone had stolen three toes. Simple hand-modeled wax could replace the exposed bone. Lacking the supplies and tools she had back home in her studio in Saskatchewan, she was having trouble giving the remaining flesh the correct charred look.

"You think that's *her*?" Blue Rinse demanded in an offensive stage whisper.

"Odd-looking type," retorted Botox.

"What d'you expect? Lord save us, look at the time! Henry will be waiting."

The two headed as one for the side door, which led to the elevator lobby. Enid came scurrying out of the office to escort them. Hypocrisy flowed like water.

"So kind of you to let us in."

"Very happy you could come."

"Such interesting pieces!"

"Roger the guard will let you out."

Enid closed the door behind them, checked that it was locked, and came over to Avior, pulling a face.

The gallery was a single hall, about fifteen meters by twenty, but mirrors and the reflective one-way glass on the office made it seem larger. Plinths supporting Avior's sculptures were grouped around and between four big concrete pillars. Two plate-glass windows—one presently covered with plywood—flanked the street door. Only a very shrewd dealer could stay afloat in the shark-infested waters of fine art, but Enid was as sharp as a chisel, catering to both the avant-garde who shunned anything in the least bit representational, and the bourgeoisie who hankered after still lifes or smoky mountains. Normally she exhibited a few traditional pieces in one of the big windows and more abstract works in the other, while the main space was given over to one-person exhibitions.

"I am so sorry, dear," she said. "Awful people. More alimony than brains."

Avior straightened up, wiping her hands on a rag. "You're sorry? I'm the one who should apologize. But I did warn you that you wouldn't sell a single piece all week."

Enid was small and meek seeming. Thick glasses expanded her blue eyes, a mask of innocence concealing a razor-sharp mind. She smiled. "But all this publicity is worth thousands to me. I still wish you'd included a few of your more, um, conventional pieces."

"No." Avior bent to tend *Fire Walker*'s wounds again.

They had known each other since their student days. They were not friends, for Avior could never be close enough to anyone to be a friend, but their acquaintanceship went back far enough that Enid could argue with her.

"The crowds will be even bigger now. The glaziers will be here first thing in the morning, and the extra security guards. You'll sell everything you show, dear—everything in your other style, I mean."

"*No!* I told you I never mix them. You said you wanted these."

Years of dealing with artists had taught Enid to endure insanity with patience. She nodded understandingly and patted Avior's shoulder, which made the sculptor twitch with distaste. She hated being touched. And being called "dear."

"Very well, dear. Are you about done?"

"Almost," Avior said. She looked over at the boarded window. "*Dying Gaul* looks more like *Rare Hamburger.* I want to see what I can do for him. Is that possible?"

Enid hesitated only a moment. "I'll tell Roger you're here. But don't stay after dark, dear. No drapes on the window, remember. You know how to turn on the alarm when you leave?"

A few moments after Enid departed, Avior walked across to take another look at *Dying Gaul.* Her version of Epigonos's classic warrior had taken a lot more killing than the original, so that many of his internal organs were on display in putrescent color. Now falling glass had killed him several times more. These new cuts had not bled, and the internal mechanism they displayed was of wire, plaster, and papier-mâché.

"I think they got you for good this time, love," she said sadly, picking glass slivers out of his braincase with tweezers. *Gaul* had always been one of her favorites. There was no way she could repair him until she could get him back to her studio, but why even bother? No one ever bought any of her interesting pieces.

The works that Enid had called conventional, meaning commercial, Avior thought of as day jobs. She earned a living by sculpting busts of pompous benefactors and deceased founders and casting them in bronze. She also had several celebrity heads that she could take more castings from and sell for absurd sums: Churchill, Kennedy, Elvis, people like that. God, how she hated bronze! It drove her crazy with boredom. The only art that excited and stimulated her was what the paper had called obscene, revolting, and perverted.

"Excuse me?" said a man's voice.

Cardiac arrest! Avior dropped the tweezers and almost jumped clear off the floor. A man and a boy were standing in the middle of the hall, and she had no idea how they could have gotten there. Roger would have phoned from his desk in the lobby to tell her if she had visitors, and he would never have let them into the gallery unattended. They were armed with long poles, and were no doubt here to finish what the hammer maniac had started . . .

But she knew them! The tall young man was Rigel Somebody, and his boy companion was Izar Something. She could not place them, although they resembled each other enough to be related, and there was an odd familiarity to their features. Where and when had she met them, and how did she know their names? She was usually hopeless with names.

"Rigel!" she said. "Rigel . . . er?"

"Rigel Estell when I'm here, but we haven't met before."

She was certain that they had. "You scared me!"

They both wore jeans and white tee shirts, and they had the same peculiar coloring—hair and eyebrows a startling flaxen white against deeply tanned faces, and eyes that at first glance seemed blind, because the irises were white also. They were both laden with jewelry, rings, and bracelets. They had to be brothers, for Rigel was not old enough to be Izar's father. Where *had* she met them before? Rigel was as tall as she was. No, he was barefoot, so he had to be even taller—six-five or so.

"Sorry," he said, with a shamefaced smile. "We'll only stay a few minutes, and we certainly mean you no—"

"Doggy!" Izar yelled enthusiastically. "Is this real?" He ran across to *Road Kill 9*, trailing his pole, which was longer than he was.

"No, they're statues," Rigel said. "Sculptures. Watch what you're doing with your staff. *And remember your ears!*"

"Breathe slow," the boy said cheekily. "Oh, look at this! Wow!" He dashed over to *Flayed Giant* and stared up at it in admiration. He might be fourteen, but he was behaving more like a very tall nine-year-old.

"Please excuse him," Rigel said, still smiling. "You obviously have a fan there. Listen, Avior, I want to tell you a few things about myself. If they sound familiar and you want to hear more, you can ask me anything you'd like—anything at all. If what I say doesn't interest you and you want us to go, then we'll leave at once. *Poof!* You say go, we're gone. OK?"

She nodded, still racking her brains to place him.

"Everything I say *may* apply to you, but won't necessarily. Well, here goes . . . My name is Rigel, but that wasn't what my mother named me. I have no navel, because my umbilical scar healed completely, without a trace. Being male, I don't need nipples, so I don't have any." He smoothed the cotton on his chest to prove that. "My face grows no hair. I have some musical talent, and obviously you're an artistic genius. I'll bet that you dance beautifully, too. My eyes match my hair just like Izar's match his."

Hers did too. She glanced at the office's reflecting window, saw three tall people. White eyes, black eyes. White hair cut very short, her black Afro.

"I can walk on broken glass in my bare feet," he said. "I never get sick and I heal incredibly quickly. I like to swim several times a day."

Avior pushed *Dying Gaul* aside so she could perch on a corner of his plinth. It fit! All of it! How had Rigel learned so much about her? She swallowed hard and nodded.

"Sound familiar, some of it?" He was grinning now, seeing her reaction. "I go to sleep at will. I find this room unbearably hot, because my comfort level is ten or twenty degrees colder than humans'." He watched to make sure she had caught that last word. Then his gaze went past her. *"Izar!"*

Izar said, "Whoops! Sorry, Rigel." He was down on the floor, peering up at the underside of *Born of Woman.*

Avior felt certain that she had caught a glimpse of . . . of something that she was not supposed to have seen. Something on Izar's head. It wasn't there now.

"Well?" Rigel said, leaning slackly on his staff but watching her closely. "I have ordinary human ears, although they're set a little too high, and I have ordinary human teeth." He flashed them in a mock grin for her to admire. "But that isn't always the case with my kind. Most of us are very tall by human standards, but not all. Now, am I boring you? Scaring you? You want me to leave and take my horrid little buddy with me?"

She concentrated on that long staff he carried. It was finely crafted of some type of burnished wood, decorated with metal bands and emblems in a style she had never seen before, and she had thought she had seen all styles. She was avoiding his question and he was waiting. She glanced at the window again. His face and hers had a vague similarity, something about the eyes. What he was hinting would explain so much, but it also dragged up unendurable memories.

"What did you mean by your 'kind'?" Her words came out in a whisper.

"I am what they call a halfling, or tweenling." He was perfectly serious now. "I inherited a mixture of human traits and . . ." He paused.

"Well?" This time she almost shouted.

He glanced around to see where his young friend was. "Elfin. They don't like that word. Never call them 'elves' to their faces. They call themselves starborn or starfolk, but they're the inspiration for all the legends about elves, and they've been around as long as humans have. They must be terrestrial in origin, but they don't live on Earth. A halfling is the result of crossbreeding between a starborn and a human, usually a male elf and a human female. If you want to see what a purebred elf looks like, I'll ask Izar to stop dissembling. He's making himself seem human, when he remembers. It's not easy for him yet, because his magic is just starting to grow in, so he'll be happy to stop doing it. Before you answer, though, remember that Izar is definitely not human! Once you've seen him, you won't be able to deny the truth any longer. And whatever you do, you mustn't laugh at him. He's only an imp yet, but the starborn can be just as nasty as humans can; he could hurt you."

Avior rose to her feet so she could face this madman eye to eye, black to white. He didn't look crazy, but she figured he must be madder than any hatter. She was trembling, but the only way to escape danger was to face it. Ignoring it let it destroy you from the inside out. "Show me that belly button you don't have."

He shrugged, leaned his staff against his shoulder, and pulled his tee shirt up and his belt down a bit. No navel. No belly hairs, either. She'd thought she was the only freak without a navel.

But he seemed to be a nice kid and she would just have to trust him.

"Let's see the real Izar, then."

"Izar?" Rigel called, tucking his shirt in.

The boy had almost finished his tour of the exhibition. He was sniggering at *Cronus Devouring His Children*.

"What? Come and see this, Rigel! This is really *schmoory*!"

"In a moment. First you come over here and let Avior get a proper look at you."

Izar arrived like a missile. He grinned hugely. "Stop dissembling, you mean?"

"Can you just show her your teeth first?" Rigel said.

"Sure!" The boy grinned again, but this time he revealed a mouthful of ivory daggers. Avior recoiled with a gasp.

"They look just like shark teeth, don't they?" Rigel said. "Or wood saws. You can see he's no vegetarian at any rate. There's a school of thought that says the starfolk are human nightmares made real. Ready for the rest?"

She gulped and nodded.

"I've been trying to diss one ear at a time," Izar explained without removing his leer, "but I can't, yet. Hang on to your hair, lady."

His ears jumped to the top of his head. They stood erect, pointed like cats' ears, but pink, hairless, and enormous, each as large as a grown man's hand. They also sported six or seven jeweled studs along each rim. The fuzz on his head—more like short fur than hair—had taken on a faint rainbow sheen, like oil on a puddle or the play surface of a CD. His eyes, too, twinkled with rainbow fire.

Avior clasped her hands over her mouth to block a scream and Rigel caught her arm to steady her.

"All right?" he asked, looking worried.

No, but she shook him off furiously. "This is real?" she whispered. "Not just some cruel, horrible trick you're playing on me?"

Izar turned his ears outward, then inward, and grinned even wider.

"It's real," Rigel said. "I was born on Earth too. I didn't discover what I was until about three months ago, so I know how much of a shock this must be. The point is, Avior, halflings like you and me don't belong here on Earth. We don't fit properly in the Starlands, either, because we're not pure starborn. But the Starlands are better, believe me! At least people will know what you are and you won't need to hide it.

If you want a taste, we can take you there and show you. I swear I'll bring you back here any time you want—after an hour, a day, whatever. I have the queen's word on that. The change is instantaneous. We just . . . *Izar, where is your reversion staff?"*

The boy stopped grinning. "Oops! I left it over here, I think." He tore off toward *Born of Woman*, looped around that plinth and kept running. "Or maybe over here . . ."

Suddenly Rigel yelled in alarm, leaping at Avior and hurling her to the ground with himself on top. Automatic gunfire roared through the gallery, shattering glass, ricocheting off concrete, and pounding the inside of her skull. The lights went out in a shower of sparks from the circuit box on the wall while lines of bright holes sprouted across the plywood shutter. Glass shattered everywhere, clattering down on the tiles. Sheer noise seemed to shake the building.

It was ten minutes past six.

Silence.

"Izar!" Rigel yelled, still pinning Avior to the floor. *"Are you all right?"*

"I think so," wailed a very young-sounding voice.

"Don't get up yet. Lie still. You too, Avior." Then Rigel added, "Here they come." The sound of boots crunching on glass was loud in the wake of the silence following the blitz.

He rolled clear of her. To her astonishment his right hand now wore a steel gauntlet and held a glittering silver sword. *What good could that be against guns?*

Three armed men stepped in through the shattered window wearing masks, clearly intent on completing their deadly work.

Peering around the now dim gallery, they began to advance, spreading out, looking for bodies, alive or dead.

Rigel muttered, "Damn!" beside her.

Izar shouted something that sounded like, "Edasich, Edasich, Edasich!"

Rigel said, "Double damn!"

Then there was a dragon, a Chinese-style dragon as massive as a pony, but longer and lower, with bright, shiny green scales. Where it had come from, Avior did not know. It had frills and horns but no wings; its eyes bulged grotesquely. *It was growing bigger as she watched.*

The nearest man yelled a curse and swung his gun around to fire a burst at the beast. Ricocheting bullets screamed off in all directions. Seemingly undamaged but understandably annoyed, the dragon swarmed forward and loosed a great blast of white fire. The gunman, *Child's Arm*, and *Famine 9* all exploded into balls of flame. The man screamed once. The dragon swelled as big as a dinosaur.

Rigel's sword and gauntlet had disappeared. He swore again and sprang to his feet. One of the gunman saw him and aimed his weapon. A gesture with Rigel's left hand sent a ball of purple fire streaking across the room at him, but it exploded on contact without seeming to harm him. The dragon ignited Rigel's attacker with another roar of flame. The third man was already running to the window, but the dragon pursued, its writhing tail hurling plinths and sculptures aside like sticks. The man leaped through the gap, his terror clearly visible to the TV cameras outside. The monster was too big to follow, but its head wasn't, and its jaws closed on him with a crunching sound audible even to Avior on the floor. The game was over, but fire had engulfed the plywood window covering and most of the wax sculptures.

Izar arrived, crashing into Rigel and wrapping his arms around him.

"All right, imp!" the halfling said. "Up, Avior."

"Rigel, I still can't find my staff!" Izar sobbed.

Two of the burning men had escaped into the street and were rolling on the ground. The dragon was leisurely eating the third. The fire had spread to the carpet and the office was also in flames. Choking, eye-watering smoke was filling the gallery.

"Doesn't matter," Rigel said. "We'll all go on this one. Hold on!"

He took up his own staff from the floor and held it upright. Izar and Avior both grabbed it.

Shock . . . icy cold . . . an agonizing wrench . . .

Chapter 3

For a moment Avior was racked by coughing and her eyes streamed tears, but gradually she became aware of bright sunlight and a cool breeze.

She was standing on the roof of a stone tower, set among rolling green hills checkered with patches of forest and open meadow. There was no sign of habitation as far as she could see in any direction. A small pond shone like silver about a hundred yards away, under a sky of Wedgwood blue and puffy white clouds.

The tower itself was about seven or eight meters high and five in diameter. A stone bench encircled it, backed by a balustrade so massive that it looked more like battlements. A ladder protruded from a floor hatch.

"*Schmoor!*" Izar shouted. "This isn't Fornacis!"

"No, it isn't," Rigel said, scowling. "Sit down and make yourselves comfortable while I think. Sorry, Avior Halfling. I seem to have brought you into danger."

There was moss growing on the stonework, and mica grains twinkled in the stones themselves. The air had a fresh, after-rain smell. So real! This was either a nightmare or acute schizophrenia. She had to behave as if she believed it was real or she would go catatonic. She rather wished she *could* go catatonic. Obviously she had slipped completely over the edge this time—the hammer through the window, the vicious reviews, the breakup with George, and the escalating legal battles . . . She needed a drink, several drinks.

She must not stare at the boy's grotesque ears.

"Dragons and gunmen aren't danger?"

"Those too." Rigel hurled his staff down and sat on the bench. He leaned back against the wall and scowled at the landscape.

Avior sat also, though not too close to the wizard. The seat was unexpectedly high and felt damp. It must have rained here recently.

"Why'd you make all those *schmoory* bodies and things?" Izar asked. "Worms coming out of people's eyes and—"

"Mind your own business, imp," Rigel said. "Can you hear birds?"

"No."

"Me neither." That seemed to be bad news.

"Rigel, did I leave Edasich behind?" Izar asked mournfully. "Don't want to lose Edasich!"

"I don't think so, but don't call her here! There isn't room for her. I'm sure she must have come with the amulet."

"I'm going for a swim," Izar said as he headed for the hatch.

"No! Sit down."

"You can watch me."

"That pool may be full of crocodiles. You know what this building is, imp?"

The boy paused with one foot on the ladder, but he obviously knew when to listen to his older friend, or brother, or whatever Rigel was to him. "No."

"I think it's a blind. The pool is a watering hole." Rigel gave Avior a rueful smile. "Welcome to Jurassic Park."

She said, "You're joking!"

Izar asked, "Wha'sa blind?"

"A blind is a place where hunters lie in wait for animals. Blinds are usually made of wood or wicker but this one's stone and I don't like that. What's it supposed to keep out—elephants? Or worse? I don't think there were birds back in the Jurassic, so that's a bad sign. Ah! Look there. That's better."

A flock of specks had risen from some trees, swirling as birds do.

"And there's a hawk or a vulture!" Izar pointed at a very high dot.

"Right! Good. We don't know how accurate this domain is," Rigel said. "There were no starfolk around in the Jurassic, so if they were going for something prehistoric, cave bears and sabertooth tigers are more likely than T-rexes."

Avior hugged herself so the shaking of her hands wouldn't show. She was cold. "Elms, beech, oak. Those aren't Mesozoic species."

Rigel bobbed his head in a bow of tribute. "Well done. Thanks. Modern flora indicates that there's probably modern fauna. But I do think this is a safari park."

"Who are you?"

He sighed and rubbed his close-cropped flaxen hair. "I'm a professional babysitter. Babysitting can be a lot tougher than is commonly believed."

"He's my bodyguard," Izar said cheerfully, hauling himself up on the bench next to Rigel. "He kills people who try to kidnap me."

She thought Izar did a pretty good job of killing people for himself, if he had loosed that dragon. "Can you start at the beginning, please?"

Rigel glanced at the sun. "We do have a few hours of daylight left, but the beginning was about sixty thousand years ago, when Naos first imagined the Starlands. Let's fast-forward to this afternoon . . . I told you what halflings are. What I didn't say is that making them is illegal and highly immoral. That doesn't stop some starborn, though."

"Like my dad," Izar said glumly.

That remark Rigel ignored. "You were located as a lost halfling on Earth, Avior. Queen Talitha, like Queen Electra before her, insists that lost halflings be rescued. On Earth we're freaks; here we're people—second-class citizens, admittedly, but even that is better than being a freak. I volunteered to come for you, because I was raised in Canada, so we speak alike. Insanity sounds even worse when it comes in an unfamiliar accent. I'm Izar's official bodyguard, and it seemed like a safe, educational little trip for him. Also, he threatened to eat me raw if I didn't bring him along, so this afternoon we flew to Fornacis, which is the domain of Starborn Fomalhaut, the queen's court mage. He let us spy on you with a type of magic called seancing—crystal ball stuff. We watched the two fat women sneer at your work. As soon as you were alone, Fomalhaut gave each of us a reversion staff."

Rigel nudged the fallen staff with his bare toe. "The staves are a special form of amulet, and they must be longer than the person being reverted. That's because the Starlands aren't a world, they're a different 'dimensional continuum'—don't ask, because I don't know. A red mage like Fomalhaut can flip back and forth between Earth and Starlands as much as he pleases with a staff, but he had to preset them for us. We 'extroverted' to Earth and introduced ourselves to you."

"We were betrayed," Izar said.

"I was. I don't think you were."

"Yes I was!" the boy said indignantly. "We were betrayed twice. Someone else was seancing that gallery place and when we arrived they sent in men with guns to kill us. They wouldn't have bothered doing that if they'd known our staves were booby-trapped too. The staves were set to introvert us here so that something else could kill us."

How old was Izar? At times he seemed like a mere child to Avior, yet he could spout logic like an adult. His matter-of-fact way of talking about murder and betrayal was bloodcurdling, as if they happened all the time. And the sight of his ears kept ripping up half-buried nightmares.

Rigel smiled fondly at him. "That's very ingenious, and you may well be right. I agree that there must be two traitors, but it's more likely that they were both just after me. We hadn't told anyone that you were going to extrovert with me, remember—not even your mother, who will have my hide for a doormat if the Family doesn't get it first. So whoever sent the gunmen didn't know you were there. Edasich didn't come until you called her, which means you weren't the one they intended to hurt. And whether the second traitor was Fomalhaut or Mizar, he probably sabotaged my staff but not yours. If all had gone according to their plan, you would have introverted back to Fornacis and I would have come here."

Avior closed her eyes and sniffed the woodland-scented breeze. She ran her fingers over the stonework of the bench. It was all real, real, real! It was not a movie or a role-playing game. Not madness. She could remember childhood dreams of other worlds and aliens coming to rescue her from her personal hell. Maybe those dreams had finally come true. She opened her eyes and saw Rigel watching her worriedly.

"Why should anyone want to kill either of you?" she demanded.

"Well, nobody should want to kill Izar," he said. "Except because of his manners, I mean. Kidnap him, yes, because his mother is Queen Talitha, who rules the Starlands, and his father is Prince Vildiar, who wants to. If Vildiar can get his hands on their son, he can force Talitha to abdicate in his favor."

"He would threaten his own son?"

"Vildiar personally wouldn't, but Izar's brothers would."

"Don't call them that!" Izar yelled. "I'd rather be related to rats!"

"Sorry," Rigel said. "The Family."

"But where *are* we?" Avior demanded, shocked at how shrill she sounded.

"I don't know. In some domain in the Starlands. See those?"

He pointed to a herd of about a dozen deer that was cautiously emerging from the trees, sniffing the air, edging steadily closer to the water hole. Even with only trees to judge their size against, Avior could tell that the adults were very large, and the buck flaunted enormous antlers. Bigger than Izar's ears . . .

"They look a lot more appetizing than we do," Rigel said. "I think we should start exploring while we still have some daylight. Go look for snakes at the bottom of the stairs, imp."

Needing no further encouragement, the boy vanished down the hatch. Rigel frowned at Avior's city shoes. "Did you get human or starborn feet in the lottery, Avior Halfling?"

"I can walk on nails, if that's what you mean, but I want to go home, please. You said—"

He pouted. "I know I did, but I don't have the magic needed to reset my reversion staff. It might dump you back in a burning art gallery and a murder case. Or it might do much worse, because it was sabotaged to trap me here, so it won't likely be set to get me out again. We're in a totally new situation. Sorry."

It made sense. She kicked off her shoes and reached down to pull off a sock.

"Shouldn't we stay here to be rescued?"

"No. My enemies know where I am; my friends don't."

He had an answer for everything. Men always did, of course. She could only hope that Rigel's answers were right more often than George's had been. She followed him to the hatchway.

The first ladder took them down to a room as appealing as a dungeon. Barren of furniture of any kind, it was dimly lit by narrow slits in the thick stonework. The ground floor was identical, except it had piles of leaves on the floor and a doorway leading out to the grasslands. The pivots for a door were still there, but the door itself was gone, and the implications of that were nasty. Avior took note of Rigel's worried frown but said nothing, because Izar was waiting just outside, within earshot.

As they set off across the meadow in line abreast, the deer at the watering hole raised their heads to study them, but did not seem alarmed. The breeze was slight, but brisk enough to make Avior shiver as the wet grass chilled her feet. Izar removed his tee shirt and tucked it into his belt, and a moment later Rigel did the same. Not a nipple between them. How old was Rigel? About half her age, she decided—out of his teens, but not long out. She was amazed at the trust she was putting in him, but perhaps that was a natural reaction to all the impossible things that were happening. His calm acceptance of their situation was all that stood between her and screaming hysteria.

Besides, she had no choice.

If she failed to respond to the court order by Monday, George's lawyer . . .

"A lesson in how to fight sabertooth tigers, please?" she asked.

Rigel exposed perfect human teeth in a grin. "As long as they don't sneak up on you, they shouldn't be a problem." He stopped and tugged at the rings on his left hand, eventually freeing a gold one with a blue stone. "Put this on. Either hand, doesn't matter. Now turn the stone inward. Put your thumb on it and pretend to throw something at that bush."

"I'm not good at throwing."

"Doesn't matter. The amulet is. Try."

Her clumsy gesture sent a ball of purple fire flying straight from her hand to the bush, which exploded in flames, then vanished in a cloud of smoke and drifting ash. She said, "Oh!"

"Now turn it so that the gem's facing outward," Rigel said. "That's the safety catch. It will certainly scare the stripes off a sabertooth, if saberteeth have stripes. And I see that discretion is the better part of venison, too."

"What?"

"We've scared the deer away." He started walking again.

His childish humor was presumably intended to calm both her and his young ward. Or perhaps just her, because Izar seemed more annoyed than frightened about being marooned in this strange place.

"Seriously," Rigel said, "there's no need to worry. The starling and I both have Lesaths. At least I hope his dragon is still with us. Try calling her now, Izar."

Izar stamped his left foot twice and said, "Edasich, Edasich, Edasich!"

The dragon appeared, strolling alongside him, no larger than a Saint Bernard dog now, rolling its globular eyes independently as it scanned the countryside for trouble. It had dried blood around its mouth.

"Good girl!" Izar said happily. He patted the scaly neck. "Edasich, go home!" The dragon vanished. The boy grinned at Avior and did a little dance so he could point at a jade bangle on his left ankle. "That's where she lives."

"Edasich would snack on mastodons," Rigel said. "As for people, see this bracelet of mine? It's old and very powerful and legendary, what the starfolk call 'ancestral.'" He held out his right arm. "Saiph!"

Back came the gauntlet and sword that she had glimpsed in the art gallery.

"Rigel fought Hadar and Tarf and Adhil with Saiph!" Izar said excitedly. "Hadar has a Lesath called Sulaphat and Tarf had one called—"

"Let's leave out the gory details," Rigel said. He lowered his sword and it disappeared. "Saiph saved your life from the gunmen. Just before they opened fire, it yanked my arm so hard that I fell to the floor. Fortunately I guessed what was happening and grabbed you on the way down. I'll have a bruise on my wrist tomorrow, see?"

It sounded as if her life had been saved by Rigel rather than his gadget. *He must have incredibly fast reflexes.*

"A Lesath is a magic weapon?" Avior asked. If anyone had told her an hour ago that she would be seriously discussing magic . . . Well, it did keep her mind off bat ears.

"A Lesath is an amulet with massacre potential. Amulets are recorded magic, like stored programs in a computer. It can take days to frame a complicated spell, so even high-rank mages store their spells in amulets, where they're readily available. The greatest Lesaths have their own names. They're illegal, but Izar and I have royal license to wear ours. That ring I gave you could kill someone, but it's trivial magic and most starfolk wear protection amulets. There's virtually no defense against Saiph or Edasich."

They reached the pond, which was bigger than she had realized. The edges were muddy and trampled. She didn't search for recognizable tracks among the weeds, afraid of what she might find.

"I don't see any crocodiles," Izar grumbled.

"Dive in and maybe we will," Rigel suggested. "No, I don't mean that." He peered all around. "Starfolk adore water. If there's a house anywhere in this subdomain, then it will be on a lake or a river. Now, physical laws don't necessarily apply here, but we seem to be in a main valley. There's a stream running into this slough here, and I expect there's one running out at the far end. Starling Izar, if you were going to put a nice, clean swimming hole somewhere in this country, where would you do it?"

The imp preened at being asked his opinion. He pointed. "That way."

"Upstream? Good thinking. Forward, then. We head upstream!"

Avior suspected that Rigel had just flipped a coin.

Chapter 4

They walked until Avior's legs ached and the sun stood unpleasantly close to the treetops. Hard-pressed to keep up with her younger companions, she discovered just how out of shape she was. She was also chilled to the bone, so Rigel gave her his tee shirt to pull on over her blouse. He obviously had things to say that he didn't want Izar to overhear, but although Izar ran circles around both of them, investigating every rock and bush, those enormous ears were always pointed in their direction and he was probably missing little of their conversation.

Rigel told her of his own rescue, which had involved an even larger massacre than hers, and she told him what she remembered of the news stories about it, although she paid little attention to such things.

"I'm an unusual halfling," he said, "in that my starborn part came from my mother. She extroverted to Earth to have her baby in secret and then lost me through no fault of her own. She spent the next twenty-one years hunting for me."

He was fishing for Avior's story, but she wasn't going to tell it. Not yet anyway.

"His mom was the queen!" Izar shouted from the sidelines, where he had been examining a heap of dung that would not have shamed an elephant. "And she admitted it before the whole court!"

Rigel rolled his eyes at this unwelcome revelation. "Queen Electra. It created a terrible scandal, but she was dying and wanted to make it up to me."

"Is that why you're so hated that people want to kill you?"

"Some people, yes. They think I ought to disappear. It's more than just racial prejudice, because elves and humans are different species. Halflings are supposed to know their place and keep to it; royal halflings are a galactic disgrace. Queen Talitha has shown me favor by appointing me head of Izar's bodyguard, so there's that, too."

"He's her sweetie pie," Izar sniggered, having come close.

"No, I am her kennel master." Rigel's fist grabbed the boy's ear.

"Ayhihhh!"

"When I get you back to Canopus, imp, I am going to make you stand on the Star and repeat that remark."

Obviously Izar did not enjoy having his ear twisted, because he yowled and struggled and threatened. "I'll burn your jeans off! *Yeeee!* Stop, stop!"

"Not until you apologize to Halfling Avior for lying to her."

Izar retorted that he did not apologize to halflings and Rigel took hold of his other ear as well. Uncomfortable with the scene, Avior walked on, leaving them to it. Rigel won, because a few moments later Izar appeared in front of her, forcing her to stop. He bowed, stretching his arms out sideways, but when he straightened up he did not meet her eyes. His ears were pinker than usual.

"Avior Halfling, I am truly sorry that I lied to you. My bodyguard and my mother are not lovers and never have been, and I am very ashamed that I insulted them both."

"That is a gallant apology," she said. "I forgive you. What's the Star that Rigel mentioned?"

He fell into step beside her, still sulking. "Star of Truth, in front of the throne. If you tell a lie on it, your tongue goes on fire."

"Then I think you made a very wise decision."

He scoffed angrily and ran off to examine a hollow tree. Rigel arrived at her side again, red faced and silent. He possessed an interesting ruthless streak she had not suspected. He was not the queen's lover, but any woman would know that so much smoke required some fire. Most men would be happy to encourage a rumor like that. How did the queen feel about him? If he was the son of the previous queen, how closely were he and the present one related?

The countryside stayed monotonously the same. The tiny stream was rarely visible, playing peekaboo in swamps or long grass. There were birds, including parrots and toucans, which were not normally found in beech woods or their like. Izar found spoor of ungulates and big cats and ostriches. The castaways were marooned in a game park, just as Rigel had guessed.

"Not every elf has his own domain," he told her, "far from it. And many of those who do have inherited them, because only high-magic starborn, red or orange grade, can imagine their own domains or extend others'. Starfolk like to think they're great artists, but ninety percent of what you'll see is copied from Earth. Tal . . . The queen says she knows of at least fifty Romes, eighty Angkor Wats, and a hundred

Versailles. A domain can have scores of subdomains. The royal domain itself is enormous, like a small continent."

Suddenly weary, Avior put the big question into words. "Do you have any guarantee that there's a house here for us to find?"

"No," he admitted. "In fact it's quite likely that there isn't. If I were imagining a hunting park, I would certainly put the livestock in a separate subdomain, so that I wouldn't find tigers in my pajamas. Then I would come and go by portal."

He shrugged. "By now the queen must know what happened, and she'll shake the Starlands from one end to the other to find out where we are. There were only two starborn in Fornacis this afternoon—Fomalhaut, who's the queen's court mage, and Mizar, his apprentice. One of them must have perverted my staff, so she'll frog-march both of them to the Star of Truth ASAP.

"They know that," he went on, "so they'll probably come and rescue us themselves and pretend it was all a mistake."

Izar had moved farther away to inspect a termite hill, so she could speak her mind.

"You're covering up. If the queen's reaction is so certain to reveal the truth, why would they risk angering her in the first place?"

Rigel sighed. "The plan was never to harm Izar. Nobody knew he was going to be with me. The plan was to kill me. Not because I'm so dangerous or hated myself, although a great many starfolk resent the favor the queen has shown me. The real problem is this Lesath of mine, Saiph. I can't take it off. It's the most dangerous weapon in the Starlands, and it will stay on my wrist until I die. The writing on it bears the names of the people and creatures it has killed, scores of them.

The Family is terrified of Saiph, and the Family is almost certainly behind this somehow. I expect the plan was, and probably still is, to pit me against a company of archers and fill me full of arrows. Then I die. Hadar—he's the chief goon—gets the bracelet, Izar either goes safely home or is held for ransom, with the throne itself as the asking price. What happens to you, I don't know. Aren't you sorry you asked?"

"No!" she said.

He smiled so disbelievingly that she was tempted to start describing some of her suicide attempts, but Izar veered close again and they talked of safer things.

Shortly after that, the faint game trail they were following led them into the thick and brambly undergrowth of a stand of aspen. Rigel went in front, using Saiph as a machete to clear the worst of the tangles. Suddenly Izar, bringing up the rear, bumped into Avior, who had bumped into Rigel, who had stopped in his tracks, his sword still in hand. The other two peered around him to see what the holdup was.

The game path was blocked by a naked man holding a spear and shield. His skin was a burnt-umber shade wherever it was not daubed with red, green, and white war paint, and his hair hung in long braids, decorated with fetishes of cloth, bones, ivory, fruit, and bright ribbons. He was young, powerfully built, and human. At least a score of warriors just like him were rising out of the undergrowth.

"You stop!" he said. "You not to go this way any more. The starling will come with us and you halflings must go back."

Rigel dismissed his sword and put his hands on his hips. "Or what?"

"Or we are to kill you!"

Rigel laughed. He peered around. "Izar? Come here." He put the boy in front of him and regarded the warrior over the imp's head. "Izar Starling, did you hear what this mudling just told me?"

"Yes I did, Halfling Rigel," Izar said with rare courtesy.

"And what do you have to say to that?"

Izar, it turned out, had plenty to say to that. "You know who I am, mudling? I am starborn! I am the son of Queen Talitha and Prince Vildiar! Look at my hair! Look at my eyes! I am Naos! Do you dare to give me orders and threaten my halflings, you crawling, mud-eating worm? I will burn you to ashes. I will eat your children. I will have my Lesath tear you to pieces. Drop your weapons! All of you! Throw them down now!"

Spears and shields dropped.

"Now grovel!" Izar yelled, growing louder but shriller. "Grovel with your faces in the dirt. Eat grass! Go on, eat it like the animals you are!"

At that point Rigel clasped his shoulders. "I think you have made your point. Well done." He stepped forward to the spokesman, who was indeed biting the vegetation. "Up on your knees, you."

The man rose nervously, weeds dangling from his mouth.

"What domain is this, mudling?"

"Alathfar, noble halfling."

"Who owns it?"

"The mistress, noble halfling," the man said blankly.

"What's her name?"

"It is forgotten. The old ones—"

"What's your name?"

"Chief Tracker, noble halfling."

"And who ordered you and your companions to parade around naked, Chief Tracker?"

Horrified pause.

Rigel said, "Saiph!" and the sword appeared to do his bidding. "I killed a minotaur with this. I have also killed a sphinx, a cockatrice, and several halflings. You think I would hesitate to—"

"A noble lady, halfling."

"Where is she?"

"At the station, may it please the halfling."

"You will lead us to her at once." Rigel waited a moment to see if there would be argument, and there wasn't. "The rest of you can stop eating now, but you are to stay there, on your knees, until the sun has set. Then you can go home. Understand? Lead on, Chief Tracker."

As soon as the trees gave way to open grass again, Avior moved up to walk alongside Rigel. Izar was out in front, keeping an eye on the unhappy guide, and occasionally chivvying him along with a stick. She noted that Rigel's expression was bleak, so perhaps he wasn't truly ruthless after all.

"Was that necessary?" she demanded.

"They were armed and terrified. I doubt they would deliberately harm us, even under orders, but there might have been an accident." He sighed. "I know, I didn't warn you that there were humans in the Starlands. There are millions, maybe billions, of them. They're field workers, servants, drudges . . . They're supposed to go around fully dressed to hide their non-starfolk deformities, and I've never seen any of them completely naked like that. I expect this tribe has been set up as part of the game park scenery to amuse starfolk visitors. Elves never die, so boredom is their biggest problem."

"They massacre 'natives' for sport?"

He pulled a face. "I don't think it would go that far. Mudlings are property and too valuable to slaughter out of hand. The point is, I've never heard even a rumor of a mudling threatening an elf or a halfling. This lady, whoever she is, is going to have to answer some sharp royal questions about giving her serfs weapons."

"They're slaves!" Avior said furiously.

"Not quite. Do you know the difference between wolves and dogs?"

"Of course!"

"Well, just like dogs are domesticated wolves, mudlings are domesticated earthlings. Their ancestors were brought here tens of thousands of years ago to serve the starfolk, and all the pep has been bred out of them. While wolves were skulking around our ancestors' campfires waiting for scraps, mudlings' forebears were learning not to anger their elfin masters. Slow learners died or were neutered. Now, like dogs, mudlings live only to please. They're not very smart and they're never aggressive."

Izar had certainly been aggressive enough, and Rigel had encouraged him.

"Why did Izar call himself Naos?"

"Because he is a Naos. That rainbow sheen on his hair is the mark of Naos. By the time he's adult—that won't happen until he's forty-one, by the way; starfolk take the time to enjoy childhood properly—it will be fully opalescent, and he'll be designated a prince. The mark means he's developing a special form of magic, also called Naos, which the ruler of the Starlands needs in order to keep them from vanishing into the void. So one day Izar may even be king. Naos runs in families, but not predictably, and it also crops up at random. You smell wood smoke?"

After a few more minutes, they spotted the source, a village of wattle huts. Chief Tracker gave it a wide berth, while women and children watched from a safe distance. A couple of dogs barked and were quickly hushed. Dusk was falling.

"Theme park!"

"Exactly. But it's probably thousands of years older than Disneyland. It may well be based on the way their ancestors lived, back in the Pleistocene."

A couple of kilometers beyond the tribal village they came upon a small lake fed by a waterfall. Beside that stood the station, a sprawling complex of single-story wooden buildings with verandas, shade trees, and close-cropped lawns. It appeared to be deserted; the windows were all dark.

"Why no palisade?" Avior demanded. "If the blind had to be built of stone, then why does this place have no defenses?"

"I'm sure it has magical defenses," Rigel said absently. He was looking around very warily as their guide led them into the complex. Izar was staying close now. "The blind is scenery, so it has to look right. Chief Tracker?"

The mudling turned. "Noble halfling?"

"How many people live here?"

"People?"

It took several questions to establish that there were no halflings or mudlings living in this part of Alathfar, not even servants. Starborn ladies were seen occasionally, but Chief Tracker had no idea whether they lived there or just came visiting. No other starfolk had been seen since he was a boy.

"So who told you to threaten us with spears?"

A starborn lord he had never seen before, but he didn't know where the great lord lived.

Rigel dismissed him and told him to make sure all his men got home safely.

"Now what?" he mused. "Beat on all these doors? Go over to that big building in the middle? This stinks of an ambush. Starling, burn that cabin." He pointed at a small cabin off to the side.

Izar looked up at him with wide eyes, unable to believe that he'd received such wonderful instructions. "Burn it?"

"Throw fire at it. Set it alight. Reduce it to . . . Yes, like that. Keep throwing. Make a real bonfire of it."

Avior was stunned. *There might be people in there.*

Izar's barrage of fireballs quickly turned the building into an inferno. Flames roared up into the darkening sky.

"Very good!" Rigel said. "To continue your arson and vandalism training, let's go over there and raze another." He led the way farther into the complex, following their shadows.

The light behind them dimmed, the noise of the crackling flames stopped. Avior turned just in time to see the fire vanish. The cabin was badly damaged, but it was no longer burning, not even smoking.

Rigel said, "Aha! And somebody is home, see?"

Lights had come on in the windows of the central building and smoke drifted up from its chimneys.

Chapter 5

Rigel was trying to appear a lot more confident than he felt. He didn't believe that Hadar was behind the kidnapping, because the Family were all halflings and halflings never progressed above low green in magic, usually only reaching blue—Rigel himself seemed to have none beyond his ability to read names. Only an elf with high-ranking magic could have sabotaged his reversion staff. Prince Vildiar certainly had enough talent, but he had refrained from killing Rigel before when he had the chance. Why dirty his own hands with violence when he had bred an army of halflings for that purpose?

Almost certainly the culprit was Fomalhaut, the court mage. He could be loyal to the queen and still disobey her orders if he saw a higher loyalty in ridding her of her half-breed retainer and rumored lover. This morning, when he had learned that Izar would be joining the excursion, it had been his idea to give the imp a reversion staff of his own, even though Rigel's staff was quite capable of moving three people.

Seen that way, the plot made sense. Talitha's popularity with the more puritanical starborn would soar; Rigel could live out the rest of his five-hundred-year lifespan in this game park as lord of the mudlings. Talitha might rage and threaten, but she needed Fomalhaut too much to dismiss him. Only the fluke of Izar's losing his staff had spoiled the plan.

Also, Fomalhaut had prophesied several times that Rigel would die within months if he remained in the Starlands. Rigel had ignored that dire prediction, except to ask that he be given one week's advance warning. If the mage foresaw that the halfling would enjoy a longer lifespan if exiled to Alathfar, he might have rationalized the kidnapping as a kindness.

But now it appeared that there might be starborn living in this subdomain, and that did not fit any of those theories. Anyone, even mudlings, could use amulets, but if the fire had been extinguished by extempore magic rather than an amulet, then the visitors were about to be confronted by at least one angry elfin mage. Rigel did not truly expect violence, which was not the starfolk's way, but even if he were wrong, there would be no time for their adversary to generate extempore magic in a fight. It would be decided by amulets, and his were the best the royal collection could provide.

Halflings were another matter. If Hadar or other members of the Family were lurking in there after all, then Rigel Halfling would die, and he couldn't even guess what that pack of sadistic half-human brutes would do to Avior. She was doing amazingly well just by staying sane, for her unexpected introversion to the Starlands had been even more jarring than his own. Everyone had limits, though, and there might be more shocks just ahead.

Izar he could trust to withstand almost anything, because Izar trusted him completely and would follow his lead. Feeling the starling edge closer to him, he put a hand on his shoulder.

"Izar, we need you to protect us. Please stay between me and Avior, all right?"

"I thought you were the bodyguard?" Avior said harshly.

"I'm starborn," Izar said loftily, "and he's just a halfling. Starborn never dare hurt one another, because then they die too. That's the guilt curse."

"And it doesn't apply to halflings," Rigel added. "You and I are fair game."

They reached the steps and the main door swung open of its own accord, spilling golden light that seemed singularly unwelcoming. They all stopped.

"What happens now?" Avior asked.

"Heads we go home to Canopus and the queen," Rigel said. "Tails, we go home to Canopus and the queen." He wondered how many other sides the coin had.

They mounted the steps, crossed the veranda, and went through a doorway wide enough to take them in line abreast. They entered a very large room that, like so much of the Starlands, was clearly based on a terrestrial model. In this case, the theme was an old-world hunting lodge. Logs blazed heatlessly in a massive stone fireplace. Under a high open-beam ceiling, stuffed animal heads stared down glassily at overstuffed leather furniture and skins on the floor. It was at once cozy and imposing, barbaric and homey. Rigel had no trouble imagining it filled with talk and laughter, scores of noble guests in dinner jackets and crinolines discussing the day's hunt as servants offered them glasses of champagne and Viennese waltz music tinkled from the concert grand piano that seemed so small over in the corner.

Their hostess stood in the center of the room, with fists clenched and chin raised in anger. He wondered what Avior would make of the first adult starborn she had seen. Her name was Shaula. She was as thin as a fashion model, and looked to be two meters tall to the tips of her ears. Her ears, wrists, fingers, and ankles glittered with jewelry, but her only garment was the usual brief loincloth of shimmery, half-translucent moon cloth. She had no navel, but very definitely did have nipples and admirably high breasts. Her skullcap of short fur was the same blazing blue as her eyes.

Rigel and Izar stopped in their tracks. Avior took one more pace, then backed into line with them. She ran her fingers through her Afro, an unconscious gesture she used often. Izar pulled free of Rigel's hand and stepped forward so he had room to spread his arms as he bowed, clearly on his best behavior.

"May the stars shine on you forever, Starborn Shaula."

"May your progeny outnumber the stars, Starling Izar. You are welcome here in Alathfar, and may stay. Your servants will go and dwell with the mudlings."

Determined not to leave the negotiations to the starling, Rigel stepped around him and walked closer to Shaula, a deliberately provocative act. He stopped when she raised a hand in an elfin gesture that threatened magic.

"With respect, my lady, that cannot be. I am charged by Her Majesty to guard her son at all times. I demand that you speedily provide us all with transportation to the royal domain."

"Demand?"

"Yes. In the queen's name, I demand."

"That cannot be." Shaula smirked with worrisome confidence. Her arrogance filled the room like a bad smell. "There are no links to Alathfar, and it has no subdomains. I am a very solitary person. I live alone and tolerate no visitors. The starling will be safe here. I order you and that hairy monstrosity you brought with you to leave this house instantly. The mudlings will give you shelter. Go!"

He was used to elfin contempt by now and did not raise his voice. But he didn't cower, either. "Every domain must have a root portal, or it will cease to exist."

"Ours was sealed up centuries ago."

"I have the queen's warrant to use any force I consider necessary."

"You dare threaten me, mongrel?"

Saiph leaped into his hand, its point angled against Shaula's throat. She screamed, and Izar squeaked in alarm.

"Lady!" Rigel said. "Don't even think about whatever you were starting to think about. This is Saiph, the king of swords, and I am armed with many other royal amulets besides. All I meant was that I have an amulet to identify magic, so I can find the portal. I can, and will, break the seal on it. Or, if you prefer, I shall continue burning your property, and I think my young friend and I can ignite faster than you can quench. You are already in the queen's disfavor. You must know that you risk years in the Dark Cells if you hold her son here by force. I know that you're lying about there being no way in or out, because you didn't have to ask how we got here. Someone told you we were coming or had come. Perhaps you travel by means of an illegal reversion staff? I don't care how you do it, but deliver us to the royal domain at once, and I will ask Her Majesty to be merciful."

He lowered his sword to dismiss it, but Shaula was trembling with suppressed fury, and he felt his bracelet shiver as a warning to stay within reach of her. Then she nodded grimly.

"Very well. As you say, there is a root portal. Follow me."

She turned on her heel and headed for a door at the far side of the room. Rigel gestured his companions forward and all three of them followed the starborn. The interesting question was not why Shaula had changed her mind so rapidly, but why she had glanced over at the piano before surrendering—very much as if she were asking permission. There was nobody over in that corner that Rigel could see, although that did not mean that there was nobody over in that corner.

The starborn led her unwelcome guests through to what was obviously the kitchen area, large enough for a dozen cooks to prepare a banquet. There she opened what appeared to be one of a set of drawers, wide and deep. It was a safe bet that anyone else opening it would find it full of pots or bowls, but for her the front of the drawer vanished completely, leaving a gap. Light shone through, and a cool breeze wafted out, carrying the scents and sounds of animals.

"Camels!" Izar said, bending to peer out. The opening was about knee high to waist high, fitting him better than the halflings. In a trice he slipped a leg over and slithered out. "Looks like Canopus!" he shouted. "I can see the lighthouse. Harpy!"

Detecting no warnings from Saiph, Rigel let Avior precede him. Then he nodded respectfully to Shaula. Anything more formal would have been mockery. He backed out, following the others.

The moment he was clear of the opening, it vanished, leaving him facing a wall of massive ashlar, black with the dirt of centuries. He invoked his sword and made a scratch on the block that hid the portal. Then he turned to study the stable yard and the camels, a dozen of them. They had been eating their evening feed at mangers on the far side of the clearing, and looked no more pleased to see him than Starborn Shaula had. A couple of them decided to come and investigate the visitors.

"Imp Izar, I have no desire to be spat at by that ruminant monstrosity. Short of setting the place on fire, what procedure do you recommend?"

Izar grinned. "Itching ring?"

"An excellent choice, if it works on camels. Try it."

The imp pointed his left pinky at the closer of the two inquisitive bulls and scratched the back of his hand. The camel roared and began dancing and biting itself in obvious discomfort. Camels being smarter than they looked, the other remembered it had a meal to finish and swiftly reversed its course.

Then Rigel registered that Avior was glaring at him.

"What's wrong?"

"You threatened that woman with your sword, that's what's wrong! Bully! Monster!"

He shook his head. "I didn't do anything; Saiph did. Saiph is a defensive amulet. She was about to use some sort of magic against me. Starfolk go around armed very close to their teeth. Shaula had amulets on her fingers, in her ears, in bracelets and anklets. She hadn't counted on a halfling being so well protected." Which suggested that neither Hadar nor Fomalhaut had been behind the plot. Both were well aware of Saiph.

"You speak of it as if it were alive."

"It very nearly is. On Earth you have computers that are able to scan a financial document and tell you if some of the numbers have been faked. Well, Saiph can detect threats out of thin air."

He led the way across to the paddock gate and vaulted over it, into a predictably squalid alley. Avior ignored his offer of a helping hand. Izar tried to copy his hero and almost fell. They passed two buildings and turned a corner, emerging onto Small Harbor Street in Canopus, which Rigel knew well.

More daylight lingered here than in Alathfar, but the dhows in the harbor were all tied up and the roadway was almost deserted, compared to its usual hubbub. A bedraggled bird the size of a turkey flopped down on the top of the seawall. It had a diminutive human face and breasts.

"Where d'you think you're going?" she screeched. "You're supposed to stay where you are when you call us. You think I have time to follow you all over the city? Oh, it's you, midget. Well, you should'a stayed in the camel shit, because that's nothing compared to what you're going to be in when your screechy mother gets her claws in you."

Normally Izar enjoyed a slanging match with a harpy and could often hold his own, but this evening he was tired and hungry. "Shut your beak, crow! Go and tell my mother where I am. Zac'ly where I am!"

"And tell Commander Zozma, too," Rigel said.

"Eat dirt, mule," the harpy said. "The runt called me, not you. I can't listen to both of you spew puke at the same time. And what are you doing parading around with your deformed ears showing? Your sponsor will have something to say about that, I shouldn't—"

"Go!" Izar shouted.

Still grumbling, the smelly bird launched itself and flapped away over the water. Rigel also wore a harpy amulet. He shouted, "Harpy!" to summon another.

A troop of young human males strode past, just getting off work and chattering about their plans for the evening. They wore head cloths and long robes, Arab style. A half-naked elf rode by on a camel, then another on a unicorn.

Avior started to laugh. A snigger rapidly became giggles and hiccoughs and a rising tide of guffaws. Rigel grabbed her by the shoulders.

"Stop that! Stop! It's all right. The danger's over. You're safe and among friends. If you want to go back to Earth, that can still be arranged."

She clamped her mouth shut and stared at him with wide, horrified eyes. Then wailed, "Ears!" as if the word hurt.

"You'll have to get used to big ears if you're going to stay here." He put his arms around her and squeezed her tight. He wasn't sure if that was the right thing to do, and it wasn't. For a moment she seemed to accept the embrace, but then she screamed, fought loose, and swung a haymaker at his face.

It connected and he reeled back, colliding with Izar and fighting madly to control Saiph, wrestling down his gauntleted right hand with his left. Avior seemed about to follow up with another punch, but the sight of the shining sword between them stopped her.

Rigel managed to lower it, and it vanished. Blinking back tears and rubbing his cheekbone, he said, *"Lady!"*

"She tried to kill you!" Izar squealed.

"No, of course she didn't." But she must have intended serious injury, or why else would his amulet have sprung to his defense?

She stuttered. "I . . . I'm sorry. I don't like to be touched."

"I'm sorry too," he said grimly. "I certainly won't do it again." Fortunately his healing amulets would probably save him from developing a black eye. "And you're doing wonderfully well. This has been the worst day of your life, and you've come through fine. Pretend you're in a foreign country. Or Disneyland! You'd see Mickey Mouse ears everywhere in Disneyland and think nothing of them. We need to relax and eat. And sleep. There's nothing for you to worry about now that we're back in Canopus."

"Your harpy's here," Izar warned.

Rigel turned to see a male one with a straggly mustache sitting on the seawall, smirking. "Well! What's our hot little queen going to say when she hears that her pretty-boy half-breed has been brawling in the street with a mongrel trollop? You want me to call the guard, bawd?"

Rigel rejected a temptation to bring back Saiph and strike off the brute's head. "Go tell the duty officer of the Palace Guard where I am and that I need transportation for three right away. Go!"

The harpy departed with a shout of, "I'll tell him about the attempted rape."

Avior was still gasping. "I'm sorry, Rigel. I never behave like that!"

He sat on the seawall and beckoned for her to sit near him—Izar was already there, reedy legs dangling.

"Don't hyperventilate," Rigel said. "I'm amazed you're doing as well as you are. Just seeing Izar and me appear in the art gallery would have put some people into therapy for weeks. Truly! And no one listens to harpies."

"I do," Izar said innocently. "Lots do."

"Only people with nasty dirty minds," Rigel retorted.

The imp sniggered. "She sucker punched you!"

He was right, and the story would be all over Canopus by morning. The scandal about the queen's halfling lover would grow.

More starfolk were passing by in their moon-cloth wraps, both male and female.

Avior sniffed. "Does everyone parade around naked all the time?"

"Starfolk do, yes. Like I mentioned before, though, halflings and humans have to hide their 'deformities.' In public, I'm supposed to cover my ears and keep my mouth shut. By the way, the palace guards are sphinxes, with a SWAT team of centaurs. Can you survive that?"

"Thanks for the warning."

"I know I promised to take you home the moment you asked," he said carefully, "but that's not so simple now. The fire department must be hunting for your body in the remains of the gallery and if you turn up unharmed, the police will certainly want to interview you. I'm not saying you can never go back, but it will take some planning. Your friends must be worried sick. Perhaps we could get a message to them."

"Friends?" She shrugged.

Startled, he said, "How about the woman you were speaking with just before Izar and I extroverted?"

"Enid? We went to art school together. She's twenty years older now and wonders why I'm not. You wouldn't want to let her near a camera with that story, would you?"

"Not unless you want your face all over the *National Enquirer*."

He didn't ask her if she had a husband or lover. If she did, it was up to her to mention him. Or her. He caught himself rubbing his face where she had hit him, and pulled his hand away.

Hooves drummed on the pavement and a centaur came cantering into view, pedestrians hastily clearing out of his path. Menkent looked like the top half of a college wrestler grafted onto the shoulders of a bay stallion. He wore a curly red-gold beard and a permanent grin. He clattered to a halt and saluted, all without losing the grin.

"Marshal Rigel! Welcome back, sir. Where in the stars did you get to, you dumb biped? Hail, notorious Imp Izar! Welcome to Canopus, Avior Halfling."

"We were waylaid by treachery," Rigel said, "but I expect you know that by now. Where's the queen?"

"*Saidak*'s bringing her. Let's go down to the quay. You too, imp."

Izar charged the centaur. Menkent caught him, threw him up in the air with a twist, caught him while he was facing the other way, and turned him overhead in a somersault to land on his back, facing forward again. Izar whooped with glee, grabbed the centaur's jewel-studded elfin ears, and beat a tattoo on his ribs with his heels.

"Gallop!"

"Yow! You're hurting."

Izar drummed harder. "Gallop, I said!"

Rigel rose from his position on the wall. Avior was starting to look calmer, but obviously her nerves were still tauter than the strings on a jazz guitar. He held out a hand and she flinched, reluctant to accept even that small contact.

"Come and meet the queen, my lady," he said. He now knew that Avior must have been a very disturbed woman even before he had put her through several hours of pure nightmare.

Chapter 6

Saidak turned out to be the royal barge. But the next shock of Avior's interminable day was that the barge came gliding in over the rooftops like a silver blimp in the gathering purple twilight. It circled the harbor uncertainly until Menkent waved up at it from their position on the jetty. The mermaid figurehead waved back and the barge sank vertically to dock alongside them.

"Welcome back, Rigel dear," the mermaid said. She sat on a shelf at the bow and was enormous by human standards. Bare-breasted and bosomy in nautical tradition, she had elfin bat ears as big as dinner plates. "We were all worried about you."

"Thank you, Beautiful. I was worried, too. I was afraid I might never see your legendary blue eyes again."

The mermaid preened. "Oh, you flirt!"

Avior took an even fiercer grip on her self-control. Disneyland, Rigel had told her. He was right. She had to pretend this was all TV or a video game, or she would fall apart.

"How do I know their names?" she whispered to Rigel. "I knew yours, too."

"It means that you have some magic. Most tweenlings can reach blue grade with training. I'm studying hard, but not making much progress."

A gate opened in the railing, and a gangplank folded down. Izar, who had been forcibly removed from his steed by the steed himself, went racing up ahead of everyone else.

"Noble Starling Izar has boarded!" the mermaid boomed in a voice like a foghorn. All around the harbor, the last late-working sailors and dockworkers were watching the action.

"I wanna sit in your lap again," Izar announced, clambering over the rail to reach the figurehead.

"Mermaids don't have laps!"

"Yes they do. Make room!"

"That imp has amazing resiliency," Rigel murmured as he and Avior mounted the plank. It was narrow for two, and he went first. "You'd think he would at least want to tell his mother about the gunfire."

"Noble Rigel Halfling, marshal of Canopus, royal officer in charge of security," announced the figurehead. *Surely such proclamations were superfluous when everyone's name was somehow perfectly obvious?* "And Halfling Avior," she added as a quieter afterthought. Hooves clattered. "Menkent Sphinx of the Guard."

The welcoming party on the barge comprised two sphinxes, female Kalb and male Zozma, who was twice Kalb's size and had a beard shaped like a black icicle. They bowed to Rigel, giant cats stretching their front legs.

"You had us worried, Marshal!" Zozma purred in a register almost low enough to be classed as subsonic.

"I had myself worried, Commander. Saidak, is that brat bothering you?"

The mermaid craned over the rail to look at him. "No, Marshal. If he does, I'll just drop him overboard."

"Excellent idea. Let's go, then."

He gestured Avior toward a hatch that opened onto a stairway, which wound down into what turned out to be a saloon occupying the entire vessel. A bench upholstered in red velvet extended all the way around, under a continuous line of sloping windows, which Avior had not noticed from the outside. Everything was red and gold, warm and bright under the glow of golden chandeliers.

At the bottom of the stair stood a female elf named Ancha, who was just as grotesquely tall and slender as Shaula had been, but with hair and eyes of a striking auburn. She wore the same skimpy topless beachwear, but also bore a disk collar of silver and pearls as wide as her shoulders that draped down almost to her breasts. It had to contain hundreds of pearls, perhaps a thousand if it continued around her back. Ignoring Avior, she smiled thinly at Rigel.

"Welcome back, Marshal. We brought this for you." She offered him a bronze helmet with a brush of white horsehair along the crest. It looked like a prop from a Hollywood toga turkey.

"Ah, thank you, Companion. That's exactly what I need. You know, I've grown accustomed to this absurd thing?" Rigel donned the helmet. He would probably look good in it if he were wearing something more appropriate than jeans.

"It suits you, Marshal," Ancha said, with all the sincerity of a boa constrictor's welcoming hug. But then she stepped aside and Avior saw Queen Talitha on a throne in the center of the ship.

It was a modest throne of gilt—unless, of course, it was constructed of solid gold—but a throne nonetheless, and yet the queen of the Starlands sat there barefoot and wearing no more than Ancha, except that her disk collar was of diamonds, glittering brighter than the lamps themselves, and her hair and eyes burned with all the colors of the rainbow, the mark of Naos. She seemed impossibly young to be Izar's mother and would be truly gorgeous if one could look past the grotesque ears and shark smile. Rigel's infatuation was understandable, provided he shared the usual male ability to concentrate on certain specific organs.

He walked forward and bowed with arms outspread. Already aware of how he felt about the queen, Avior studied Talitha's face, which was guarded like a fortress. Too guarded! The other attendant present, Starborn Matar, was also watching the queen, and her lip had curled into a hint of a sneer. If elves' expressions were anything like humans', then the Rigel-Talitha infatuation was mutual, and a source of contempt around the court. Izar's slander and the harpy's slurs might not be true in action, but they were certainly true in wish. If even trusted confidants despised the frustrated romance, how must the queen's political opponents feel?

"Welcome, Marshal," Talitha said. "Congratulations and my deepest thanks for bringing Izar safely home. I want to hear all about it, but first tell me this . . . Were the gunmen human or not?"

"Halflings," Rigel said. "I saw ears on at least two of the three as they came in through the broken window."

The royal collar flared in opalescent fire. "*Schmoor!* as my son would say. Well, if we are lucky, one of them may have been Hadar himself. We must recover the bodies, though, before the earthlings start a worldwide panic about aliens. Fomalhaut and Mizar say they are willing to deny on the Star that they had anything to do with the attack or your booby-trapped reversion staff. I will hold court tomorrow, and I've summoned Vildiar to appear as well. We may get some truth then."

The two sphinxes came padding down the stairs. The centaur had stayed on deck.

The queen looked past Rigel. "Halfling Avior, you are most welcome to our realm. I apologize heartily for all the violence and treachery. It is not how we usually do business." The royal smile shone with charm; even the great disk necklace seemed to glitter in a warmer shade.

Avior bowed, but did not attempt the arms-out gesture. "Your Majesty is very kind."

"I hope you will choose to stay with us, but the decision is yours. We starborn appreciate art and sponsor it generously. Meanwhile, I hope you enjoy our hospitality." Her smile seemed genuine enough—it was an expression she had not dared direct at the marshal, Avior noticed. "Please sit down, all of you. Marshal, I want you there," she said, pointing. "Report. Matar, record this."

The throne pivoted so that the queen could face Rigel on the nearest part of the bench. Starfolk and sphinxes gathered in, but Avior stayed in the background, trying to be inconspicuous. She desperately needed a drink.

Rigel said, "Your Majesty, Commander, Companions: You know that we extroverted to the art gallery and were ambushed. At least two of our attackers were halflings. They arrived only minutes after we did, and their guns must have been acquired on Earth, meaning that they had set up an attack team long in advance. They must have been stalking Avior for some time, perhaps in the hope that I would be the one sent to approach her. They couldn't have known I would take Izar with me."

"I didn't know either," the queen said with menace.

Rigel wisely ignored that remark and went on to tell of the other treachery, the Alathfar game park, and the meeting with the hermit Shaula. Glancing out windows on the far side of the saloon, Avior realized that the barge was slowly floating over a great city. The buildings gleamed pale in the last wisps of dusk, but there were few artificial lights.

"Shaula?" the queen said with a frown. "I don't recall a Shaula. Recorder Matar, that is your specialty."

The green-haired elf played with her collection of bracelets for a moment, seemingly pondering. "Many starborn bear that name. What coloring, Marshal?"

"Bluish."

"Mmm . . . Four blue Shaulas. I recall the subdomain Alathfar, though. I was a guest there a few times, back in the reign of King Procyon. It belonged then to Naos Kurhah, who acquired it from a greatfather of his and extended it enormously and with great skill. Kurhah faded about nine years ago, just short of his thirtieth century. He had inherited several large domains, but instead of leaving them to his children, he divided them between all the starborn with whom he had ever paired." Matar toyed again with her bracelets. "And one beneficiary was a Shaula Starborn, so that fits. She's in about her fourteenth century and is thought to rank yellow or borderline orange in magic."

"How far was the burning cabin from the main house?" the queen asked.

"About a hundred meters . . . elfin paces," Rigel said. "Maybe more."

"Even a high orange could not put out a fire at that range impromptu. A wood-built complex like that would be protected with fire-fighting amulets. We must summon this Shaula to court, too. We shall need to force the root portal. Can you direct Commander Zozma to it?"

"Yes," Rigel said. "But who will force it for you?"

The queen grimaced. "If I cannot trust Mage Fomalhaut, then I am lost."

She paused, and the glow of her aura darkened to more bluish tones. The other collars did not shine in the gloom as hers did. Or change their hues. So the queen wasn't wearing a collar—her own skin must be glowing. Was that the true mark of Naos?

"We have bad news, Marshal. Chancellor Haedus drowned this morning while windsurfing."

Rigel said, "Oh, damn!" His eyes said more, which Avior could not read.

"My cousin Celaeno has agreed to take over his duties pro tem."

"Brave lady!"

At that moment a window in the bow swung open and Izar slid in over the sill. "We're there, Mom! And I'm hungry."

"Council adjourned," Talitha said. "Marshal Rigel, will you please remove this intruder and see that he's put safely to bed? Safely for the rest of the Starlands, I mean."

Back on deck, Avior realized how astonishingly quiet the Starlands were. With no traffic and no wind, the only sounds were a faint hiss from some of the nearer torches and a mutter of voices. Overhead the stars were dazzling in all their glory. Even the clear prairie air of Saskatchewan never let them shine like that.

The barge had come to rest in a large rectangular pool within an excessively formal, rectangular courtyard of Egyptian style.

Statues of animal-headed gods stood sentry along looming stone walls covered in inscriptions. Half a dozen living sphinxes and two centaurs stood guard at the foot of the gangplank, and a dozen human youths held aloft torches that burned brighter than five-hundred-watt light bulbs. Six or seven elves waited in the background.

Avior stayed close to Rigel as he described the location of the root portal to the big sphinx. Then he tentatively offered his arm to her with a sympathetic smile that she would normally have blasted right off his superior-male-juvenile face. But this was not a normal situation, and Rigel seemed to be the only thread of sanity in the nightmare. Besides, it might be the custom of this place. She forced herself to accept, and together they followed Izar down the plank. Running over to one of the statues, which stood at least ten meters high, he slapped one of its enormous toes.

"Open for Starling Izar!"

The statue reached an arm sideways and pushed back a section of wall to make an opening that would have admitted an elephant. Izar went skipping through and the great door closed behind him.

Then Rigel tapped the stone toe. "Halfling Rigel and a trusted visitor. Touch this and say your name, Avior. Good. Now you're authorized."

They walked through the gap into a room that seemed like a bizarre combination of office and stable, with filing cabinets, very high desks, an animal scent, and heaps of straw for napping.

"That was a portal," Rigel said. "Most portals are not kept locked like that one. To go between domains you must travel by air, but you can use portals to go to any other portal within the same domain. We didn't need the barge to get here from

Small Harbor, except that there was no portal close to it. Sometimes short journeys take longer than long ones. May the stars be with you, Officer Praecipua!"

The sphinx he addressed bowed to touch his beard to the pavement. "And with you, Marshal. We were worried when you failed to return."

"I was a lot more worried than you were. Halfling Avior is newly introverted to the Starlands, but has not yet applied for status. Give her a security rank of three for now."

Four sphinxes and two centaurs were scattered around the guard room in various states of repose, but they all rose as if to honor the visitors as Rigel escorted Avior to the far end, where a very large, gilt-framed mirror hung on the wall. Izar had already disappeared.

"Alula," Rigel said, and the mirror dissolved, revealing a carpeted, paneled corridor, lit by hanging lanterns. "How are you for vertigo? Prone to seasickness?"

"I have an iron stomach!" Avior declared confidently.

"Don't your digestive juices corrode it? The reason I ask is that this subdomain is officially known as Alula, but I call it Escher Castle or Vertigo Villa. It takes a little getting used to."

They stepped through the doorway into a wide, luxuriously carpeted and decorated corridor. Rigel paused and diffidently pried her grip off his forearm. She had left white marks there. She had been digging her nails in, too, and must have hurt him.

"Sorry," she muttered. "I didn't realize."

He grinned. "No harm done. I'll grow another. Come along."

The corridor ended at a balcony overlooking a large hall. There were other galleries and several staircases in view, but the sight lines were insane—carpet on the ceiling and windows in the floor, and two great staircases that didn't seem to know if they went up or down. Even as she was trying to make sense of it all, Izar went racing along another balcony in the company of a large and woolly dog—except that they were running on the underside of the balcony, upside down.

Rigel said, "Close your eyes if you have to."

She kept them open. He led the way along another balcony and through a door.

"All this is supposed to be for Izar's protection," he said, "but it's also for mine. There is only the one entrance, and that has five layers of security on it. The building itself sits on a rock in a very turbulent ocean. Can you feel the wind? Sometimes it makes my ears pop. There's a permanent hurricane blowing outside."

"But . . . How far are we from the palace?"

"That question means nothing here. You enter by the portal or not at all. The wind and the changes in orientation make it impossible to come in by air, as much as anything is impossible here."

"But who wants to kill you so badly?"

"The Family. I'll explain more over supper. Hungry?"

She nodded, then wondered if Escher Castle turned nods into shakes. They went along another corridor, which turned left six times before leading into a courtyard. It had to be open to the sky, because she could smell the sea, and hear wind and crashing surf, yet she felt no draft. She was standing at the bottom of a very long flight of stairs, overlooking a wonderful enclosed garden, with winding paths, fruit trees, humped bridges, paved grottoes half-hidden in flowered shrubs, and an Olympic-size swimming pond, in which the imp was flailing along with his dog paddling close behind. The only problem was that the landscape was all vertical. Izar was swimming straight *down*.

"We go up these stairs," Rigel said, leading the way, "although usually it's down. Don't worry about the twists. If they bother you, just close your eyes and wait a few minutes and it will all change. You get the Newcomer Suite, which is as close as we can make it to a first-class earthly hotel. Your maid's name is Tshuapa. Be gentle with her. One word of criticism and she'll cower like a scolded dog. I expect you'll want a swim—"

"No! I'm cold."

"Cold? That's your human half showing. Well, Tshuapa will draw a hot bath for you and find you whatever you want in the way of clothes. When you're ready, I'll meet you by the pool. Get Tshuapa to bring you down. Or up, as the case may be."

Chapter 7

Tshuapa, despite her African-sounding name, turned out to be as Nordic as a glass of akvavit and little more than a child, pathetically eager to please. Avior forced herself to relax, lolling in her titanic veined-marble bathtub, carefully brushing her hair—firmly declining Tshuapa's pleas to be allowed to help. And the sensory magic worked, helping her bury the terror, the insanity. She could feel the knots untie, the coils unwind, and she felt much better by the time she was ready to dress. Tshuapa had laid out no less than eighteen outfits for her to consider and seemed worried that it might not be enough.

Swathed in a cosy, long-sleeved gown of blue velvet and a gypsy-style head cloth, Avior was ready for her date with Rigel. When she peered out the door she was happy to discover that her room was now on the ground floor and she could stroll out into the courtyard without help from Tshuapa or anyone. The path winding between night-scented shrubs was lit by spluttering flaming torches on poles. It led her to a secluded, tree-roofed grotto at the edge of the water, furnished with a table, three chairs, a bronze helmet, and a red bathrobe. She sat down.

She was being manipulated, obviously. Attempted assassination, surreal adventures, and finally the sort of luxury enjoyed by vacationing billionaires. This went far beyond kindness or charity. What did Rigel want from her?

Don't worry. Enjoy.

Out in the water two heads surfaced and disappeared again, apparently in a race. One had elfin ears and she recognized the other's white hair.

Izar and another starling of about the same age were sitting on a rock on the far side of the pool, intent on eating a fish as long as a man's arm—they were tearing chunks out of it, apparently raw. Now Avior knew what those shark teeth were for. Worse, they were sharing their snack with a dog, letting it take bites also. All three seemed very happy with this arrangement.

A liveried human waiter bowed and asked what the noble halfling wished.

"What can I have?"

He looked blank, as if no one had ever asked that question before, and said she could have anything she wanted.

"Rum."

"White or dark?"

"Dark. Make it a triple."

"Anything with it, halfling?"

"A twist of lemon."

He disappeared along the path. The race in the pool was still on, and Rigel appeared to be well ahead. They had not completed another lap before the waiter reappeared with her drink.

She drank half of it in the first gulp and felt it burn its way down inside her, the smoothest lava she'd ever tasted. Before she could take another swig, Rigel erupted from the water, grinning and puffing. He wore only one of the shiny loincloths that seemed to be the national dress. He wiped his face with his hands, put on the helmet, and plopped down on a chair.

"Hope you don't mind," he said. "'No shirt, no shoes, no service' doesn't apply in the Starlands."

"I can stand it." She couldn't imagine how *he* could. She was shivering despite her woolen gown. She should have worn another under it. "Why the Julius Caesar impersonation?"

"The hat, you mean? This is Meissa. It's another amulet. It makes me invisible to magical tricks and booby traps. It's almost the only one of its kind."

The waiter appeared again.

Rigel said, "Beers, please. Two."

"Lager? Ale? Stout? Light? Dark? Small? Bitter? What temperature—"

Rigel ordered a cold lager and a cool dark ale. As the waiter left he glanced at the pool. "Loser does two more laps," he said smugly. "Before Tyl gets here, let me tell you about him. He was one of the Family, but he defected. He's sworn allegiance on the Star of Truth, so he's completely trustworthy. What he did took mega courage, because he was the second defector. The other was a lad named Graffias, who appealed to Regent-heir Kornephoros for asylum, but the regent was an idiot and terrified of Vildiar. Believe it or not, he sent the poor guy back to spy! They spotted his change of allegiance right away, of course. I rescued Graffias but Hadar got to him before he could testify on the Star. Killed him, I mean. So Tyl's . . . Here he is."

The other man surfaced and clambered out. He had Izar-style cat ears and shark teeth, combined with eyes and irises of alizarin crimson, but from the neck down he was all human: nipples, navel, and ample body hair, which was also red-orange.

He looked about thirty, and was shorter and huskier than Rigel, with a beak nose. This, Avior decided, was the best thing she had seen in the Starlands so far, and she watched approvingly as he rubbed excess water off himself with his hands and then pulled on the waiting robe.

He noticed her attention, of course. Men were appallingly predictable.

"Welcome, Halfling Avior," he said between puffs, crimson eyes promising to make the welcome as warm as ever she fancied.

"Pleased to meet you, Halfling Tyl."

By the time Tyl had covered himself, buttoned to the chin, the waiter had returned with the beers, being much speedier than any waiter Avior had ever set eyes on.

"Let's order," Rigel said, taking a gulp of the ale. "I'm famished. What do you fancy?"

"What is there?"

"Anything you want. Vegetarian?"

"Not usually," she said.

"Good. The elves think that's a really bizarre diet, because their teeth aren't much good at it. They never get fat or diabetic and they have no religious prohibitions. Let your imagination soar."

"Why don't you order for all of us?"

"Antipasto, gazpacho, roast suckling pig stuffed with oysters, a selection of vegetables, and a bottle of *blanc de blancs* from Le Mesnil-sur-Oger. We'll decide on dessert later."

Tyl smacked his lips, Avior nodded, and the waiter departed. Was this really how halflings lived in the Starlands?

"Suppose I asked for dragon ribs?" she asked.

"We'd need a bigger table," Rigel said solemnly. "Let's get the business done before the food arrives. Tyl, she knows about the guilt curse and Naos magic. I haven't told her much about your father or the Family."

"Nasty story," Tyl said and drank some beer. He let the loose sleeves of his robe fall back so she could admire the red thatch on his thick wrists. "You understand that starborn never die? Eventually they fade. After a few thousand years they lose interest, give away their domains, are seen less often, and finally never. But when the ruler goes, he or she has to bequeath the entire Starlands realm to a successor, who must be another Naos. With me so far? Usually there are thirty or forty Naos around to choose from, but V—that's my father, Naos Vildiar—was very anxious to succeed Electra when she eventually faded. Not liking the odds, he decided to kill off all the other claimants. He didn't dare do it himself because of the guilt curse. Mudlings can't be used as assassins because they're tools, and the guilt for their crimes falls on those who command them. But halflings have free will and the guilt curse has no power over us, whether we kill an elf or vice versa. That's why we're the bodyguards and assassins of the Starlands."

Rigel held up his—hairless, slender—right wrist to reveal the Saiph bracelet and Avior nodded.

So did Tyl. "Even so, V has to be careful not to issue a direct order to kill anyone. He needed halflings. He also had, or cultivated, a fetish for human women. He set out to breed himself an army."

She had already guessed that the Family must be something like that. "How long has he been at it?"

"A couple of centuries. Hadar, the current leader, was born in 1851, but he looks no more than thirty by human standards. We tweenlings have hybrid vigor, and we live six or seven times as long as earthlings."

Although Avior was accustomed to compliments on her youthfulness, she had never considered celebrating her five hundredth birthday.

"We're also sterile," Tyl added thoughtfully.

Yes, she already knew what he was hoping for.

"We knew all this, generally speaking," Rigel said, either missing or ignoring the code under the plaintext. "But Tyl brought us a lot of new details. Phegda, Vildiar's domain, is enormous. He must own hundreds of millions of mudlings, so we just assumed he raided his slave barns to make his halflings."

"The product wasn't good enough," Tyl said, pulling a face. "Mudlings are insipid compared to earthlings—human wild stock, I mean—and their crosses rarely yielded the savagery that V needed. They lacked drive and passion."

He did not, of course. With the merest roll of her eyes to acknowledge his continuing hints, Avior emptied her glass. She could feel the alcohol starting to work, but a refill would be welcome.

Tyl smiled. "My job all last year was seancing Earth, looking for pretty girls who slept alone. Just about every night, V extroverts there and rapes one or two. None of them can resist his magic. None see him as he truly is. Even if he only visits a girl once, there's another department of the Family who keeps watch to see if she bears a halfling child. Miscegenation is rarely successful, but he harvests a few halflings a year. They're exchanged for mudling babies from Phegda."

"That's the old legend of changelings come true," Rigel commented as the waiter delivered the antipasto and an ice bucket.

Tyl drained his lager. "And then the mudling mother and her foster baby are moved to the crèche at Unukalhai, one of his subdomains. When the child is five, the mother is sent away and the child is reared by its half sisters and later half brothers."

There was a pause.

Avior was quite certain that she was being manipulated and this was payoff time. "You told me that the Family 'seances' the world, if that's the right term, for halflings."

Tyl nodded. "And we're distinctive. Once you've seen one of us, you can't mistake the rest—something about the eyes. Once in a while one of V's victims moves away and the supervision squad loses track of her. So unless she aborts the fetus, she will bear a halfling child unknown to us. Unknown to the Family, I mean."

"We found you," Rigel said, "because Tyl knew that the Family had located a halfling in Saskatchewan, but was just ignoring her. It took us a couple of months to find you. The Family had still done nothing about you. We decided, if you will pardon the insult, that you did not look sufficiently savage for their needs. You had missed out on their monster training."

She found that funny, or perhaps the rum did. The boys at art school had called her the black widow, although she was neither black nor a widow. Or the Dragon Lady. Many had accepted her challenge; most had gotten much more than they'd bargained for.

Rigel looked puzzled by her amusement, but when she did not comment, he went on. "Now I suspect that Hadar was trolling you as bait for me, and I bit when I decided to rescue you." He paused expectantly.

There it was again, and not very subtle, either.

"All right," she said. "I'll tell you. Very briefly and just once. I have no idea who my father was. My mother belonged to a rich ranching family in Argentina. When she became inexplicably pregnant, they quickly married her off to a visiting Venezuelan, who could have given your Vildiar lessons in sheer nastiness. I was born in Caracas. So, yes, Halfling Tyl, I may very well be one of your half sisters. As far as I am concerned, I have no family whatsoever. And I will not discuss it again." After a lifetime of trying to forget, she would not start digging up corpses now. She lifted her glass with a shaky hand and remembered it was empty.

The waiter appeared with the champagne and three flutes.

Tyl nodded sadly. "It's very likely. What V has been doing is a major crime. He ought to have been sent to the Dark Cells for it a thousand times over. No other starborn does it."

"Tell her about your childhood," Rigel said. "What she missed."

Avior protested. "I don't want to hear!" She drained her champagne.

"You don't," Tyl agreed. "The three Rs taught at Unukalhai are Ravishing, Reliability, and Ruthlessness. The insufficiently vicious are used for practice." He reached for a handful of olives. "About twenty years ago, V decided his army was large enough, and the slaughter began."

"They killed these Naos people?"

"Some faded, a few may have died in genuine accidents, but the others were all killed except for Talitha and Izar—and Vildiar himself. V never orders a criminal act, you understand. He can still proclaim his innocence on the Star itself. Hadar and Botein pick up on his hints and know what's needed. When Queen Electra was dying of the guilt curse, she had to choose between Vildiar and Talitha, who is still in her first century and far too young for the job. But Electra knew Vildiar was an unthinkable choice."

"Rigel!" Izar announced, slouching in. "I'm tired!" A very large, smelly, wet dog came bounding after him and was intercepted by Tyl just before it pillaged the antipasto.

Rigel laughed. "Does that surprise you? Come on, then. Excuse us, all." He scooped Izar up and slung him over his shoulder in a fireman's lift. "Heel, Turais." The dog followed, wagging vigorously.

That left Avior alone with Tyl, who grinned at her and raised his champagne glass in a silent toast. Laying Rigel would be cradle robbing, but Tyl was available as her *lover du nuit.*

"So you and I are brother and sister?" she murmured, laying down her empty glass.

He refilled it. "Who knows?" He shrugged and smiled. "Who cares?"

How old was he? Twenty-ish like Rigel or forty-ish like her? Who cared?

"Not me." She offered her glass. He clinked it with his. Deal made.

"What else can I tell you?" he asked.

"What made you decide to defect? How could anyone who was raised as you were develop a conscience?"

"Rigel." Tyl chewed and swallowed. "Rigel's arrival changed everything. One day, out of the blue, we heard that the legendary Saiph had turned up on the wrist of a wild-stock halfling. That would be a deadly combination even with a lesser man than he. Hadar decided to steal it, although he knew perfectly well that a defensive amulet like Saiph cannot be stolen without killing its bearer first. Hadar tried to do just that and very nearly killed Talitha and Izar in the process. Talitha was so impressed with Rigel's prowess that she appointed him to be Izar's bodyguard.

"The Family had ruled the roost for twenty years with hardly a bruise to show for it. Then within a couple of days, it lost eight people, thanks to Rigel. Now it's started again—this afternoon they set up an ambush to kill him and lost three more."

"But Rigel didn't kill them! Izar's dragon did." She could see Rigel and the dog walking up a wall.

"I didn't say he did. He didn't kill all the eight, either. Starborn Fomalhaut is the ranking mage in the Starlands. He gave Imp Izar a Lesath amulet. That was an insanely irresponsible, criminal act!"

"The dragon, Edasich?"

Tyl chuckled. "No, a dog named Turais. The present Turais is just a dog; the first one, his namesake, was a nightmare. But why in the stars did Fomalhaut do that? I think it was because of Rigel. Like most starfolk, Fomalhaut despises halflings as part animal, but he's a red mage and probably has a powerful prescience. He sensed this new boy was a mover of mountains. Rigel is as deadly as the queen on a chessboard. Avior, the kid has worn Saiph all his life! Literally since the hour he was born. That amulet has shaped him, made him into the warrior it needs. If you want to see what reflexes and agility are, try him on the squash court. Or tennis. My brother Thabit's a fantastic tennis player and I'm just as good, but Rigel can beat the pair of us together. I could break him in half in hand-to-hand, except he'd have a lock on me before I touched him."

His reflexes hadn't saved him from her punch on the dock.

"Rigel soon proved that he was a game changer. The day he arrived here in Canopus, he stormed V's house on Front Street singlehandedly and took on Tarf, Adhil, Muscida, and Hadar. All of them wore top-rated sword amulets, but the new boy with the sword gave Hadar the worst fright of his life and killed the other three. Hadar only barely escaped, and Rigel almost got him the next day. Hadar claims to fear nothing, but he's terrified of Wonder Boy."

Avior tried to equate this blood-and-thunder story with the diffident youth with whom she'd spent the afternoon. Tyl was not on the Star of Truth now, but he seemed sincere, and she could not imagine Rigel arranging to have his praises sung this way. The testimony was genuinely felt, if not necessarily correct. The constant reminders of Rigel's youth were just to keep her from changing her mind about the late show.

"He seems very loyal to the queen," she said.

"Ha! The rumor has it that the court mage, Fomalhaut, has prophesied that he will die very soon if he remains in the Starlands, but he won't leave Talitha."

"How does she feel about him?"

Tyl's leer was answer enough. He took a sip of champagne. "She certainly keeps anyone else's hands from getting too close to him."

The hints were coming at her like snowflakes in a blizzard. "She's the queen, isn't she?"

"Yes, but even queens can't indulge in gross indecency, which is what balling a halfling would be. The starfolk can accept him as Izar's bodyguard, because they all know why the imp needs a bodyguard and why an elf would be no good. They are deeply resentful that she made him marshal of Canopus, but most of them can see that he's doing a good job. The sphinxes and centaurs worship him. But not in a thousand years will the starborn ever tolerate a half-breed as the queen's gigolo."

"His mother was the previous queen?"

"Yes, but she only confessed to copulating with a mudling when she was minutes away from dying. It was the scandal of centuries, and it has made them all watch Talitha that much more closely. And since the guilt curse doesn't apply to killing halflings, very soon it will be bye-bye, Rigel Halfling. I think that today the court mage tried to fulfill his own prophecy."

Then the loyal, lovesick superman in question came trotting back, closely followed by laden waiters, and conversation took a backseat to the best food Avior had ever tasted, bar none. They finished the champagne, with her doing most of the work, and Rigel ordered another bottle. When talk resumed, it was about travel plans that needed to be postponed because court would be held on the morrow. Avior had gathered by then that Tyl and the unseen Thabit were Rigel's deputies in guarding Izar, and that the starling's instructors were educating Rigel as well.

"He'll throw a tantrum at missing the buffalo roundup," Tyl remarked.

Rigel grinned. "So will I. Let's tell him that someone's going to tell lies on the Star of Truth. That'll reel him in."

"Or that he may be called as a witness. The little terror would love the attention."

Avior waited for some discussion of her future. It did not come, so she asked.

"You haven't told me the real reason why you rescued me, and what you want of me."

"Just like I told you; we try to save all the halflings we can find." Rigel was not a good liar.

"Stack of bibles?"

He grinned. "Small stack. That was reason enough, I swear."

"But . . . ?"

"But I have to kill Prince Vildiar. On Earth he would be called a psychopath. He's a serial killer with a private army, and he's also the strongest starborn mage alive. I've done quite well in the past against his goons, but Vildiar himself is in another class altogether. I had my sword at his back once and his defenses were too strong even for Saiph. Maybe if he were to attack me—because Saiph is a defensive amulet, not an assassin's weapon . . ."

"Why you?"

He grinned. "I'm a megalomaniac. I know it has to be me."

"What happened to the person who was windsurfing, the one the queen mentioned?"

"Her prime minister, Chancellor Haedus," Rigel said, pulling a face. "Elves don't die unless they meet with nasty accidents, and they do tend to take risks that would be absurd for humans. But they can be murdered. The queen and I have been wondering what Hadar's next move will be."

Tyl said, "Oh, crap! You think Hadar's starting in on the cabinet?"

Rigel emptied his glass. "We expected it, and even if he didn't order Haedus's death, this'll surely put the idea in his head. If the queen's ministers start dying in quick succession, the rest will flee. Starborn are just not built to withstand violence; it's too foreign to their thinking. The ruler's duties are amazingly light, but Talitha cannot govern alone. So I'm running out of time to rid the Starlands of Prince Vildiar."

"And me?" Avior asked. "Where do I fit into this bloodbath?"

He evaded the question with a shrug. "You make your decision first, to stay or go home. There are no conditions on the offer. You can decide tomorrow or wait awhile. If you do stay, you might be able to help us—nothing risky or violent. The court tomorrow should be interesting. I'll call for you when it's time."

Perhaps he didn't trust Halfling Tyl quite as much as he said he did. He had certainly not told her everything, far from it. But suddenly she was struggling to choke back a yawn.

"'Scuse me," she mumbled. "I think today has gone on quite long enough."

That was the signal to open the rutting season. Tyl brightened and gripped the arms of his chair, but Rigel was already on his feet.

"All's well that ends well. I'll see you safely to your room."

Chapter 8

After all that champagne, Avior was disinclined to risk the journey by herself, for her door was now in the roof. She had not been offered a choice of companion, but she flashed Tyl a wink behind Rigel's back to let him know that she'd still be interested in exploring orange body hair just as soon as she disposed of the beanpole American Express logo in sandwich wrap.

Seemingly unaware, Rigel led the way. He was careful not to touch her, and the world duly rearranged itself around them. They arrived at her door without any embarrassing incidents such as her falling flat on her face. Overhead, the waiters were clearing the table they had just left and Tyl was in the pool again, floating on his back, staring down at her.

"See you in court tomorrow," Rigel said, smiling inside his absurd helmet. "It should be very educational."

"I have nothing else on my calendar." She reached for the handle. "You don't want to come in?"

What she meant was, *I need a man now, and you know you're only a boy, don't you?* It might have been the champagne, or maybe it was the rum, but the words didn't come out with quite the emphasis she'd intended, and Rigel beamed a huge smile.

"Love to!"

He advanced eagerly. She backed up. He closed the door while he still had his back to it and she heard the lock click, so perhaps he was not quite as unobservant as she'd believed.

Now she had to deal with a blinding close-up of gleaming, pearly teeth, as Rigel waited politely for her to confirm what she had just implied. But his eyes were no longer white to match the teeth; they were all black iris, and bright as diamonds. He had his chest out, chin in, and his already flat abdomen was pulled in against his spine. Fists rested on his hips to display his arm muscles, and he was standing much closer to her than before. Possibly this was all unconscious, but she was an artist, an observer. Whether he knew it or not, Rigel Halfling's body was announcing in fanfares that it was now available for DNA transfer.

Where are you when we need you, Queen Talitha?

So be it. Despite his schoolboy looks, he was a killer, no cherub. He could, presumably, hold his own. He'd shown an interesting streak of ruthlessness earlier, and a lesson in humility wouldn't hurt him, if that was all he was going to get. She had to outweigh him by fifty pounds.

"Just wanted to ask a personal question," he said. "If you don't mind. Why do you wear a wig?"

Whatever she had expected, it wasn't that. "I do mind."

"Oh. Sorry. Well, pleasant dreams, then. Mustn't keep Tyl waiting." He was actually blushing, and she could not remember when she had last seen a man do that. The body language had all been unconscious.

"Wait! You invited yourself in. I'm going to be powerfully insulted if you just turn around and walk out."

He smiled nervously. "A goodnight kiss, then?" He pulled her into his meter-long arms and kissed her as she hadn't been kissed since she'd deflowered virgins in middle school. She bit his lip hard and raked his back with all ten nails. He yelled and broke loose, staring at her in dismay.

"Jesus, lady! What was that for?" He rubbed his back with his hand and examined the smear of blood.

"For not knowing how to kiss a woman. Come here."

He backed off. "I'm sure Tyl will appreciate the lesson more than me."

Never mind Tyl. This promised to be fun.

"Then I'll answer your personal question if you'll answer one of mine." She dragged off her wig to show him the scar tissue around the auditory canal openings high on her head.

Most men reacted with revulsion, but Rigel just nodded. "I suspected something like that. What did they do to you, for God's sake?"

"He cut them off. Every time they grew back, he cut them off again. Later he burned them, and that worked better. My mother held me down."

Rigel shuddered. "It's illegal to make a halfling look like a starborn, but healing injuries is okay. I think magic could make your ears grow back—elf ears, of course, not human. If you decide to stay. We can ask." He hesitated. "What was your question?"

She took hold of his waistband. "You're very tall. I want to see if you're well proportioned." She investigated. The bulge already felt promising.

He detached her hands but did not release them. "I'm sorry. It would be really fun, but I am promised elsewhere."

Who wrote his script: Jane Austen?

"One kiss, I insist! You owe me that much. But dump that bucket first!"

"Just one. Kissing 101, but no further than—" He removed the helmet. "Oh, hell! No! Sorry, gotta go."

Then she saw those celebrated reflexes in action again. Faster than a cat he had unlocked the door and disappeared.

Chapter 9

He slammed the door on Avior's spray of abuse. Tyl was still nursing a drink on the patio terrace, halfway up one wall. Giving him a wave to indicate that the coast was now clear, Rigel tore off along the balcony, hoping the gashes on his back weren't too visible. The alarm ring on his left index finger burned like fire. He gave it a twist to end the signal. When Avior had asked him about his stealth helmet earlier that evening, he had mentioned its name, Meissa, and that had activated it until the moment he took it off.

Why had he been naive enough to step into Avior's bedroom without realizing what she would expect? To add injury to humiliation, his frustration was already showing up as a sickening ache in his groin, just like when he'd tried to pass as a human boy with human girls. It had never worked. And although nothing more had happened this time, he felt a barrel-load of guilt. He had betrayed Talitha, despite all his protestations of love. They had sworn no oaths of celibacy, but the understanding was there. Her council was still trying to bully her into pairing with a highborn elf just to quash the rumors. So far she was still refusing, but why should she keep that up if he was going around kissing female tweenlings?

Avior was seriously weird, but that was forgivable, given her background, and her weirdness was exactly what might make her useful in his campaign against Vildiar, assuming that she would want to help him after tonight.

He sprinted all the way to the roof exit, which happened to be downstairs at the moment. Out on the roof, the wind struck him like a tsunami. The sea itself was a vertical wall, with waves rushing upward to break on a dark and rocky sky, but the wind at his back swept him along to the corner turret at the far side of the castle in about eight seconds flat.

The door knew him and opened for him. With a blast of rain and storm he burst into Izar's bedroom and wrestled the door closed. Turais sleepily thumped his tail on the floor. Izar was curled up in a tiny ball at the far end of his bed, eyes wide with fright, keeping as far away as possible from Thabit, who was sitting on the chair, obviously having little success in calming the imp.

"You weren't there!" Izar cried. "The parrot started screaming and I used my signal ring and you didn't come!"

Rigel wiped rain off his face with an arm and picked his way through the inevitable clutter. "I'm here now. Go back to sleep or put your wrap on. What's the trouble?" he asked Thabit. He could hear the parrot still squawking downstairs.

Thabit rose and yawned. "She wants you," he said. "Won't respond to me."

Thabit was Tyl's identical twin, and just as hairy. He had a towel wrapped around his loins, but that wasn't enough; he knew better than to let Izar see him like that. The imp's irrational dread of body hair dated from the childhood years he had spent with Hadar and his innumerable other half brothers. Male starborn were no hairier than their female counterparts, but tweenlings could take after their mothers' male ancestors.

Rigel cursed and descended the spiral staircase by balancing on his hands on the rails and sliding. He almost fell flat on his face when he reached what was officially his bedroom, although either Tyl or Thabit occupied it when he wasn't there. This was the first night he hadn't been and, of course, the first time Talitha had ever called for him.

On a gold stand in the corner the mechanical parrot was shrieking his name and flapping polychrome wings. Anywhere else in the royal city of Canopus messages were carried by harpies, but even harpies could not fly to Vertigo Villa.

"I'm here," Rigel said.

The parrot stopped flapping. "Where were you?" Its voice was that of Queen Talitha in a towering rage.

Thabit and Izar had come hurrying down the stairs after him and would hear whatever he said. Even Turais was with them.

"I was with a friend, Your Majesty. What can I do for you?"

"You can guard my son as you swore you would!"

Thabit laughed softly and threw himself backward, landing on the bed spread-eagled.

"I'm all right, Mom," Izar said in a voice of innocence, leering at Rigel. "And he doesn't look as if he's come to harm." The imp clearly thought he could guess what Rigel had been doing with the friend, and was amused that his guard had been caught playing hookey. "'Cept for the blood on his back. And his lip's all swollen."

"And the hickeys," Thabit murmured, although Rigel knew there were none.

"What're hickeys?" Izar the Terrible asked loudly.

"I'm at Fornacis," the parrot snapped. "Come here at once."

"No!" Rigel protested. "You can't trust—"

The bird closed its jeweled eyes and tucked its cloisonné head under a silken wing as if going to sleep. Rigel glanced at Izar's shock and Thabit's frown.

"Don't go!" Izar squeaked. "We were betrayed there yesterday."

"Maybe," Rigel conceded, wondering what Talitha was up to now. She was prone to making snap judgments, but a queen must be obeyed.

"Don't leave me!" Izar moved closer while keeping a wary eye on Thabit.

"Get dressed!" Rigel snapped at Thabit. He would have ordered the twins to shave their chests if the Starlands possessed any grooming aids other than cutthroat razors and ordinary soap. Elves did not even need combs. "No, wait."

He must make his own snap judgment. One beer and one glass of champagne should not be enough to warp his judgment much. Yesterday a trap to dispose of him had been sprung in Fornacis; today there might be another complicated plot to separate him from Izar for good. Taking the imp along would be doing the unexpected, always a good idea. Besides, Saiph and Edasich were an unbeatable combination of defenders, and Izar would do what Rigel told him, which he wouldn't for anyone else. Made sense.

"All right. Let's go, Izar. *Turais, stay!* You're off duty, Thabit." Rigel headed for the door, Izar trotting along at his heels.

He did not suggest that Tyl might need help, but the thought crossed his mind.

Out in the musty-scented guard room, Kalb Sphinx and Muhlifain Centaur crouched on the floor, playing chess. Other guards of both species lay dozing on straw, but all heads rose as Marshal Rigel and Imp Izar trotted through. Rigel called out their destination on his way past them. Since Saidak was almost certainly at Fornacis with Talitha by now, he opened the portal to Mabsuthat and stepped through into one of the strangest places he knew in the Starlands.

The sky was starlit but moonless, so the land should be dark, but trees in Mabsuthat glowed with a silvery phosphorescence. The grass underfoot was as soft as mohair, the breeze bore scents of exotic spices, and the massive boulders and menhirs that dotted the glade took turns at humming sad, uncanny melodies. In short, Mabsuthat fairly crackled with magic, as befitted the royal hippogriff ranch. Even stranger creatures were reputed to lurk in the woods, so that wandering far from the portal was unwise, but Rigel had never needed to.

The great dark shape pacing forward to meet him was Kitalphar, the hippogriff who usually consented to transport him and always seemed to know when he needed her. She was capable of refusing, just as she was capable of biting his head off or ripping him apart with her talons.

He bowed to her. "Imp Izar and I have been summoned to Fornacis, Your Ferocity, and would be greatly indebted if you would consent to transport us."

Kitalphar bowed her eagle head in gracious acceptance. She turned her tail to him, spread her great wings, and crouched so that he could scramble aboard and lift Izar up. Her front half was eagle and her rear half horse, both halves a glossy black, but no horse ever foaled or bird ever hatched could have contributed parts of adequate size. Hippogriff riding was a dicey sport. Kitalphar's great beak would bite through any girth, and probably take off the hands of anyone stupid enough to try to saddle her; she would certainly snap a steel bit like a pretzel. She had no mane on her great neck, only plumage, which she would not allow a rider to grip. Fortunately a crest of tough hair along her back provided a precarious handhold. The posture was a wide straddle for even Rigel's long legs, and Izar preferred to kneel in front of him.

Luckily Kitalphar's ride was as smooth as a boat on a pond. Without ever flapping her enormous wings, she soared up into the night like a balloon, buoyed up solely by magic. Silent and graceful, she banked slightly as she turned to the east.

"How come," Izar grumbled, leaning over dangerously, "I can see stars *below* Mabsuthat? It has an *edge*, see? You don't have to hold me so tight. Why can't I see daylight down there if the sun goes there at night?"

"Dunno," his guardian countered. "You're the expert on magic. Is that a lake?"

"It's either a lake or a hole right through," Izar decided. He wriggled around to peer past the other side of the hippogriff's great feathered neck. "*Stop* squeezing my arm!"

"It's either that or flying lessons, imp," Rigel said.

The presence of a direct highway between Canopus and Fomalhaut's Fornacis made the journey brief, but it crossed a significant boundary, because Fornacis was rooted in Prince Vildiar's domain of Phegda. That made Fomalhaut one of the prince's underlings. While the starfolk insisted that the relationship between overlord and underling might have mattered eons ago but now was merely ceremonial, they continued to recognize it. They could all recite their own overlords all the way up to the queen herself, and they deferred to them. Talitha was convinced that her court mage was totally loyal to her, but either Fomalhaut or his pupil Mizar must have rigged Rigel's reversion staff to trap him in Alathfar.

Starborn with highly ranked magic competed to see who could imagine the most fantastical yet convincing domains, and Fomalhaut was a mage of the red who had been at the game for thousands of years. From the outside, Fornacis was a scattering of ancient-looking stone buildings perched on the rim of a volcanic caldera. At first glance the grouping appeared unimpressive, a deserted hamlet of peasant hovels, but that was deliberate—a sort of reverse snobbery. What afficionados would notice was that it was convincingly natural, as if the buildings had grown out of the slaggy black landscape. That artless look ironically took great skill to create. Even the obligatory swimming hole did not seem as improbable as a lake on a rocky mountaintop should. Eastward the huge dome sloped gently away to a distant ocean, where stars were starting to vacate the sky in expectation of dawn. On the other side was a sheer drop into a vast crater, whose flat, basalt floor was home to dragons and salamanders. Glowing fountains played in the central lava lake.

As Kitalphar glided in, a pair of patrolling griffins swung close to inspect the newcomers, then veered away again. That was evidence that Talitha was indeed there, and soon Rigel made out the royal barge on the pond, and then a couple of sphinxes patrolling the enclave. He felt hungry and sleep deprived. That thought made him yawn.

"Who were you humping?" Izar demanded. "Avior Tweenling?"

"Mind your own business!"

"Thought so. Pretty fast work! Good ride, huh?"

"That does it, Potty Mouth! No buffalo roundup for you today."

Izar moved one bony shoulder in a half-shrug. "Good. I wanna go to court and watch Mom fry whoever tried to squidge us yesterday. Why're you laughin'?"

Chapter 10

The landscape was all black lava, rugged and sharp, and at first glance completely barren, although closer inspection would reveal myriads of tiny orchids hiding in the crevices like colored stars. The buildings were low and as dark as the rocks.

Izar leaped down. Dismounting more gracefully, Rigel thanked Kitalphar for the ride. She acknowledged his gratitude with a dignified nod and launched upward, soaring into the pearly dawn sky. Saidak would take him back to Canopus.

Commander Zozma came bounding toward them, massive paws throwing up spurts of black sand. He stopped abruptly, staring at Rigel.

"You smell of blood."

"It's my own." Probably his medical amulets had healed his scratches already, but he should have taken a minute to swim.

Izar sniggered.

"Her Majesty is impatient, Marshal," the sphinx growled. "I recommend haste." He spun around and loped off at a pace that made the two bipeds run to keep up with him. He led them to a small, windowless shed built of undressed lava rocks with a low slate roof sagging badly in the middle. The kennel-height plank door swung open on its own. Even Izar had to duck under the lintel; Rigel needed to bend double to fit through. When he straightened up, reality had suffered another dimensional twist, for he was now in what Fomalhaut called his laboratory, which was really a showroom, filled with wonders to impress visitors.

Whether it was indoors or outdoors was debatable. The space was as large as a football stadium, open to the breathtaking moonless night sky of the Starlands. Even at noon yesterday there had been no sign of sun in here, and yet the interior was always bright as midday. The walls comprised a circle of massive stone monoliths, topped with a ring of capping stones, like Stonehenge only much larger. Every gap looked out on different scenery—beaches, jungle rivers, snow-capped mountains, village streets—some in bright sunlight, others at night or under monsoon rains. The floor was a polished mosaic of cabalistic symbols that changed surreptitiously, like the writing on Saiph.

Jaded by terrestrial technology, Rigel found it all rather juvenile, but Izar thought it was a wonderful place to visit. He laughed aloud as he saluted a suit of golden armor standing just inside the door and it returned the gesture. A dozen or so of these metal guardians stood scattered around, and once in a while they would trade places in a stiff, clanking march.

Talitha was visible over at the far side, in the seancing court, and Rigel herded Izar in that direction, keeping to the perimeter to avoid some less trustworthy wonders on display. The pool of black water periodically swirled as if large things swam just below the surface; the pentagonal hearth burned with dark blue flames cold enough to make even a starborn shiver; and so on. The centerpiece was a stupendous pendulum that

Fomalhaut called the Time of Life, a crystal disk about five meters across, suspended on a rod that hung from the night sky. It should have been possible to calculate the height of the pivot from the period of the pendulum, but this was not Earth and the period seemed to vary. At the moment the rod was close to vertical, the bottom edge of the disk near the ground and imperceptibly sinking.

"Come away from that!" Rigel yelled.

"Aw, just a peek . . ."

"No! Come here, *starling*. You heard what the mage told you yesterday."

They had an agreement: When Rigel called him "starling," Izar had to obey instantly. Any other time he was free to choose and, although he might still be punished for any wrongdoings, disobedience would not be listed on the charge sheet. He accepted the terms because Rigel never abused them.

The seancing court was a circle of multicolored mosaic, surrounded by a low parapet, a toddlers' paddling pool without water. In the center a sphere of crystal about a meter and a half in diameter was mounted on a silver plinth that put its top at about head height for an elf. A male starborn stood beside it, embracing it, hands and forehead pressed to the crystal. His unusual sea-green hair identified him as Mizar, one of Fomalhaut's assistants. Standing beside him with her eyes closed and a hand on his arm was Queen Talitha. Izar ran forward to join the group.

Rigel followed at a slower pace, but found his way blocked by the menacing figure of Fomalhaut himself, a tall golden-haired elf wearing his court mage's disk collar of opals and pearls in honor of the queen's visit. Fomalhaut was a starborn of the old school, although that meant very little because they all were, and he had disliked Rigel since the day they first met in a Wal-Mart store. When he learned that the halfling was Queen Electra's by-blow, dislike had ripened into loathing. And when the new queen appointed the mongrel to one of the highest offices in the land, loathing had become abhorrence.

Rigel halted and bowed, arms out. "May the stars shine on you forever, Starborn Fomalhaut."

The mage did not offer the customary formal reply. "Halfling, I just want you to know you that I did not tamper with your reversion staff yesterday."

This was an astonishing concession for him, almost an apology.

"I thank you for telling me, my lord."

"I will so testify today on the Star of Truth."

"For me that is not necessary. I would never doubt your word."

For a moment the elf just stared down at him with his lip curled in distaste. Then he said, "Then why do you not believe me when I tell you that I foresee imminent death for you if you remain in the Starlands?"

"Within months, you said. I did extrovert yesterday. Has that changed your prediction?"

"No. You returned. Your fate will be the same."

"Still months?"

"Nearer weeks."

Not good news. "Thank you, starborn, but my answer must remain that I am bound to serve Her Majesty and Imp Izar. A long life has no appeal if it is to be marred by shame."

"Idiot!" Rejecting the suggestion that a half-blood could have a sense of honor, the elf spun on his heel and strode back to the seancing court. He laid a hand on Mizar's arm. A moment later Rigel arrived, spoke his name for the benefit of the others, and connected to the seance by grasping Fomalhaut's shoulder.

As soon as he closed his eyes he was back on Earth, hurtling along a street roaring with busy traffic, a disembodied and invisible presence flying just above head height. Mizar, who was directing this trip, was following a black SUV, which slowed for a green light, then swung around to make a dangerous left turn through a gap in the oncoming traffic. The move caught Mizar by surprise, so the perspective wavered unsteadily, passing through a furniture van—whose interior was predictably dark—before speeding forward to catch the disappearing quarry.

Rigel heard Izar say, "Wow!" as if from very far away, barely audible over the sound of traffic.

"About time you got here, halfling!" That was the queen. "Identify this location."

Rigel knew he was deep in the skunk pen when she called him that. He looked up at the buildings whizzing by and then over at the street signs. It was early on a hot summer morning, and the road reeked of exhaust fumes. There was a plane coming in overhead.

"It's Calgary," he said, "where Izar and I were yesterday. Heading east. If you're following some members of the Family, I'd guess that they're skipping town. I wonder why they didn't leave right after the art gallery disaster."

"They had some business to tidy up," Talitha said angrily. "Tell us where they're going."

"Back to Saskatchewan, likely. If they were staking out Avior as bait for me, their headquarters must be in or near Regina. That's the city where she lived. When she brought her work to the show in Calgary, they would have followed. Or at least some of them would have."

There was silence for a while. The road widened as it emerged from the older section of town, beginning to look more like a highway. A turnoff sign to the Deerfoot Trail confirmed Rigel's identification of the route, if not necessarily the destination.

"Mintaka's the passenger," Talitha said. "I don't know the driver. Pull right inside and let Izar have a look at her."

The SUV had sped up and was passing all other traffic, weaving in and out. Mizar tracked it closely, and Rigel found the effect dizzying. He wondered if starfolk were immune to motion sickness.

"First," he said, "can you give us a look backward, please, starborn?"

The mage ignored the halfling's request. The point of view continued to race after the SUV, moving steadily closer to its back window.

"Why do you want that?" Talitha demanded.

"Because I think I can hear a siren. The Mounties are . . ." No, this was still inside city limits, so the Mounties might be assembling somewhere ahead, outside the city. "The police may be after them."

"Worse!" the queen said. "Much worse. Show us, mage."

"What Your Majesty requests is not easy," Fomalhaut muttered, and the scene lurched and spun several times before Mizar had them racing backward along the highway. Even then, the ground sloped sharply to the left.

Yes, there were flashing lights in the distance. "They won't give chase," Rigel said. "It's too dangerous. They'll radio ahead and close the highway. What have they done—the halflings, I mean—to get the cops on their tail?"

Silence. Seancing Earth was legal, unlike actually extroverting there, because seancers could do nothing to influence events or make themselves known. As genuine reality TV, it was a popular pastime with some starborn but that didn't mean they always understood everything they saw. The scene twisted around to a forward view again, but the fugitives had drawn a long way ahead. Mizar jumped the view a kilometer or so and started to close in on them again.

"What have they got in the vehicle, then?" Rigel asked.

"Guns," Fomalhaut said. "They stopped at a place with many small houses around a yard, and they loaded up with guns. At the time we thought someone in the guardroom was watching them."

Not a guardroom, more likely a motel office. The survivors of the attack on Rigel were destroying evidence of their crime; being machinery, guns could not be introverted to the Starlands.

The SUV's back window loomed in front of them, and they were once again surrounded by the sound of tires on the asphalt and a stench of exhaust. The luggage in the back was hidden under a blue tarpaulin, and the man in the passenger seat had twisted around in an attempt to extract something. He wore a red turban to hide his ears, but his face had a Nordic pallor and his eyebrows were gold. Given the way the vehicle was weaving in and out of traffic, Mizar was having trouble stabilizing the point of view, but Rigel recognized the passenger instantly.

"That's Mintaka!" Izar said. "I hate him, hate him!"

"So do we all, love," his mother said. "He's very bad."

Mintaka succeeded in throwing off the cover, revealing a heap of automatic or semiautomatic firearms. What he was after was underneath them and he had to rummage to find it. "Got it!" he shouted, his voice sounding abnormally loud to the watchers in the seance court.

"That's a reversion staff!" Rigel said. "They're going to blow."

"Blow what?" asked Izar.

"Introvert out of there. Can they use a staff sitting down?"

When Mizar did not answer, Fomalhaut said, "They may try. But if they can't straighten out parallel to the staff, they may leave bits of themselves behind."

Their vantage point crept forward and twisted to show the driver's face, which was screwed up in a rictus of concentration or just plain terror. A Starlands halfling could not have much experience driving a car and she was well over the speed limit now, tearing along the highway. Her features were nondescript and quite human-looking, but she had the unmistakable something-about-the-eyes that spelled "halfling." Whether or not she had a navel or iron-hard feet, her lack of obvious elfin features would make her especially useful to the Family for extroverting missions. She might be a resident agent, or just part of a team assembled to collect the weaponry and prepare to ambush Rigel.

"That's Alkes!" Izar said. "I never liked her much, but she wasn't as bad as Mintaka, or Hadar, or Botein, or . . . *Huh?*"

The view swung around to check on Mintaka, who had just reclined his seat so he could stretch out, his body approximately straight if not flat. He was holding the reversion staff on top of him.

"What're you doing?" Alkes shouted, frantically dividing her attention between the road and her companion.

"G'bye, sister. Gotta fly."

"Bastard! You wait for me, you—"

She reached a hand for the staff. Brakes squealed. She screamed; he swore. The SUV vanished as the watchers' perception shot out through the windshield. The shriek of brakes ended in the nauseous sound of one impact, then another.

The point of view twirled madly as Mizar looked for the crash. When he found it, he had to soar back along several hundred meters of highway. The SUV had left the road, rolling across the median ditch and into the oncoming lane. Two cars, a van, and a bus had brought it to a halt.

Then another car plowed into the tangle.

"Stop!" Talitha shouted, apparently forgetting that she had only to open her eyes to break the contact. But the mage did stop, and Rigel was suddenly back in Fornacis too. The realism of the crash had left him sweating and shaking.

"Did they both make it?" he asked. "Did anyone see?" How many innocent victims had been killed or harmed in the other vehicles? He felt sick, but he was not at fault and there was nothing he could do. Survivors with cell phones would be calling for ambulances already.

"I didn't see," Talitha said.

"Nor did I." Fomalhaut scowled at Rigel, rubbing his shoulder as if it had been soiled by the halfling's touch.

"I shall add Mintaka and Alkes to the summons that has already been sent to Prince Vildiar," the queen announced. "If he cannot produce them when court assembles at noon tomorrow, we shall ask why."

She would never get Vildiar to testify on the Star of Truth and no one in the Starlands would dare to arrest a Naos, but she had apparently decided to provoke a confrontation of some sort. She showed her youth sometimes by refusing to listen to her advisors' counsel. Only rarely did she pay attention to Rigel's views; he was a foreigner, a mere babysitter, and not much older in years than Izar. All he could do was hope that she wasn't making a horrible mistake.

"However badly Mintaka got mangled," he said, "they'll never mistake him for human. I wonder if yesterday's three bodies survived the fire?"

"Enough of them did," the queen said. She turned and walked away, so Rigel and the two mages necessarily followed. "We have identified two of them, Aludra and Benetnash. The third was unrecognizable. Starfolk Mizar and Achird were keeping watch over the gallery, and when the bodies were removed, they trailed the vehicles."

She came to a grouping of sofas and armchairs outside the seance court. Achird, another mage trainee, was stretched out there, fast asleep. Whereas Mizar was a typical halfling-despising snob, Achird was the closest thing to a friend Rigel had among the adult male elves. Mizar came from a family blessed by high magical talent, in which reds were commonplace and even Naos cropped up every few generations. By way of contrast, Achird had few relatives above yellow grade, which was the Starlands equivalent of being poor. He was the first red his family had produced in centuries. He was no taller than Rigel and his scalp fur was a sandy shade that would not have seemed out of place anywhere in northern Europe. He even had a sense of humor, unlike most starfolk over the age of a hundred.

Talitha sank into a chair, but did not invite the others to sit. The smile she directed at Rigel was not a sharing smile. It made him think of tigers and young ladies of Niger.

"They also kept watch on the room where the bodies were stored. A few hours ago, Hadar, Botein, Sadalbari, and Mintaka extroverted in. They proceeded to steal the bodies and introvert with them. Mintaka left the building on foot."

"But now the denizens of Earth may have two other cadavers to categorize," Fomalhaut proclaimed. "Mizar, return to the seance court and determine whether the tweenling twosome extricated themselves from their vehicular contraption before it impinged on the other traffic."

His apprentice ran off. Talitha dismissed the problem with a flick of her fingers. She had lost interest in the extroverting halflings now that there was no urgency to find out what they were up to. The Light of Naos that glowed around her neck and shoulders was sparkling much redder than usual. Rigel had rarely seen her truly enraged and never before had her fury been directed at him. Perhaps now he would know better than to drink champagne with a promiscuous woman. Or not.

"He had an access amulet, I suppose?" he asked. Earth's best locks could not withstand magic.

"Of course. But he set off alarms. That's how the city guard was alerted, I imagine. Halfling Alkes was waiting outside with that big vehicle while he and Mintaka drove off to collect the guns. Mage Mizar was still watching, and he seanced after them. That's when I tried to call you, halfling. And where exactly were you?"

Fomalhaut sneered in the background.

"I was with a friend, Your Majesty," Rigel said.

The starry glow had spread up her chin and down almost to her breasts. It glowed even redder. "It could only be that hairy halfling hussy, I suppose?"

This was going to be their first lovers' spat, and the fact that she was choosing to start it in front of witnesses made him all the madder. "And what if it was?"

"Your duty is to guard my son!"

"All day and all night? No time off at all?"

"Not without my permission!" She glared at him. Time off was not the problem, of course. Avior was.

Rigel discovered that he was perilously close to losing his temper. Either they were lovers or they weren't . . . and they weren't. They could never be lovers, at least not for fifty years or so, when the starfolk grew more accustomed to having a child queen. He had been stupid to drink champagne when he had so little experience with it, but was he really supposed to be on duty 168 hours a week? "Then I ask your permission to take a night off once in a while. That doesn't seem an unreasonable request. And I can safely leave your—"

Your what? Rigel looked down, around . . . *Bloody gizzards!* The imp had disappeared. He bellowed at the top of his lungs, *"Starling!"*

But he could guess exactly where the brat had gone. Ever since their first visit to Fornacis, several months ago, Izar had been dying to inspect the Time of Life, and the many times Fomalhaut had warned him away from it had only made him more determined. Rigel took off at a sprint. Now that he was listening for trouble, he could hear Izar screaming, far away.

Chapter 11

Rigel hurdled a marble lion with centimeters to spare. It came to life roaring and tried to bite him, an instant too late.

"I'm coming!" he yelled.

It is the Time of Life, the mage had said. *It is as dangerous as the Star of Truth itself and an even greater magic.* That last bit was doubtful, because it had obviously been inspired by the earthly invention of the pendulum clock, which was only a few centuries old, whereas the Star was ancestral. Nor had the mage ever explained what the Time did. Possibly nothing except impress Fomalhaut's friends.

Rigel was approaching the great disk edge-on, and something was moving inside it. The curved crystal distorted the view too much for him to be certain, but it had to be Izar. Somehow the machine had swallowed him. And now the disk had passed its low point and was very slowly rising. It might be hours before it swung low enough for the imp to be rescued.

Having leapt over a toothy mouth that opened in the floor and dodged a vine whose tendrils moved to intercept him,

Rigel reached the disk, a meter or so out of reach above him. Now he saw that there was a hole in the bottom edge, apparently the start of a narrow vertical shaft. Izar's feet and legs were visible just inside, on the lowest rung of a crystal ladder.

Izar was screaming more from glee than terror. He was yelling for Rigel to come and join him, so they could explore together.

"Drop!" Rigel shouted. "Let go and I'll catch you!" He had to repeat his command several times before the imp heard him. Even then, the shaft was so narrow that Izar could barely look down to see who was shouting.

"Come on!" Izar insisted, scrambling up a few rungs.

"Izar! *Starling!* Come down now."

But he obviously wasn't going to listen, and the disk was rising relentlessly. Rigel crouched and sprang. His fingers caught nothing and he dropped back. He backed away several paces and took a running start.

This time his left hand caught a cold glass bar. He swung, got his other hand on it too, and dangled there for a moment. The others had arrived below him.

"Rigel, come down!" Talitha shouted.

"Not until I get Izar. Find us something soft to land on." He hauled himself up a couple of rungs, so that his head was just below the mouth of the shaft. He thought he would fit in there, but only just.

"Izar! Come back down here."

He heard a very faint treble laugh from much higher up the shaft. "This is doggy! Come on, Rigel!"

"Go no farther, halfling!" roared Fomalhaut. "The starling's continuance is incommensurable, but the measure of your ephemerality may be divulged unto you. Drop now, while you hazard only moderate corporal impairment."

All very well for him to say that. What he meant was that Rigel would just break an ankle or two if he jumped down now. That might not be true, and he was certainly facing humiliation. It was barely an hour since he'd failed Talitha by not being on immediate call, and failing her twice in one day was unthinkable. Besides, his arms were being pulled out of their sockets. He began hauling himself up, rung by rung.

"Stop, halfling!" the mage yelled. "Your rationality cannot tolerate cognizance of your predestined expiration."

Talitha was shouting also, but soon Rigel was completely inside the disk and could rest his toes on the bottom rung of the ladder. Then he couldn't hear what they were saying.

Izar had disappeared into the darkness above. Rigel turned on the light amulet on his helmet. The rungs of the ladder seemed to be made of glass all the way up, and the inside of the shaft was shiny black, like obsidian, but his helmet prevented him from tipping his head back far enough to see very much. He couldn't tell if the starling's feet were still in sight. Likewise, he couldn't look down well enough to see his own. He turned off the light while he thought.

He could take off his helmet, but he couldn't lay it down anywhere, and he still wouldn't be able to see past it.

He shouted for Izar a few times without result. Stars alone knew how far the little demon would go before he saw that Rigel was not following. Knowing him, he'd probably just continue up alone.

Rigel would be stuck in this hellhole for hours. On his first visit to Fornacis, he had estimated that the pendulum's period from vertical to vertical was less than a day, but not much less. So if old Fomalhaut didn't fetch a very long ladder very quickly, Rigel and Izar would have to wait that long before they were safely returned to ground level.

He might as well go on up until he caught the little bastard and could deliver a blistering sermon on obedience. He started to climb into the darkness.

The swing of the pendulum was too slow for him to sense it. Nor could he detect any tilt away from the vertical, at least not yet. But there was something very fishy about the tube. He could barely bend his arms enough to move up, banging an elbow for every rung gained, and he couldn't lower them below his shoulders. Yet he could bend his legs far enough to advance his feet up from one rung to another, and legs were much longer than arms. It was almost as if the damnable machine kept changing the tube's diameter to accommodate him, in a sort of mechanical peristalsis. He wondered if Izar was as cramped as he was.

A whole day with his arms above his head was not going to be pleasant. The strain on his feet and ankles was not insignificant, either. In short, he might cramp up until he lost his grip on the ladder; if that happened, he was going to fall a very long way. Or he might get struck on the head by a descending Izar.

Putting such thoughts aside, he concentrated on working out what Fomalhaut had been trying to tell him at the end there. When he got excited, the old pedant drowned in his own vocabulary. "Your rationality cannot tolerate cognizance of your own predestined expiration." That meant something like, *Foreknowledge of your own death will drive you crazy.* Very likely, but how was that relevant to his present situation? What did the damnable contraption actually *do*?

He was getting very tired of climbing this fecal ladder. He tried calling Izar's name again, but there was no response. The acoustics in the tube were horrible.

How far up could this wormhole go?

How high had he climbed already? He should have counted the rungs.

There was a light above him, very faint. His helmet prevented him from seeing where it came from. Spurred by the hope that he might soon find himself somewhere more pleasant, he kept climbing.

The light grew steadily brighter, and then suddenly became very bright. There was a window behind the ladder, a peephole about the size of a sheet of paper. It seemed to be unglazed, because he could hear sounds of rustling and vigorous breathing from behind it.

He found himself looking into a room, a bedroom. His viewpoint seemed to be where the headboard of the bed should be, or behind it, but both the headboard and the wall were transparent. A man was stretched out on the bed; his face was tipped downward, but Rigel could make out human ears and a bald patch. All that could be seen of the person underneath him was the tip of one elfin ear.

Rigel had never considered himself a voyeur or a Peeping Tom, but he could not tear his eyes away from the couple's frenzied copulation. He even knew the room, with its heavy nineteenth-century furniture and overpowering wallpaper, for it was where he had enjoyed the only genuine conversation he'd ever had with his mother, the night before she died. That was her bed. The male covering her was no human, but a halfling, old Wasat—court archivist, curator of the royal treasury, and Electra's secret lover for longer than several earthly lifetimes. By a freak event that almost never happened, Wasat had sired a child with her. That was obviously what he was in the process of doing now. Rigel was viewing his own conception. As he realized that, Electra began to cry out in the ecstasy of climax. Wasat increased his efforts.

Of course the Time of Life would begin at the beginning.

Had Izar seen this on his way up? Certainly not. He would have been shown the ancient voluptuary Prince Vildiar, with the barely nubile Princess Talitha as his reluctant partner. They would have been engaged in the same act as Wasat and Electra, and Izar was certainly old enough to know what it meant. Given how much he feared and detested his father, it must have been torture for him.

Oh, Izar! Rigel resumed his climb up the shaft. He dared not shout now, lest the sound pass through the magical window and into his personal history. If he somehow interrupted his own creation, would he fulfill old Fomalhaut's prophecy by vanishing in a flash of paradox? The light faded away below him. He climbed through darkness again until he detected another faint glow above. He paused to think.

His conception . . . and then his death? But surely there ought to be more than just the beginning and the end. How many windows would there be between them? One for every birthday? He set off upward again.

The second view was of another bedroom, one without grandeur, just peeling walls, rickety furniture, and a floor of cracked linoleum, slummy and base. A blizzard howled beyond the window, a Canadian winter at its worst, and the woman giving birth on the blood-soaked bed was Queen Electra of the Starlands, hiding her shame in voluntary exile. This time she was the visible one and her companion was out of view. Rigel just saw the occasional glimpses of grizzled hands holding towels in an effort to staunch the hemorrhage. Of course it must be Wasat again, a terrified old man desperately trying to save his lover and unborn child.

Somewhere in the paraphernalia littering that room must lie a collection of amulets borrowed from the royal armory, including an engraved silvery bracelet best known as Saiph, the king of swords. When Wasat succeeded in hauling out the bloody babe, he would grab that murderous Lesath in place of the amulet he had intended to use, and place it on his son's tiny wrist.

Rigel shuddered at the gory scene. He wanted to shout out the good news that mother and child would live, but he dared not. He resumed his climb.

He could run barefoot over sharp gravel, perhaps even walk on nails, as Avior had bragged, but continual standing on the ladder's cylindrical rungs was a different sort of stress, and it was starting to cramp his feet. He recalled reading about the dreaded Chinese form of bastinado, where relentless gentle tapping on the soles of the feet eventually produced a hyper-sensitivity that sent fearful spasms of pain through the entire body. Muscles he had not known he had were starting to shriek complaints.

Was it time to give up?

The answer had to be no. The climb down would be just as bad as going on, magnified by a sense of failure. He had a mission. He had been given custody of a child and he had failed in his trust. He had to honor that responsibility. But must he suffer so? His helmet was another legendary amulet. If he invoked Meissa, he would become invisible to magic. Then the Time might just vanish, leaving leave him a hundred meters in the air above the mage's workshop, and he would not see the prophecy of his death.

The worst part about this was that he knew he *wanted* to see more. He would want to even if he didn't have the excuse of rescuing Izar. Fomalhaut had warned him once that the hunger for knowledge grew by what it fed on. He had seen his own conception, then his birth . . . What next? Boyhood?

Manhood? He forced himself upward until he came to the third window.

Another bedroom was what it showed. Were bedrooms all that mattered in life? Well, perhaps so. Surely that was himself he was seeing, that sweating, gasping, pounding male animal? He couldn't make out the woman because there were pillows in the way, and this did not surprise him; only one participant was shown in each of these erotic visions. He did have a good view of her legs, though, for they were pointing straight up, and he could hear her gasps of pleasure. She was certainly not Avior Halfling.

Whoever she was, if the rest of her matched those legs, she was worth all the effort his future self was providing. This was the next stage in the Time of Life—conceiving a child of one's own, for children were the only possible down payment on immortality. For a human-starborn cross, it was a gloriously welcome sight, because halflings were normally mules. Ever since he learned that his father was a halfling, he had been hoping that three-quarterlings like him would be fertile too.

Rigel stayed and stared at the pornographic vision until it faded away and the window itself disappeared. What next? One child only? Or a large brood and a new window for every conception? One generic conception might stand for many, in which case the visions would jump straight to the last bed, the death bed. For a mortal there could be no other ending to this series. Izar might be up there already, staring at his own corpse. Or at the stars, the final home for which old starfolk yearned. Hopefully it was the latter. Despite what the mage had said, elves were mortal, for even their lives could be cut short by violence.

No one ever wanted to view his own death. Rigel now suspected that catching Izar was a magical impossibility. And a physical one, too. Not only did his shoulders ache from the strain of holding his arms high, but there were only so many places on the soles of his feet that would support his weight on the polished glass rods. Standing still was rapidly becoming more torturous than continuing to climb.

He had barely started again when he thought he heard Izar cry out. Rigel shouted, but there was no reply. The imp might have fainted. Or worse. Mustn't think that. He twisted his head to look up the shaft, and spotted the next window only a meter or so above his head. A man chuckled.

It sounded like Hadar.

The light filtering in through the spyhole was very faint. When Rigel reached it and peered through, he saw no bedroom this time, but a forest of giant conifers—cedars, perhaps, although Starlands flora was no more realistic than the fauna. Trees this size never grew so close together on Earth.

Flakes of snow floated in the air and there was snow on the ground, too, although not much. That was reasonable, because the canopy overhead would be thick enough to catch most of it. Snow was rare in the Starlands. When he had asked Talitha why that was, given the elves' preference for cool temperatures, she had told him that it was hard to imagine realistic snow, snow that would take footprints, and even harder to get it to return to its artistic, pristine state later. Too much bother, in other words. The snow in this vision had many patches of conifer needles mixed in with it. Token snow.

There was Halfling Rigel, leaning against an especially huge trunk. He was barefoot, wearing only his usual wrap and bronze helmet, but that was quite credible. He had no need of clothing until the temperature dropped well below freezing, although he had wrapped up on Earth to avoid drawing attention to himself. He must have walked on the pine needles on his way to the tree, because he had left no footprints. He looked quite relaxed, but he was holding his sword.

"I am in no hurry," he announced. "I'd like to talk about men and women who make war on children."

Who was he talking to? In contrast to the dense forest behind him, the ground before him was empty, just snow and needles and exposed roots.

A man said, "Boss, I'm worried the prisoner may escape. Shouldn't we sort of fix him there somehow? I mean, nail him in place with an arrow?" He sounded as if he was standing in the pendulum, directly behind Watcher-Rigel.

The reply came, unmistakably, from Hadar. "I don't think one arrow would do it. We'll start with one and work our way up. Scheat, pin his left shoulder."

A bowstring cracked, Saiph blurred, and an arrow sprouted in a trunk about a meter from Target-Rigel. He shrugged. "That the best you can do?"

Hadar said, "No. Schemali and Sadalbari. On the count of three. One . . . two . . . three!"

Bowstrings cracked. Again Target-Rigel's right arm and sword blurred, and this time two arrows struck the trees behind him. A shower of snow fell off a low-lying branch.

Several people laughed: mostly men, but women too.

Back on Rigel's second day in the Starlands, Regent-heir Kornephoros had mockingly asked how anyone could go about stealing Saiph, and Talitha had told him they could send a regiment of archers against it. That was what Hadar had somehow managed to do. There must be a whole gang of Family members lined up against Target-Rigel.

Why didn't he escape into the forest? Once he started dodging away through those trees, they would never hit him. The answer must lie in that remark he had made about making war on children. They must have taken Izar hostage. Rigel would never desert him.

"Seems we must try targets that are farther apart," Hadar said. "Scheat, the shoulder again. Sadachbia, dear, you're a good shot. You try for his balls. On the count of three. Stop that, maggot!"

A child cried out and tried to say something, but the words were cut off.

"Prepare to fire when this brat turns blue," Hadar said. The Family laughed. After a moment, he added, "Going to behave yourself now?"

Izar mumbled something.

"Very well, on the count of three."

Watcher-Rigel tried to close his eyes and couldn't.

That time the victim did cry out. One arrow fell in two pieces, but the other pinned his left shoulder to the tree behind him. Just one cry, then a hard swallow and silence. He went very pale and clearly could not move without hurting himself more.

There could be no doubt that Rigel was watching his own execution. Fomalhaut had warned him that the sight might drive him crazy. He should go now, before it got any worse. His feet wouldn't move. He wanted to scream, and couldn't make a sound.

"What's going on here?" said a new voice, the horribly familiar voice of Naos Vildiar.

"Just softening him up a little, Your Highness," said Hadar. "We got the brat here, too."

"Good. Hold him tight. He's a slippery little devil. Have you any last words, Rigel Halfling? I concede that you have caused me more trouble than I would have believed possible. But this is definitely the end. You are about to die."

"I won't bet against it," Target-Rigel said. "But let Izar go, please. He should not have to watch this." Blood from his shoulder had run down all the way to his feet. His face was chalky white.

"No, it is educational for him to view punishment and see the penalty for insubordination."

"As soon as we've disposed of you," Hadar barked, "our favorite little brother here will be going on to Unukalhai to begin his manhood training. This is nothing compared to what he'll have to watch there . . . and learn to do himself!"

"Carry on, Hadar!"

"Yes, my lord. When I call out your name, shoot. Try to avoid vital areas, so that we can all have a chance to do our bit for the great cause."

Izar screamed, "No!"

"Quiet!" his father said. "Or I will have you gagged. Proceed, halfling."

Hadar shouted, "Diphda, Sadalbari, Schemali, Phact, Sadachbia, Rotanev!" A fusillade of bowstrings cracked.

The condemned man screamed. Some arrows had missed or been knocked aside by Saiph, but two had hit their mark: one through his right elbow and another in his belly. He screamed again. And again.

His sword and gauntlet disappeared, unable to help further. Only the silver bracelet remained on his immobilized arm. He tried to speak but there was too much blood in his mouth.

Watcher-Rigel was sobbing, and still he could not drag himself away.

Hadar said, "Hand around the bows so some of the rest of us can have a share of the fun. Maaz—"

"Stop!" Izar yelled. "Stop! Stop!"

"Izar." That was his father. "If I tell them to stop torturing Rigel, will you promise to do what I tell you in future?"

"Yes, yes! Anything!"

"You promise?"

Again the dying man tried to say something and only blood came out of his mouth.

"Yes," Izar sobbed. "I promise! I'll do anything you say, Father."

"Kill him, Hadar."

"Yes, Your Highness. Rotanev, hold the brat for me and give me your bow. This is my job." Brief pause. "Bye-bye, sucker!"

The scene went black. The window disappeared, leaving Rigel in darkness, clinging to the ladder, gasping and shivering. This was why Fomalhaut had warned him. Now he knew his own death. Nothing he could do would change that. Somehow he must try to remain sane while knowing how he would die. It wouldn't be very long, though, for Izar had still been a child in the vision.

The last words Rigel would ever hear would be Hadar's mockery.

Could a prophecy be defied? If we know the future, can we not escape it?

After a few moments he tried to haul himself up another rung. He wasn't surprised when his helmet thumped against the top of the tube, a flat plate. He had reached the end of his life. Yet now there was a dim light far below him. He started descending and it grew rapidly brighter. The way down seemed only a fraction as long as the way up, and he could detect a slight tilt to the shaft. In a few moments he emerged into the brilliance of the crystal disk and heard voices shouting below him. Some of them were definitely telling him to jump, and the shrillest one was Izar's.

The advantage of knowing that he must die at the hands of Hadar's henchmen was that nothing else could be too terrible. Rigel let go.

He shot out the bottom of the disk and landed on a giant cushion, which broke his fall as if it were filled with soft dough. Izar, Talitha, Fomalhaut, and the apprentice mage Achird were all standing around watching him. Izar came running even before Rigel could struggle to his feet.

"What'yu see?" he demanded excitedly.

Among the onlookers, Talitha's anger seemed less convincing than before, Fomalhaut's sneer was more arrogant than ever, and Achird just looked relieved. Mizar must have still been at work in the seance court.

"You went first," Rigel said. "What did you see?" *And how had he returned first?*

"I saw *him*," Izar said disgustedly. "So I just climbed down again."

Fomalhaut raised golden eyebrows, but said nothing. Rigel glanced at Talitha, who also looked suspicious. Despite his elfin childishness, Izar Imp could be as devious as a Mafia boss. He certainly hated and feared Vildiar quite enough to have just turned around and left after catching a glimpse of his father in the conception scene. But he might equally well have gone on to view the highlights of the rest of his life. Time itself was distorted inside the Time of Life; otherwise he could not have managed to bypass Rigel on the way back.

"And what did you see, tweenling?" Fomalhaut demanded of Rigel. "If you presume to arrogate my occult contrivances without leave, the least you owe me is a detailed report of the consequences."

"How accurate are these so-called prophecies?"

"They have never been wrong in four centuries."

"That's a relief," Rigel said, smiling sweetly. "I assume if Izar had climbed all the way to the top he would have seen nothing but stars?"

"He would have heard the music of the spheres, but I'm certain that you did not!"

"No, I didn't," Rigel admitted. "But I did learn that I am not about to fulfill the last of the prophecies for a long time." Not until after he had sired a child, in fact. Viva chastity! As long as he remained a virgin and stayed away from snowy forests, he could not die.

He had two prophecies from Fomalhaut now, and the last cancelled out the first, at least in terms of timing. Perhaps they were both utter lies, charades concocted by the mage in order to scare the unwelcome tweenling upstart into scarpering back home to Canada.

"Come along, all of you!" Talitha said angrily. "Izar should have been in bed hours ago. We have a busy day ahead of us."

Her court mage ignored her. "Did you learn the name of your father, halfling?"

Rigel shrugged. "I already knew that, starborn. My mother told me before she died." *My mother, the queen,* of course. He smiled blandly at the old elf's annoyance and followed Izar and Talitha as they headed for the door, the royal barge, and Canopus.

Chapter 12

Avior Halfling, the former Mabel Bonalde, was scalding her mouth on her fifth cup of strong black coffee when shrill screams drove through her head like iron spikes. Izar and a couple of slightly larger imps cannonballed into the far side of the pool in simultaneous eruptions. Where Izar went, could Rigel be far behind? She cowered over the table, trying to will herself invisible.

No such luck.

"Good morning, tweenling!" he caroled, striding in along the path. He stopped, towering over her. "Something wrong?"

"No," she said. "Morning," she conceded. She was not about to mention a pounding headache, a million bruises, nor certain intimate places that had been rubbed almost raw—all in a very good cause, admittedly, but hard to bear in the cold light of day.

He sat down, clattering the chair like a kettledrum. "Waiter! I want a tall glass of grapefruit juice and bring the lady a morning-after pick-me-up.

"They do their best," he added softly when the mudling had gone, "but I did warn you about their intelligence. You have to ask specifically for everything you need."

A pick-me-up sounded promising; she turned a bleary eye in his direction. The Starlands were packed with surprises. Rigel had not been gone from her room two minutes last night when Tyl had walked in with a full bottle of rum, which he had handed to her without a word. While she was taking her first swig, he had dropped his robe and climbed into bed, uninvited but welcome. He had assessed her needs very rapidly and proceeded to go one better than his Unukalhai three Rs training, Ravishing her Ruthlessly and Repeatedly with astonishing Reliability for the rest of the night, until they ran out of rum.

"Rigel!" Izar bellowed from the pool.

"The monster calls." Rigel was disgustingly cheerful and hangover-free. "We do have time for a quick swim before court assembles, if you want. No? Well, here comes your fixer-upper. It will make you feel much better. By the way, you'll do better to cover your head and leave off the wig. Excess hair offends the elves, because their own never grows long. It's like chimpanzee fur, but don't tell them I told you so. Halflings Tyl and Thabit will be joining us. Thabit is another of Hadar's assassins who came in from the cold right after Tyl. They're twins, the only twins in the Family. Excuse me." He laid his helmet down on his chair.

He was gone with barely a ripple on the water.

The tonic arrived. Avior pulled a face at the smell of it and swallowed it in one gulp. It went off inside her head like a nuclear blast. When the fireworks stopped, she opened her eyes and watched the world spin slowly to a halt. *Crispies!* The pain had disappeared. A hangover tonic as effective as that would be worth billions on Earth.

She had company again. Rigel's helmet was now on the table and Tyl was sitting on the chair opposite her, a satisfied sneer on his elfin face. He wore a pale long-sleeved robe, fastened to the throat, and at least a dozen sparkling studs in his cat ears.

"Good morning, Avior."

"No, but it's better than it was," she admitted.

"I trust you slept well? The ugly wretch behind you is my brother, Orang."

The man in the chair wasn't Tyl, she suddenly realized. His name was Thabit. She looked up in alarm, not having realized there was anyone else present. Tyl was behind her, wearing a blue robe.

He said, "Shut up, Utan."

Orang? Utan? . . . Red body hair . . . Right.

The twins were exact duplicates, alizarin eyes and all.

"Pay no attention to Utan," Tyl said, smiling down at her with dentition stolen from a great white. "Ever since he finally reached puberty, he's been insanely jealous of my superior prowess."

"As well as being practically impotent," Thabit retorted, "my brother is an outrageous liar. We are both very happy that you're here, Avior Tweenling. We are eager to make your welcome to the Starlands both warm and memorable."

"I have a trained eye for detail," she said, "but I admit that you two are astonishingly alike, even for twins. Fortunately, I have the starborn trick of reading names, so I can easily tell you apart."

Tyl said, "Why does it matter?" and Thabit, "Who cares?"

The palace was built on a cyclopean scale and seemed to cover more ground than a major airport. The giant statuary that loomed everywhere caught Avior's professional interest, but mainly because it displayed such a weird medley of styles. Even when the figures were posed with stiff arms, left foot forward, and both heels on the ground, they were neither quite Egyptian nor Greek. Elfin ears showed up everywhere: on Buddhas, togaed Romans, Hellenistic goddesses, Aztec warriors, Chinese dragons. The building itself was constructed of pink granite and black diorite, miles of walls covered with the alien script that adorned Rigel's amulet. Her eyes' inability to comprehend it properly reminded her of Frederick Catherwood's frantic efforts to draw Maya ruins that were so alien to his experience. Below all this gigantic grandeur teemed near-nude starfolk and draped mudlings, but there were also halflings, sphinxes, centaurs, even a few lumbering cyclops. Almost all sported bat ears, and the rest had their heads covered.

Tyl and Thabit brought her at last to a gap in a high wall, where their way was blocked by a menacing sphinx. He gave them a sudden smile just as she learned that his name was Algenubi.

"Tweenling Avior!" His voice was not as subterranean as Zozma's, but it was deep enough. "The marshal mentioned you. Follow me. Better still, hang on to my tail."

He padded through the opening into a corridor, whose opposite side was an endless wall of towering monoliths, and through the nearest gap into a solid mass of starborn. Most of them were facing to the left and Algenubi turned in that direction, but there were many thousands of starfolk assembled there. Having no elbows, he began a low, never-ending, bloodcurdling growl, which seemed to be the Starlands equivalent of a police siren, for the elves stopped their twittering and jostled aside with angry grumbles. Algenubi treated any who were too slow to react much as a snowplow treats obstinate drifts. Avior, towed along, tried to apologize at first and then just gave up. She assumed that Tyl and Thabit were following.

This enormous courtyard was evidently the court itself, and the crowd packed into it was waiting for the queen. The roof was a cloudless ultramarine sky, and the walls were granite slabs, four or five stories high, like god-sized dominoes set on end. Each one was a backdrop for an Egyptian-style animal-headed colossus, with the jackal-faced Anubis the favorite, but also many others, both male and female, clad or unclad. Avior could spend days exploring this courtyard alone. Not today, though.

She hated people in crowds; to be honest, she hated people, and the more of them, the worse. Yet starfolk did not repel her as a human mob would. Lacking signs of age or wear, they flaunted their bodies shamelessly and unerringly; they were gracile and entrancing, each of them glittering with gems. She felt that she was plowing through a field of tall flowers. Earthlings stank, but the starfolk smelled of grass and blossoms, not the overpowering chemical stench of scents from bottles. Their chatter was as musical as the chirruping of birds or the murmuring of doves. Their smiles were Komodo nightmares.

Algenubi brought her at last to the front of the crowd, where the foremost row of starfolk struggled mightily against the pressure of the crowd behind, which was threatening to push their bare toes across a thin blue line on the mosaic floor. The line itself was almost invisible, but two sphinxes were patrolling it, and those massive padding paws kept the elves from trespassing. Occasional howls of pain served as a reminder.

Beyond that lay a wide, mostly empty expanse, containing in its center a black inlaid star that had to be the notorious

Star of Truth. Did it really have an ominous aura, or was that a product of her imagination?

On the far side of the gap, seven wide, shallow steps ran the full width of the court, the topmost holding a throne that was the most alien thing Avior had seen yet, a mass of gold and colored stone so subtle and complex that her eyes could not trace its lines. It repelled her and yet held her gaze hypnotically.

Either Tyl or Thabit poked her in the back. "Don't stare too long at that thing. It's neither elfin nor earthly, and it can sprain your mind."

"Thanks," she said, raising her gaze to the plain black monolith behind it, taller than any other. Flecks of golden light like fireflies moved slowly within it.

The sphinx delivered her and her escort to a small group standing off to the right, at the base of the lowermost step—elves and a few self-effacing halflings. Most were wearing jeweled disk collars and seemed to be officials. They glanced with disapproval at the three newcomer half-breeds and turned to continue their conversations.

"Wait here, halfling," the sphinx commanded. "You may be called near the end, but Marshal Rigel thinks there will be too much official business today for them to get to you."

"Good turnout," Tyl remarked.

The sphinx turned his head to appraise him for a long moment with the studied stare that must characterize patrolmen everywhere in the galaxy. Eventually he said, "You have been here before?"

"I accompanied Prince Vildiar once, back in Queen Electra's time."

"How long ago?"

Tyl shrugged. "Forty years? Maybe fifty."

Algenubi nodded and stalked away. Tyl had to be a lot older than he looked. But so was Avior, and age certainly had not blunted his prowess.

"How many thousands?" asked a nearby starborn wearing a collar of sapphires and emeralds.

"King Procyon told me once it can hold twenty," said her companion, peering around. His name was Hyadum and his collar was of rubies and onyx.

"Must be close to full. I expect they've all come to get a look at her, this being the first time she's held court."

"Naw, they've come to sneer at that halfling lover of hers. And because the word got around that Vildiar's commanded all his underlings to attend. They think he's going to challenge her for the throne."

Sapphires' name was Azmidiske; she tinkled an effete laugh that set Avior's teeth on edge. "*Democracy*? In the *Starlands*? Will he try, do you think?"

"Not a hope," Hyadum said. "Not yet, anyway. But you heard that Chancellor Haedus went windsurfing and was returned by the tide facedown, right? I was told this morning that several other ministers are thinking of handing in their collars." His voice dropped so low that Avior couldn't hear it through her head cloth.

She returned to studying the scene.

Her two guards were standing very close on either side of her. Tyl tried to take her hand and she shook him off.

"What happens if I'm called?" she asked, realizing for the first time that she was terrified.

"Nothing much," he said. "You have to prove that you're a halfling, not a mudling, and you can do that by uncovering your unbuttoned belly. Then a starborn has to sponsor you, and the queen's going to do that, Rigel says—"

"Why?" his brother interrupted. "The queen herself? That's unusual."

Since he seemed to be asking Avior, she said, "I have no idea." Rigel had hinted that she might be able to assist him in his vendetta against Vildiar, but she could not imagine how.

The rumble of the crowd paused as a matronly human woman wearing a skirt and head cloth walked out from behind the throne. Carrying a gilded chair, she marched to the right until she was directly in front of where Avior was standing, then descended one step, and there she set the chair. She turned and retraced her steps. The crowd went back to its gossiping.

A few moments later, two sphinxes, one of them the huge Commander Zozma, stalked out from the same concealed door and took up positions on either side of the throne. Then came Rigel in his classical Roman helmet. He went to stand directly behind the chair—and the crowd's avian murmuring changed flavor, from bland to acid.

"Well, I can see why she fancies him," Hyadum said. "As long as he keeps the bucket on his head."

"Oh, my dear, how could you?" Azmidiske declaimed, her voice poignant with angst. "Have you seen Starborn Ruchba's anthropoid gardens? He has some male *Paranthropus robustus* who will undoubtedly appeal to you."

Izar came out. With chin raised, lips tight, and eyes focused straight ahead, he strode past Zozma, descended one step, and moved over to the chair. He paused before it, then shot his arms out sideways and bowed to the court. To Avior's astonishment, the assembled starfolk burst into cheers and applause. He sat down and turned his head to grin up at Rigel behind him.

"Stars! A standing ovation?" Tyl muttered. "Little bugger'll be impossible now."

"He always is," his brother retorted. Neither sounded serious.

"Oh, isn't he a *darling*!" Azmidiske said. "I do *adore* imps!"

Hyadum said, "Try playing with boys sometimes, dear, and maybe you'll get one of your own."

Her reply was drowned out by a deafening blast of trumpets in a key Bach's clavichord never knew. Avior winced.

Tyl leaned even closer. "Smile for Daddy," he whispered to the place where her ear should have been.

She spun around and stared toward the rear of the long courtyard. A jade-and-silver throne was approaching, floating with eerie grace over the courtiers' heads. Its occupant was unusually tall, even for an elf, and as he drew nearer she saw that his hair and eyes showed the same rainbow opalescence as the queen's, the mark of Naos that Izar was starting to display. His fish-belly-pale features were set in a brooding, heavy-browed scowl that made her think of Easter Island statues. So this was Prince Vildiar, the elf who thought he should be king, Tyl and Thabit's father.

Very probably he was her father too. In one of the calm spells during the night, she and Tyl had discussed incest, agreeing that since they had met as adults and were both unquestionably infertile, the possibility was nothing to worry about. Only the stud book at Phegda could confirm or disprove it. That had given them an excuse for a celebratory rematch.

The discordant trumpets fell silent. The courtiers had necessarily stopped talking, and now some loyalist voices tried to raise a cheer for the prince. It died for lack of support. Showing no signs of noticing this mass snub, he floated his throne up the steps until he was level with Izar, one down from the royal throne itself and on the far side. There he settled.

Izar jumped to his feet and snapped into another of his jerky, arms-spread bows, this one directed to his father. Vildiar nodded in acknowledgment. The court exploded in applause, as if the imp had performed some sort of feat. Avior realized that if she were one of Vildiar's illicit offspring, then she was Izar's half sister, as well as Tyl's and Thabit's. She put that thought aside for later consideration.

More trumpets. A woman wearing a silver collar emerged from behind the throne's giant black backdrop and advanced to the front of the uppermost step to address the congregation.

"Celaeno!" Hyadum whispered. "She's crazy to be doing this after what happened to Haedus. She's got a lot more courage than I do."

"Not difficult, dear."

Chancellor Celaeno pronounced a wordy proclamation summoning all starborn within the sound of her voice to attend their rightful sovereign, Talitha the Thirteenth, Queen of the Starfolk, and witness her judgment on diverse grave matters. There was magic involved, because Celaeno seemed to speak in a normal conversational tone, and yet it cut quite clearly through all the whispering. Even close whispers became very difficult to hear.

Queen Talitha emerged to take her place on the throne. The group of officers and witnesses around Avior all bowed, but given the thousands who were gathered at the front of the court, only those in the front row had room to do so.

"Starborn Elgomaisa, come forward," the chancellor said.

A male elf detached himself from the front row of the congregation and walked forward to stand on the Star of Truth.

"Fires of Hell!" Tyl whispered. "What's he supposed to have done?"

His surprise seemed to be universal. Izar looked astonished and Rigel puzzled. Azmidiske and Hyadum sounded as perplexed as any, and quite scornful of the elf himself. He was probably ugly by conventional elfin standards—no taller than Avior, stocky in build, his hair an earthling black. If he was in peril of having his mouth set on fire, why was he grinning?

"Starborn Elgomaisa," the chancellor said, "Her Majesty is mindful to appoint you her consort, to share her bed and favors, to provide her with support and companionship. Are you willing to accept this appointment?"

"I am."

"Are you, and will you always be, loyal to Her Majesty, her person, and purposes?"

"I am now and will be evermore."

Evidently the appointment was a popular one. As the new consort strode up the long steps, the court exploded in roars of approval.

"So Pretty Boy's out!" Tyl said.

"She was really mad at him last night," his brother said, having to shout in his ear, "when she discovered he wasn't in his own bed."

They both knew whose bed Rigel had *not* been in, because Avior had told Tyl about the attempted kiss, and Tyl had laughed so hard that he would certainly have passed the story on to Thabit. If the queen had learned of Rigel's failure, she evidently regarded the intent as more important than the result.

But if Rigel was now out of favor, why wasn't he upset? For he clearly wasn't. He wasn't grinning, but he was taking the news with remarkable good cheer. Izar, the ultimate Rigel supporter, had twisted around to look up at him in outrage, but his guardian just gestured for him to turn back to facing the crowd.

Starborn Elgomaisa bowed to the queen, kissed her hand, and took his place, standing by her side between the throne and Commander Zozma.

"Ha!" Azmidiske said. "He can't be a day over fifty. I suppose they can play hide-and-go-seek together."

"Or ball?" Hyadum suggested.

"No, he's too young to have any."

Chapter 13

Rigel felt hurt that Talitha hadn't warned him in advance, but otherwise the news about Elgomaisa was actually a relief. The appointment of an official consort ought to squelch all the vicious gossip that the queen was sleeping with a halfling, which should in turn deflate any trial balloons Vildiar might be floating among the starfolk. Yes, Rigel still yearned for her and probably always would. The thought of her making love to someone else was torture, but his impossible love ought to be more bearable the more impossible it became. Until now only willpower had held the lovers apart, with the constant threat that one sip of wine too many might burst the dam of their self-control at any time. Now she had locked and barred the door, so he was free to look around for a more accessible partner, probably a halfling, although certainly not Avior, that crazy S&M pervert.

Pay attention! Fomalhaut was on the Star, being questioned by Counselor Pleione under the watchful eyes of the chancellor and the queen herself.

And Rigel had the Time of Life prophecy in his hip pocket, figuratively speaking. He could not die until he had fathered a child! Those outspread legs he had glimpsed in the third vision had looked too suspiciously perfect to belong to any earthling or mudling. The thought that they might be Talitha's had been fighting to be released from his id ever since. Now he could dismiss it as wishful thinking. Perhaps one day he would sire a child with a female elf, but not in the present century, thank you very much. Male halflings were so rarely fertile that they were universally believed to be sterile, but even Halfling Wasat, chief curator of the royal treasury and proof to the contrary, agreed that female halflings absolutely never conceived. Wanted: curvaceous halfling female, objective cohabitation. Then he wouldn't have to worry about his date with destiny for some time.

Concentrate!

The mage was saying that, yes, he was aware that reversion staffs were illegal, but he had special royal permission to own and use them, for certain purposes that he was not at liberty to reveal. Yes, he had prepared the staff for Rigel Tweenling's extroversion, and when the halfling had arrived with Starling Izar as his traveling companion, Fomalhaut himself had prepared a second staff for the imp as a favor to the queen's son. Yes, he had preset both to go to a particular spot on Earth and return to his laboratory in his domain of Fornacis. No, only a mage of the red or high orange could have overridden his settings. No one else had been present in his laboratory, to the best of his knowledge, except for his two apprentices, starfolk Mizar and Achird.

He was told to step aside for a moment. Mizar and Achird were called forth to testify. Achird had been elsewhere during the times in question. Mizar had not tampered with the staff and had seen no one else in Fornacis at the time of the sabotage.

Rigel had watched Counselor Pleione in action before. At that time he had thought that she must have either an amazing memory or a very swift mind, but now he knew that almost no device or convenience ever invented by humans had not been anticipated centuries earlier by the starfolk's magic. Undoubtedly one of her amulets was some sort of prompter.

The audience stayed silent as they listened to the evidence, trying to guess where it was leading and what crime had been committed. Talitha had summoned only the first four branches of starfolk to court, meaning those whose domains were rooted in the royal domain, plus owners of domains rooted in theirs, and so on. All starfolk were free to come, though, and obviously many more had done so.

Fomalhaut was recalled.

"You chose your words very carefully when answering my last question, Lord Fomalhaut, as did your two apprentices when asked the same thing. So now I require that you be more specific. You agree that somebody must have tampered with the staffs after they left your hands?"

"After I finished with them, somebody must have changed the settings on the staff wielded by Rigel Halfling, because it did not introvert him back to Fornacis. And because Starling Izar had lost his staff on Earth and the halfling used his to extrovert himself, the starling, and another halfling, all three went to another domain."

Shock! The audience had now learned that the queen's son had been abducted. Such crimes were unheard of in the Starlands.

Rigel was growing impatient. The problem was not who had booby-trapped his reversion staff—he thought he knew that now—but how to get Vildiar on the Star of Truth and ask him where his missing halflings were.

Pleione plodded on. "And how did this unknown someone change the settings without your knowledge?"

"One possibility, Counselor, is that the staff was changed while on Earth." Fomalhaut shot a look of dislike in Rigel's direction.

Damn! That clearly would be his cue. Sure enough, Pleione summoned Rigel Halfling, marshal of Canopus. She did not demand that he remove his helmet. It was not currently activated, but all he had to do was speak its name while wearing it and it would be. He took it off and tucked it under his arm, for he had no intention of testing the strength of the Star of Truth's power to detect lies against Meissa's ability to conceal him from its magic.

As a non-elf he was required to kneel.

Yes, he was Rigel Halfling, born on Earth, son of the late Queen Electra, and now marshal of Canopus. He testified that the staff had not left his grasp during the few moments he had spent on Earth, and no one else had touched it there except the two persons who had introverted with him. He spoke softly, knowing that he would be audible the whole length of the enormous space. He was allowed to withdraw. This could take days.

Again Fomalhaut was asked to explain the miracle. Even he was in danger on the Star, and Rigel was amused to see that his habit of speaking in convoluted syntax and sesquipedalian vocabulary deserted him there.

"It is possible, Counselor, for mages of very high grade and training to render themselves virtually invisible, although only for brief intervals, because the strain is considerable.

When I say 'virtually,' I imply that their presence can be detected by extreme means, but they wouldn't be noticed by casual observers. I am forced to conclude that some such mage trespassed in my laboratory yesterday and sabotaged the halfling's staff."

Shock! again.

"How many starborn are capable of this trick?" Pleione demanded. Her show of anger suggested that she was not one of them and had never heard of it before.

"I do not know," Fomalhaut said. "Thousands of starborn have inherent red skill and many hundreds of them have taken mage training in their time. The ability I mentioned is most commonly associated with, although not always limited to, Naos."

Talitha jumped to her feet, startling Elgomaisa and her sphinx guardians. She came striding down the steps to the Star, which Fomalhaut hurriedly vacated. She took his place, facing the assembly.

"I, Talitha, testify that I did not meddle with the reversion staff." She began to turn away and then decided to add to her testimony, "Had I been present, I would have forbidden my son to be included on that expedition, which I regarded as far too risky for a child."

She went back to her throne while the elite of the Starlands sniggered at the way the offensive Halfling Rigel had been so thoroughly put down twice in less than an hour. He wasn't the queen's unofficial consort now; he was nothing.

But what of Prince Vildiar, lounging his great length on his throne? He was the only other Naos left other than Izar, who would not be recognized as such until he reached his majority in another twenty-two years, and whose powers were still rudimentary.

Vildiar yawned. "I wasn't there, either. Anyone who wants to call me a liar may do so on the Star."

"The court thanks you, my lord," Pleione said. "If you will be so kind as—"

"No." He laughed softly at the ensuing silence. "You must have forgotten, Counselor, that a Naos is not required to testify on the Star except to answer a direct accusation made on it by a starborn. Do you wish to proceed on that basis?"

Rigel had not known that law. Talitha had never mentioned it. Clearly caught off guard, Counselor Pleione fumbled with her finger rings for a moment before she nodded. It seemed as though today's battle plan had just sprung a very large leak: Who would bell the cat? Who would risk a horrible death? Talitha looked concerned, as well she might. If she failed to call Vildiar to account after assembling such a large crowd, she would lose whatever respect she had gained.

Pleione kept going, dismissing Fomalhaut and bringing Rigel back. Again he tucked his helmet under his arm; again he knelt.

"Tell the court why you reverted and what happened."

"I went to Earth to rescue a halfling, whom I believe, but cannot prove, to be an illegitimate daughter of Vildiar Naos. Starling Izar wished to accompany me, and I agreed because I expected the extroversion to last no more than ten or fifteen minutes and foresaw no danger."

Here was his chance to upset Vildiar's applecart.

"I did not notice my reversion staff being sabotaged, although I believe I now know who did that. The starling and I arrived at—"

Pleione barked, *"Stop!"*

The witness certainly had the court's attention now. Even Vildiar had dropped his air of amused boredom and was staring hard at Rigel. He held all tweenlings in contempt, but he knew that this one was dangerous.

"Whom do you accuse of sabotaging the staff?" Pleione demanded.

"I do not know the person's identity for a fact, Counselor. I can only give you my suspicions and my reasons for them."

"Do that."

"Since I will be speculating, may I do so outside the Star?"

The counselor scowled, then nodded.

Rigel rose and stepped out of the danger zone. "The staff introverted us to a domain called Alathfar, claimed by Star-born Shaula. I have been informed that the domain was largely imagined by, and until recently owned by, Naos Kurhah. During my discussion with Lady Shaula, I had a feeling that there might be someone else present." He glanced at the queen, who looked as angry as he'd expected. She would be wondering why he hadn't told her this before. He barged ahead. "Star-born Shaula allowed the three of us to return to Canopus by means of the root portal. Commander Zozma reported to me that last night his officers tried to open the portal, but its lock was proof against the strongest amulets in the possession of the Palace Guard."

For a moment Prince Vildiar showed his teeth. Rigel understood why; when you had spent twenty years murdering all the Naos in the Starlands, it must be quite annoying to learn that one of them had escaped. If their voices had not been magically quenched, the rest of the court would have been in an uproar.

Talitha was flushed and glaring, but Rigel hadn't been sure enough of his suspicions to share them with her beforehand. In the past he had seen her use her own ability to vanish from sight, although not completely, but until he heard Fomalhaut link this skill specifically to Naos magic, he had not made the now-obvious connection to Kurhah.

Talitha made her decision. "Court Mage Fomalhaut! At the conclusion of this meeting, you will accompany Commander Zozma and his officers to this root portal and—"

Trumpets blared at the far end of the court.

Chapter 14

Rigel was probably the only person other than the queen and Consort Elgomaisa who did not look around. He saw Izar's elfin eyes open impossibly wide and that was all the confirmation he needed. He put on his helmet to conceal an irrepressible grin and strode back up the steps. There was going to be a precedence problem in a moment. There were going to be all sorts of problems in a moment, but only one concerned him. Although Izar should not be present at all by the normal protocol of protocol, the sovereign could make and unmake rules as she wished, and Talitha had her reasons for putting him in full view, with Rigel as his guard. But now the imp had to make way for an adult Naos, whose rank would be infinitely greater.

Any words Rigel spoke on the steps would be broadcast throughout the court, but fortunately Izar was sharp enough to guess what Rigel's gestures meant. Grinning broadly, he walked forward to his new place, one step lower, and Rigel brought his chair down for him.

The court buzzed with excitement and approval. The appearance of another Naos changed the situation completely. In the eyes of the starfolk, Talitha was centuries too young to rule and she had accepted the throne only because Electra had refused to give it to the odious Vildiar. Now she could give the Starlands to Kurhah. He would expect as much. At an age of around three thousand, he would be quite acceptable and could rule for a few centuries until Talitha matured. Vildiar would become his problem, not hers. No one would notice or care if she slipped away to enjoy a private life in some quiet domain to raise her son and cherish her tweenling lover.

The approaching jade throne floated close enough for Rigel to study the elf aboard. Naos Kurhah had opalescent hair and eyes, of course, and wore his three millennia well. No starborn would ever look old, yet there was a gauntness to him, a weariness, but also a serenity that others lacked. He did not steer his throne to the place Izar had just vacated, but to the far side, the place of honor, presently occupied by a furiously scowling Vildiar.

"Your manners were shitty when you were an imp, sonny," the newcomer said. "They haven't improved one bit. I am six times your age, so make way."

In smoldering silence, Vildiar floated his throne across to the other side and Kurhah took his place.

The older Naos rose and bowed to the queen, then sat down again.

Talitha gave him a regal nod. "You are most welcome, starborn. We had thought that you had faded."

"Very close, my dear," the Naos said. "But then distinguished starfolk began dying like earthlings and I became intrigued. I decided to wait around and see what would happen next. Such a mistake! Look where it has gotten me!"

"It is unfortunate that you were not present when poor Queen Electra returned to the stars." Talitha smiled sweetly and Rigel's heart dropped to the floor. She wasn't going to abdicate. Once a queen, always a queen. If anything, she probably saw Kurhah as a source of protection. She had tasted the royal jelly and she was safe from Vildiar's assassins as long as the older Naos stood between him and the throne.

"Even the most prescient of us could not have foreseen her tragic ending," Kurhah said sadly. "Or the egregious revelations that have forever blighted her memory." He glanced briefly in Rigel's direction.

"So it was you, Starborn Kurhah, who sabotaged the reversion staff?"

"It was. Of course I—"

"Why?" roared the queen. "What authority did you think you had to kidnap and endanger a senior officer of my government?"

Kurhah shrugged, seeming more amused than threatened. "A *halfling*? No halfling has ever been appointed to an office of cabinet rank in the Starlands before now, my dear. Of course one must overlook and forgive minor errors of judgment committed by one so young in the first shock of a totally unexpected accession to the throne. I sought to provide you with a face-saving escape from your own indiscretion; that is all. Naturally I did not expect your dear son to be involved. As soon as I discovered that he was, I ensured his return to Canopus. We cannot blame the child for losing his own staff, but we can, and indeed must, censure the total incompetence of the one who dragged him into extreme danger, namely that same halfbreed you—"

Gong! A blast of sound thundered through the court, making even Rigel wince. The effect on the starborn, with their more sensitive hearing, must have been much worse.

"Silence!" the queen roared. "You have admitted to several breeches of criminal law and your slanders against the throne may constitute lèse-majesté. We shall take counsel on the matter. You will wait upon us this evening at our pleasure and we shall discuss the matter further."

Talitha was flushed and furious. Kurhah was a loving grandparent tolerating a rambunctious infant with fond amusement. Vildiar yawned.

Glaring like a teacher trying to restore order in a rowdy classroom, the queen said, "Now that we have solved the sabotage problem, Chancellor, you may proceed to the next item."

Celaeno bowed and beckoned Pleione over for a quick conference.

The next item would obviously be Vildiar, who was pretending to have lost interest in the proceedings as he smiled down at Izar, one wide step below him. Izar was trying not to notice, but he was hunched over on his chair with his fists clenched, trembling. Standing directly behind him, Rigel could neither do nor say anything to comfort him. What sort of a father so terrified his own child?

Pleione was ready. "Prince Vildiar, you were required to produce halflings Alkes, Aludra, Benetnash, Botein, Hadar, Mintaka, and Sadalbari."

Vildiar's elongated, pale face turned to regard her as a keen gardener would inspect a bad infestation of spider mites. "I was, and I have complied as well as I could at such absurdly short notice. Those that we were able to locate are waiting at the back, but the guards have failed to keep a center aisle clear."

"Bring forth the halflings," Pleione commanded. At the far end of the court, a drum began to beat.

"You must understand," the prince continued, addressing her but obviously intending his words for Talitha, "that Phegda is very large, with thousands of subdomains. To find particular individuals and transport them here is bound to take time."

A disturbance at the far end of the court was approaching through the crowd.

"How many of them did you bring?" the counselor demanded.

The giant pondered. "I believe the last count I was given was eighty-six."

Now the angry flush had reappeared on the queen's face. Izar twisted around to give Rigel a look of horror. Prince Kurhah was barely veiling his contempt. Rigel tried to remain impassive inside his helmet, but he could tell that Vildiar was about to win another round.

The disturbance was now recognizable as a wedge of sphinxes driving ruthlessly through the spectators. Behind them, herded by centaurs at a fast trot, ran a pack of humanoids. By the time they emerged into the cockpit area before the steps, they were distinguishable as halflings, young and old, male and female. Those who looked most elfin wore the usual loincloth; others were shrouded like Bedouin, with only their faces showing. The centaurs lined them up in front of the spectators.

"How many of these are your own spawn?" the queen demanded.

"That offensive remark is unworthy of the high office you hold, Talitha, but if you or one of your starborn minions will dare to repeat the accusation on the Star of Truth, I will respond." When no one volunteered, Vildiar shrugged. "Hundreds of millions of mudlings live in Phegda and probably as many starborn. Halflings happen, and if they happen within my domain I see that they are reported to me and treated as the law requires."

Halflings happened because they were necessary, and not just for guard duty or violence. Halflings happened because the mudlings who did the rough work of the Starlands made competent herders, servants, gardeners, farmhands, and so on, but they needed halflings to supervise them. Halflings had more drive and intelligence and happened to be conveniently sterile, so they had no dynastic ambitions. They had few rights in law, either, and the ninety or so here presented all looked terrified.

Vildiar smiled, teeth like twin wood saws. "Alkes was the first you requested, I believe? Halfling Alkes, step forward one pace."

Three males and two females stepped forward. All elves and most halflings were born with a star name, and there were only so many named stars. Repetitions were inevitable.

"When I was forced to live in Phegda as your partner," the queen said with cold anger, "I met halflings named Alkes, Aludra, Benetnash, Botein, Hadar, Mintaka, and Sadalbari, among many others, all of whom claimed you as their father. Where are those halflings?"

"It is a wise halfling who knows his own father, my dear. I am sure—"

"Do not call me that, you insolent lout!"

"*Your Majesty.* I am sure that most of the rabble you see down there make the same claim whenever they think it's safe to do so."

"You know which halflings I mean!"

"Yes, I do," Vildiar said with a chuckle. "But I have no idea where any of them are now."

Of course not. Hadar ran the dirty tricks department.

Pleione looked helplessly at Talitha. What was needed now was for some starborn to enter the Star and announce that Vildiar fathered halflings who killed starfolk for his benefit. But no one knew enough to dare make that accusation as a matter of fact, and repeating a rumor would not count.

The queen sprang up. “Court dismissed!” She went striding off around the throne and disappeared behind the great monolith. Consort Elgomaisa strode after her like a hound.

The first court of Queen Talitha’s reign had been a total disaster.

Chapter 15

"Elgomaisa?" Izar said in tones of deepest scorn as they were going down the steps. "In all the Starlands she couldn't find anyone better than him?"

Rigel had never met the new royal consort. "Not good?"

"He calls me 'Impy'! And he plays the zither!"

"Horrible. I don't know which is worse."

"Both!" Izar said firmly.

The crowd was clearing amazingly quickly, draining out through the sides of the courtyard like water from a sieve. Starfolk crowds left no litter behind them. Fomalhaut was standing apart, on the lowermost step, and the flame in his golden eyes was a summons. Rigel sent Izar off with Tyl and Thabit and headed over to the mage.

He bowed. "My lord?"

"Manifestly the political paroxysms have abated, halfling. Another Naos stands between the upstart Vildiar and the throne. The queen's council will responsively tender its advisement that she relinquish the throne to Prince Kurhah, as a more seasoned ruler. The now-deceased Regent-heir Kornephoros grievously erred in the license he allowed Prince

Vildiar, but the new king will swiftly exact retribution for his transgressions."

Indeed? If Fomalhaut really believed all that, then his reputation as a prophet had to be based on a few lucky guesses.

"I would never question your assurances, my lord." Rigel waited, knowing there would be more and having a fair idea of what it would be.

"So the termination of your assignment to defend Izar Starling may be considered imminent. My altruistic but precipitous action in including you when I inverted our deceased honored monarch, Queen Electra, back to the Starlands fortuitously created a situation neither commendable nor propitious. I acknowledge a moral obligation to rectify the current circumstance by restoring you to the continuum of your birth with adequate provision for your future prosperity."

Just as expected. "My lord is most generous. I shall most happily accept this heartwarming offer as soon as I am assured that the Vildiar danger is truly past."

The golden eyes narrowed. "You dare to set terms? Meaning what, precisely?"

"Meaning that I must either see his lifeless body or know that he has been shut up in the Dark Cells for a thousand years or more."

"You are insolent!"

"That is not my intention, my lord. On Earth we have a word for persons like Prince Vildiar, and that is *sociopath.* To protect society, many sociopaths must be confined, because there is no treatment for their condition.

"Furthermore, I saw no sign today that Her Majesty is, or ever will be, willing to abdicate in favor of Prince Kurhah. As her head of security, and based on his recent activities, I must regard him as yet another threat to her safety. Thus I humbly ask your assistance, as court mage, in keeping a close watch on his movements from now on."

"Spy on Naos Kurhah? It is unthinkable! Seancing Earth from the Starlands is possible, but seancing within the Starlands is not."

"Truly?" Rigel asked softly. "I was told once that it was illegal. Why make it illegal if it isn't possible? Kurhah obviously has been spying on you, and he trespassed in your domain with illegal intent."

The elf bared his shark teeth, spun on his heel, and strode away.

Saddened, but trying not to show it, Rigel joined Izar, Tyl, Thabit, and Avior. The multitude was still steadily draining away through the gaps between the monoliths, and soon they would have the whole great courtyard to themselves.

"I am sorry your bonding ceremony had to wait," Rigel told Avior. "But I expect that a few more days of sightseeing might help you decide whether or not you want to stay in the Starlands."

Without the grotesque wig, with just a cloth framing her face, she was a very typical tweenling, larger than most and more muscular.

"I think I do want to stay, but I'd like to see more of the world."

"Remember, the Starlands aren't a world. They're 'a dimensional matrix transformation of the space-time continuum with conservation of supersymmetry.' Or so the Minotaur told me."

"What does that mean?"

"I have no idea." He caught himself smiling at her more widely than he should. Now that Talitha had taken a consort, his fruitless romance with her was over, and any sexy woman was of interest. Avior was extremely sexy, in spite of her bizarre hangups. *In spite of*, not *because of*, he hoped. The idea of a rape fantasy repelled him. Orang and Utan were watching with amusement, and so was Izar. Before he could think of something more to say, Avior did.

"You hinted that I could help you in your feud with that Vildiar character."

Her father.

"Yes I did. There's only one way to . . . But let's wait until you've made your decision, and gone through the formalities. There's less hurry now that another Naos stands between him and the throne."

"Hey, pothead!" A female harpy perched on the back of Izar's chair was yelling at him.

"You mean me?"

"Of course I do. Your former lover wants you to take that delinquent brat of hers to Segin right away. I hear her new consort is going to geld you, just to be on the safe side."

"Go away." Rigel turned his back on it.

"What does *geld* mean?" Izar asked.

"Tell you later. Avior, let's talk again in a few days. Tyl and Thabit here will look after you, if that's all right?"

The twins exchanged glances and one of them muttered, "Woof! That's a tough assignment, Marshal."

"I'm sure I will be in good hands," Avior said calmly.

"I'm certain you will be," Rigel agreed. Four of them.

Segin was the island of the merfolk, yet another royal subdomain. Any portal in Canopus would take them there. When they arrived, they stepped through onto an acre or so of sand as white and soft as talcum powder, baking-hot on the feet.

Segin was an example of the elves' imitation of human calendar art, in this case a cliché tropical evening. The sun had just set, leaving one side of the sky smoky red, while the other was deep indigo, speckled with a few early stars. Curving palm trees waved their fronds in a wind much too warm by elfin standards, while waters of an incredibly azure lagoon lapped at the beach. The royal barge *Saidak* floated at anchor there, but without her figurehead. Ocean surf boomed endlessly on a reef a few hundred yards out.

Yelling in agony at the heat, Izar danced down to the water and plunged in. Rigel bounded after him, always ready for a swim, although he was elf enough to find the Segin lagoon too warm. The floor was an ever-shifting mosaic of rippling light and darting, multicolored fish.

Izar headed for the reef, arms flailing. Long before he reached it, Saidak surfaced in front of him with a great bellow of welcome.

A moment after that her husband, Sertan, appeared alongside her. Like hers, his human part was at least double life size, and his fish half was as long again. Sertan had probably been inspired by some image of Neptune, because he sported a huge golden beard and curling locks that floated around his head even when they were wet. All he lacked was a crown and a trident. A shoal of merkids popped up around him, ranging from adolescents to the fishy equivalent of toddlers, all welcoming Izar with shouts of glee.

Rigel stopped to tread water and exchange greetings.

"Is the queen here?" he asked.

"Indeed she is!" Saidak boomed, oversized eyes flashing. "And Elgomaisa with her. I swear he is the ugliest elf I know. He has black hair! I'd say he had some mudling blood in him, if that were possible. He's to have visiting privileges from now on. If this means she's jilting you, tweenling, then she's even stupider than I thought she was." Saidak was nothing if not forthright.

"No, I have never been more than her loyal servant, so she's not jilting me. I swear that that's the truth, so please don't hint otherwise! Naos Kurhah?"

"We're to admit him when he arrives," Sertan said, cutting off some no-doubt toxic comment from his wife. "I think he visited here in my grandfather's time. Or perhaps great-grandfather's. And Her Majesty is coming! It will be a pleasure and an honor to have Segin acting as the sovereign's principal residence again."

Rigel had not been warned about that. Talitha had a hundred palaces at her disposal, and he and Izar would live wherever she did. Personally Rigel disliked Segin but professionally he found the news not unwelcome. In its way, Segin was as secure as Castle Escher, but Rigel would have to think about how it might be made even more so. Izar would miss Turais, but, being practically amphibious, he'd be happy enough. He had already been towed away by laughing merkids.

Rigel was growing tired of treading water. "Then if you will kindly take me to Her Majesty, I will find out what she wants of me."

"I know what she needs of you!" Saidak always had to have the last word.

Clasping Rigel's arm in a hand that easily closed all the way around it, Sertan towed him out to the reef.

"Ready?" he said, which was Rigel's cue to suck in a chestful of air. Down they went, to be swept by a returning wave through a tunnel, out into the ocean. The outside wall of the reef was a giant sponge of multicolored coral, weeds, anemones, and rainbows of fish. By himself, Rigel would have been helpless to resist the surging to-and-fro pressure of the waves overhead, but his guide held him firmly, pulling him down, down, down, into cooler, darker water. Pale blue became bluer and greener and finally almost black, but the merman knew where he was going, and before Rigel drowned—although not very long before—he was swept into the great hall of Segin Palace and released.

For a moment he stood there on the white-sand floor, gulping in what felt like air. It behaved like air, in that he could shake the water out of his ears and walk and talk. But it was water to Sertan, who floated beside him like a giant shark with an elfin grin. And it was water to the shoals of bright-colored fish that swept around, to the gently waving weeds, and to the many mermaid and merman servants. Once in a while a bubble would waver upward to the roof. Yet Rigel knew that when he stepped through the one-way exit portal to dry land anywhere else in the royal domain, no flood would accompany him.

The great hall was a cathedral-sized cavern of coral, illuminated by pale blue-green light that filtered down from openings far overhead. Even the floor was slightly rippled, so there were no flat surfaces or right angles anywhere. Its walls bore stairs and balconies for the use of landlubbers, and corridors led off to scores of rooms. Rigel had never explored a fraction of it, but he would have to become familiar with all of it, and quickly, if he was still in charge of royal security. Yet he could not imagine how Hadar's assassins would ever penetrate this palace's outer defenses. How did you bribe or intimidate merfolk?

A swirl of red fish shot past him. A starfish was exploring his toes.

"Anything else you need right now, Marshal?" Sertan inquired with a hint of a smile behind his great beard.

"Not right now, thank you, except . . . what happens if strangers come through the portal to the island?"

"If they're not on the approved list we leave them there to die of thirst."

There was no fresh water on the island. The portal up there was one-way; guests could come in but not out.

"But they might live long enough to ambush whoever arrives next?"

Evidently that had not occurred to the big fellow; Sertan was not much smarter than his wife. He frowned. "What should we do? Send for the kraken?"

"If I'm here, perhaps you could just come and tell me? I'll bring Halflings Tyl and Thabit to live here, too. They're my deputies. Um, yes?"

A young merman named Porrima was hovering nearby—literally, for his tail fins did not quite reach the floor—and staring at Rigel with very worried green eyes, almost level with his own. So, a half-grown merman.

"Rigel Tweenling, Starborn Elgomaisa gave orders that you were to be taken to him as soon as you arrived."

"Then lead the way. Sertan, my thanks. We must share a flagon of wine sometime soon."

He followed Porrima into the depths of the palace. Their route had more turns and twists than a moray eel, more stairs than a lighthouse. Doors in Segin were round, like portholes, and a label above each opening displayed the owner's name in the starfolk's ornate, many-colored syllabic script, which Rigel now read at about a second-grade level. The door he was led to stood open and the unmistakable twanging of a zither was drifting from it. Porrima floated in.

"The halfling, starborn."

The music stopped. "Good. Carry on with what you were doing earlier."

Rigel entered and found himself in a garden, walled around by multicolored coral, lit by the blue-green sea surface far above, and populated with starfish, lobsters, sea anemones, darting shoals of fish, and all the tourist-delighting denizens of a reef. He was also face-to-snout with a shark, a great white larger than he was.

"That is Halfling Rigel," Elgomaisa said. "He is permitted."

The glassy dead eye surveyed Rigel for a moment, then the monster whipped around and soared upward. Rigel swallowed his heart back down to where it belonged and bowed, elfin style, to the starborn, who was sitting in a chair fashioned from a huge clamshell. He did not appear to be armed with a gelding knife, which was a relief.

"May the stars shine on you forever, Starborn Elgomaisa."

"Halfling." The formal response to an inferior's greeting was, "May your progeny outnumber the stars," but that would be absurd when said to a mule. "The queen will be taking up residence today, and these are the royal quarters. You may inspect the areas that concern you."

Rigel thanked him politely and did so. Other than the exit, four doors were inset in the walls, all circular and made of heavy timbers. He picked out the names on each, symbol by symbol: Izar, Elgomaisa, Talitha, Guard.

Izar's door stood open, and inside Porrima and a young mermaid were coaxing starfish off the walls and putting them into a net bag. The room itself was spacious and well furnished. Light, and possibly air, entered by a dozen or so very narrow shafts. Even Izar wouldn't be able to escape through those.

"Are those stars a problem?" Rigel asked.

The merman shrugged. "They have been known to crawl on people's faces while they sleep. Starborn Elgomaisa told me to remove them in case they frighten Starling Izar."

Rigel said, "Ha! The starfish would get the worst of it."

He went out and crossed over to his own space, the guard's room. It was tiny, with one very small bed taking up most of the space. The decoration on the walls comprised four very large octopuses working their way through a symphony of colors and patterns. Wondering who had chosen these quarters, he followed the sound of the zither back to the courtyard and was left to stand and wait until Elgomaisa completed the piece. Porrima and his companion finished cleansing Izar's room of starfish and came out to do the same in the central garden.

When, at last, the music ended, Rigel said, "Are there any other exits, starborn?"

"The other two rooms have access to the sea, but the precincts are well patrolled."

"I should prefer my room to be closer to the starling's."

The un-elfin black eyes studied him for a moment. "Life is full of disappointments, tweenling."

The upstart was being put in his place. The two merfolk were listening.

"As you say, starborn." Rigel bowed and went off to explore the rest of the palace.

Chapter 16

After an hour or two, Rigel had amply confirmed that he did not care for Segin. It was too confusing, and was simultaneously enormous and claustrophobic. It contained many beautiful halls and gardens, but the windows looked out on water and nothing else. In Canopus he had friends among the centaurs and sphinxes, but here there were only merfolk, who had the conversational skills of goldfish, and the few starborn he met ignored him. Every now and again a gigantic shark would come hurtling along a corridor at him, swooping up and over his head before he could even duck, with just a puff of pseudo-air to mark its passage.

He had been the queen's confidant and platonic sweetheart. Until last night they had shared that secret and been friends. Then he had dared to look at another woman, and the romance had ended. Clearly Consort Elgomaisa was going to be making the decisions from now on, and his views of the pursuit of happiness nowhere included Rigel Halfling.

That became even more evident at the dinner the queen gave for Naos Kurhah. Or perhaps it was a welcome for her new consort, who certainly sat very close to her throughout the evening. Kurhah was not the only guest, although he obviously considered himself the guest of honor. Apparently his rudeness in the court had been forgiven, or he had apologized for it, although that seemed out of character. Eight of the starborn officers of the government were there in their glittering collars, including Court Mage Fomalhaut and the new Chancellor Celaeno. Prince Vildiar was not.

Five halfling officials were also present, people who actually worked and were roughly the equivalent of earthly bureaucrats. They, like Rigel, had to stand along one wall and watch while the elves ate and drank and twittered as elves did in company. Imps should be seen and not heard, so Izar was seated at a separate table for starlings. Normally on such occasions he would have a few friends keeping him company, but that evening he was alone, and glumly spent most of the time levitating cutlery.

Mermaids served the food and wine. Merfolk and merkids entertained the diners with music and three-dimensional ballet. The evening was a social success.

Rigel grew steadily more disgusted, and his thoughts kept returning to Fomalhaut's standing offer to return him to Earth. The mage would be only too happy to oblige him. He would provide a bag of gold and perhaps even ensorcel him with a fake navel and nipples, so he could take his shirt off without being revealed as a freak. Even he wouldn't be able to supply Rigel with a birth certificate, though, so he would still be a nobody, a nonperson, unable to obtain a passport or a driver's license.

The only problem was that he would go mad.

The worst moment came near the end, after the servants had left. Talitha raised her glass to indicate a toast and everyone fell silent.

"Naos Kurhah," she said, "we are overjoyed to know that you have not left us after all. It is no secret that Prince Vildiar has more ambition than honor, and we had begun to fear that his killers were starting to slaughter officers of our government. Your return to the Starlands is a great relief to all of us."

Was she going to offer the Naos the throne after all?

Evidently not. "We shall sleep better knowing that you stand between him and the succession . . ."

Kurhah's expression of modest pride soured to wary surprise.

"But one thing bothers us," the queen continued sweetly. "What was the real reason you invaded Starborn Fomalhaut's laboratory yesterday to tamper with Rigel Halfling's reversion staff?"

Rigel noted that he was no longer Marshal Rigel. Fomalhaut was listening intently.

Kurhah leaned back in his chair. "My memories go back a long time, my dear."

"Who?"

"Your Majesty. And I know lore that goes back even further. Any halfling wearing a Lesath amulet is an abomination. When that Lesath is the notorious Saiph, then the consequences are always dire. Always! Saiph is the most ancestral of all, a potential disaster even when it's worn by a starborn. I could tell you scores of tales about the deaths it has caused. I saw a chance to remove it from play, and took it. That was all."

His friend Shaula had been surprised to find a halfling with an amulet potent enough to read her intentions, so Kurhah was undoubtedly lying.

The queen considered his answer for longer than one would have expected. Now was the moment when she could mention that her son had twice been kidnapped and rescued by Rigel and Saiph. She might also recall that they had saved her own life from an attempted murder.

"I see," she said eventually. "But the sphinxes and centaurs do approve of him . . . Well, your real motive is slightly less treasonous than the excuse you gave in court, even if your methods remain censurable. Do we have your word that you will refrain from further aggression against our son's bodyguard?"

Kurhah hesitated, and Rigel expected a wrangle about the difference between a bodyguard and a cabinet post, but it did not come. "If that is Your Majesty's command, then of course I shall obey."

Talitha turned to Fomalhaut. "Court Mage, are you prepared to forgive Naos Kurhah's excess of zeal?"

The elf's golden eyes flicked briefly in Rigel's direction. "Absolutely, Your Majesty. Were I not sworn to obey your orders, I should have disposed of the half-breed myself long ago."

"Then, friends, let us welcome Naos Kurhah back and drink to his continued long life among us."

Imp Izar said, *"Oh, schmoor!"* loudly enough to be heard by everyone.

Rigel conducted the chastened starling to his chamber. Izar was frothing mad at the way his hero had been treated, and Rigel himself had trouble justifying it. It was, he assured the imp, no business of his whom his mother chose to be her consort, and Starborn Elgomaisa was a much more appropriate choice—fortunately Izar did not ask him to explain why. And since the nasty rumors about Rigel being her secret lover were unfounded, she must not seem to take his side in any discussion of him.

"Well, it's not fair," Izar protested.

"Life isn't fair, lad." Fortunately the starborn worshipped no omnipotent gods, so Rigel did not have to explain *why* life wasn't fair.

Izar was still far too angry to want to sleep, despite his elfin ability to turn himself off at will. Rigel suggested chess and asked the mermaid on guard duty in the garden area to fetch a board. Izar had recently taken to chess like a merkid to water and was becoming very successful at it, helped by a tendency for pieces to move themselves when his opponent wasn't paying enough attention.

After he had won three games, one of them almost honestly, he let Rigel persuade him to call it a day. Throwing himself flat on the bed, he went as limp as seaweed on a beach. Rigel headed across to his own tiny kennel. The octopuses were still exploring the spectrum in plaids and the starfish had returned, probably through the window. Wearily, he took off his helmet and tossed it onto the blanket.

There was a door in the corner that he had not seen before. From what he understood of the geometry of his suite, it ought to open to the sea, or just possibly Elgomaisa's bedroom, but he doubted that it would.

Earlier in the day, while exploring the palace, he had activated Meissa so that he could investigate some magical trickeries. He put the helmet back on and again spoke its name. The door disappeared. It was magic, but the magic worked backwards—the door was only visible when it sensed that he was there. The intention must be that only he could see it.

He removed the helmet, set it down, and opened the door. The other side was almost dark. There was just enough light for him to make out another bedroom—a grandiose state bedroom, with a monarch-sized bed, coral pillars, and much marble statuary. The slender woman sitting in the exact center of the bed was recognizable as Talitha by the glow of Naos. She was leaning back on her arms, legs stretched out so that the soles of her feet were angled toward him. She was watching him with an expression that could best be described as quizzical. There was no sign of Elgomaisa.

"Took you long enough," she said.

"Sorry. Didn't realize . . ."

She beckoned him with a toss of her head. The Naos light over her neck and shoulders had begun to surge in a kaleidoscope of shades and shapes.

He went closer, and his heartbeat seemed to rise with every step. The Time of Life had predicted he could not die before he had sired a child. If he mentioned that . . . He knew he wasn't going to tell her that. Not ever. Tonight might even be the night.

He stopped when his thighs met the mattress. "I understood that you had chosen a consort."

Her smile was gleeful. "So does everybody. Don't worry! I've known Elgo since we were imps. He's my oldest friend. Longest, I mean, not oldest. He's not even sixty yet."

"Yes, but a consort . . ."

She frowned impatiently. "Don't pretend to be stupid, Rigel Halfling. I told Elgo about our problem and he'll pretend for me. By day he's my consort. In return, I promised him that we'll have a proper pairing in a century or two and try for a child together. Meanwhile, at night . . ." She raised an eyebrow.

"You do still want me? Not that awful Avior halfling? You weren't serious about her?"

"No, no. I just . . . just wanted to ask her a question . . . I mean, like Thabit says she's a . . . I mean Tyl . . ." Every word he said was making it worse. "I didn't!"

"I knew you hadn't . . . wouldn't. But I nearly went crazy with jealousy at the thought of you with another woman. That's when I realized how cruel I was being. You do forgive me, don't you?"

"Nothing to forgive." His heart was flying around his chest like a bat.

"We won't be disturbed. You do have all night, but . . ."

He dropped his wrap and crawled across the bed to her. She spread her legs, and he realized that she was already naked. He fitted himself into that welcome until she was lying flat and he was poised above her on his hands and knees. The Naos sunburst around her neck and shoulders had fanned out over her breasts and face, brightening the room like a display of aurora borealis.

He sank down on his elbows and kissed her. Strangely, this time he needed no lessons. His lips and tongue knew exactly what to do. His chest on hers, her breasts in his hands, then his mouth on her nipples. She squirmed with joy beneath him, caressing his back, his groin. How long they played he could not tell, but eventually he could wait no longer and slid smoothly inside her.

He had not known there could be an experience as glorious as that. After taking a moment to relish it, he started to move and caught hints of even greater pleasures in store. He began thrusting; she joined in, in counterpoint, faster and harder, until they reached a mutual climax, an explosion of pleasure engulfing the world. Rigel made incoherent animal noises. Talitha cried out, "Stars!" her whole body blazing with rapture.

Rapture faded into stillness as they lay together, still joined inside and out, listening to the slow thump of their hearts.

The Starlands moved for me . . .

Whatever Hadar had in store for him, this moment with Talitha was worth it. But life seemed much more precious now than it had an hour ago.

Eventually he withdrew and rolled off her. He found his voice.

"Why not . . ." he whispered. "Why not let old Kurhah have the throne for a few centuries? Retire to Spica and build a domain. I'll help—I have a good eye for wallpaper. Then no one will care about me, and I'll shrivel up and die anyway before you have to assume the throne again."

The queen sighed.

"I'd love to. But I wouldn't last a week. Hadar cannot kill me now, because I must give the Starlands to my successor, as Electra gave them to me. But if Kurhah rules, I die. Izar dies. Then Vildiar's succession will be safe because he'll be the only adult Naos left. You would die first, of course."

He hugged her tighter. "You're right." He should have seen that. How long would Kurhah last? "One last thing. My mother . . . Electra . . . She told me my father's name, and—"

"Halfling Wasat, curator of the royal amulets. She told me too."

"She did?"

He felt her chuckle. Talitha enjoyed teasing. The Naos sunburst around her neck and shoulders was cycling through colors faster than any octopus. "It was when she told me I would have to take the Light. After all those years of searching, she had finally found you, and she was so proud of you! And so happy that you and I had fallen in love. You would be a help and guardian, she said."

"But the danger!" There were no condoms in the Starlands.

"Childbirth doesn't scare me. The possibility is exciting, but it's a very remote chance, you know. It took Wasat more than a hundred years, and if it happens everyone will just assume it's Elgo's anyway. Starfolk adore imps and all imps have white hair, like yours."

What if the child had human ears, like he did? But he was a three-quarterling, so their child would be a *seven-eighthsling,* so surely it . . . he . . . she . . . would look quite elfin.

"You haven't said the magic words, Mister Estell."

"I love you. I adore you more than life itself." Which was regrettably literally true in his case.

"Good. Because I don't feel very pregnant yet, and I can tell you're about ready to try again. Less chatter and more action, if you please."

Chapter 17

Everyone was always telling him that he was smart for his age, so it was to be expected that Izar only needed a few days to work out what was going on, really going on, in Segin. The odious Elegy—if he could call him Impy, then he could call him Elegy, at least behind his back—was always around, clinging to Mom like barnacles to a rock, and being obnoxious to everyone else, especially Rigel. But Rigel never seemed to mind and wouldn't listen to rude remarks about the consort, even when he and Izar were alone. Yet he *did* seem to mind, or he minded something, because if he wasn't kept entertained, he would sit and brood, which wasn't like him. When that happened, Izar would find something specially awful to do, just to distract him. It was a kindness.

The big breakthrough came after Dschubba came to Segin on what Elegy called a play date. Izar preferred to think of it as a learning conference, because they exchanged all sorts of useful stuff, 'specially whatever they'd picked up recently about fornication and how really disgusting it could get, and so on. Izar didn't have many buddies, and he never got to visit the ones he did have now. Ever since the Family had kidnapped him, Mom kept him chained up like a dog and insisted that he invite pals to come and see him instead of the other way around. So Salm or Ukdah or Dschubba would come for the day and sometimes sleep over. Luckily the royal domain had more entertainments to offer than any other.

As soon as he arrived in Segin, Dschubba produced a new amulet he'd picked up—he was vague about where or how, so Izar knew better than to ask. It was a pink jewel. Just clip it in one ear and you could eavesdrop on conversations that were miles away, Dschubba explained. Well, maybe not miles, but a *very* long way away. If you could see 'em, you could hear 'em. They tried it out in the great hall, which was pretty big, and it worked fine.

Obviously a royal imp like Izar needed that amulet. He needed it more than he had ever needed anything he had ever seen in his whole life, but he was careful not to seem too eager.

"What's it worth?"

"Not trading."

"Yes, you are. If I offer enough you'll trade. Name your price."

"Name your offer."

Izar bet the farm. "A ride on a hippogriff?"

Dschubba gasped. "Up in the sky?"

"High enough to see the edge of the world. It's dangerous, so p'rhaps we'd better not."

Dschubba stared hard at the gem resting on his grubby palm. He closed his fingers around it. Then he gulped and said all right, if he really, truly got to see the edge of the world.

That left Izar with the problem of producing what he'd just agreed to produce, and Rigel certainly would not cooperate. Not without wanting to know why, and that was obviously impossible. So there would have to be punishment in a certain imp's future, but no matter how bad it was, it would be worth it if he got that amulet.

The first trick was to escape from Rigel by dragging Dschubba through a portal in a fast dive, and that wasn't too hard, because Izar hadn't done anything like it since they'd arrived in Segin, and even Rigel got slack if he wasn't kept on his toes. It was Izar's duty to maintain a certain standard of deviltry, although Rigel had never bought that as an excuse after the first time, when he had exploded in laughter.

The portal took them straight to Mabsuthat.

Even in daylight Mabsuthat was a very scary and dangerous place, with humming boulders, gauzy mists, strange scents, and tales of dangerous monsters creeping about. Dschubba said nothing, but he moved very close to Izar and peered all around. The second problem would be finding a hippogriff, but all Rigel ever did was wait, so Izar waited, and in a few moments one came trotting out of the mist and halted to inspect the intruders.

But it wasn't Kitalphar; it was a young male, whose name was Torcularis Septentrionalis. Weren't the males supposed to be dangerous? More dangerous, that was. Izar really didn't know what he was supposed to do here, so he bowed, which was what Rigel always did.

Torcularis eyed him with its eagle eye, first right, then left. It advanced a few steps.

"Please, noble Torcularis Septentrionalis, will you give me and my friend a ride?"

Silence, but the hippogriff cocked its head even more, which seemed to suggest, *Why?* And it moved a little closer.

"Because I am the queen's son." Nothing happened. Izar was sweating buckets now and hoped Dschubba hadn't noticed. "I am Naos, or will be soon." Torcularis's only reaction was to clack its fearsome beak a few times.

"Because I promised my friend that you could take him up high enough to see the edge of the world."

He hadn't known that hippogriffs could shrug, but this one did. And it had come close enough now that he had to look up at it, and all he could see was its enormous razor-sharp beak.

"Because," Izar said shrilly, "I am going to get most horribly punished for coming here and asking you this, and if you won't help me, my friend will call me a liar forevermore." *Still nothing!* "Also, I am very cute. Everyone says so."

Torcularis Septentrionalis nodded, turned around, and sat down.

"You always have to butter them up a bit," Izar said offhandedly. "Climb aboard."

"You're coming too!" Dschubba said hoarsely. His forehead was shiny.

"If you're scared, sure."

So the two imps clambered onto the hippogriff and gripped the crest of hair along its back. Dschubba was shaking a lot. The beast spread its wings and soared up like a kite.

They did see the edge of the world, not to mention volcanoes, icebergs, and golden fountains. Izar got the pink amulet. He carefully rearranged all his ear clasps so that no one would notice that he had a new one.

Rigel reported his clandestine activities to Mom, who was extra furious and had him locked in his room for a whole day, with nothing to do except chase fish. That was for running away from Rigel. He didn't get fed, either, because he wouldn't say where they had gone.

But, oh, was that amulet ever going to be worth it!

His pal Ukdah came over a couple of days later, and they went dolphin riding with the merkids, heading over the horizon to find the setting sun, which they didn't; twilight at Segin went on forever. Luckily, the merfolk knew the way home.

When they got back to the island, Rigel was sitting in the ripples, arms on his knees, staring at the sea. Izar splashed over to him, Ukdah close behind.

"What'ch you doing?"

Rigel looked up with a faint smile. "Just thinking about what a beautiful place this is."

Izar glanced out at the lagoon and the spray over the reef. Yes it was, but how long did a guy need to decide that? "You didn't come looking for me!"

"No," Rigel said. "The merfolk told me where you'd gone, and they look after you."

Izar didn't want to talk about his captivity in front of Ukdah, so he said, "Ha!" mysteriously, to imply that there were times when even the merfolk couldn't keep track of him. He trotted off, buddy in tow, until they were far enough along the beach not to be overheard.

Then they sat down to discuss prospects for lunch. Ukdah didn't like the sound of raw oysters. Izar hated them himself, but couldn't admit that, having suggested them.

"What's wrong with the halfling?"

Izar glanced around, to where Rigel had gone back to brooding. "Dunno. He gets like that sometimes. Grown-ups always need someone to copulate with."

If Ukdah dropped one feather of a hint about Mom, there'd have to be a fight, but he didn't. He just sighed. "What's the absolute oldest you can get without having to do the puberty thing?"

"'Bout thirty-one."

"Gruesome!"

Izar agreed; it would be terrible to have disgusting urges like that.

But then the portal opened, like a hole in the air, and who should emerge but Elegy, alone. After glancing around, he headed over to join Rigel.

"Who's he?" Ukdah demanded, for he was too far off to sense names.

"Elgomaisa, Mom's consort."

"You like him?"

"No."

"He's ugly."

"Yes. Now shut up for a sec, I'm thinking!" Izar turned an ear—his *right* ear—in their direction.

"Halfling?"

Rigel clearly hadn't heard him coming. He started. Then he scrambled to his feet and bowed. "Starborn."

Elegy sat down in the water. "Had I been someone coming to kidnap Impy, I would have taken you by surprise."

When not ordered to sit, a tweenling remained standing. "Had you been a threat, my lord, my amulet would have warned me in plenty of time."

"Saiph? Let me see that." He inspected Rigel's bracelet.

"What're you thinking about?" Ukdah asked.

"Shh!"

"I trust you are being discreet about your new sleeping arrangements?" Elegy said.

Izar must have twitched, because Ukdah said, "What's wrong?"

"What sleeping arrangements, my lord?" Rigel asked. "If you're asking whether I find my new room somewhat cramped, then the truth is that, yes, I do, but I am well aware that it is extremely luxurious compared to the sort of billet assigned to most halflings. I have no intention of complaining to anyone."

"Tactfully put."

"My lord is kind."

The trouble with eavesdropping at this distance was that one couldn't watch faces, and Izar had a strong suspicion that Rigel meant something more than he was saying.

Elgomaisa seemed to understand well enough, because his tone sharpened. "Sit down. Now listen, boy. I would never have agreed to this arrangement if the circumstances had not been extremely unusual. You must be aware that she was paired very much against her will, while she was still a minor and subject to her father's authority. She was not a virgin, because she had previously granted me the honor of taking her maidenhead and we were enjoying a first—first in her case, I mean—romance. We starfolk prize that initial union very highly. Our poets rave about it. In our case, it was cruelly terminated by the regent's edict and she was bundled off to Phegda to provide a child for that monster."

No doubt about who they were discussing now.

"What in *schmoor* are you staring at?" Ukdah demanded.

Izar said, "Mating whales," and pointed at the horizon.

Elegy was still spouting. "The ordeal she endured there continued to haunt her for years afterward. We—her friends, I mean—were all very concerned. She behaved erratically, hanging out with some highly unsuitable people. She even refused offers of relationships from starfolk with the highest possible reputations as skilled and satisfying lovers."

"That would certainly be unnatural," Rigel said.

After a pause, Elgomaisa said, "What do you mean?"

"Oh, beg pardon, my lord. My experience is all with earthlings, as you know. Among them, an unusual or unnatural sex life is often a sign of emotional instability."

"Starfolk do not suffer from 'emotional instability,' as you call it."

"How about Vildiar?"

"That is Prince Vildiar to you, halfling. He is Naos and immeasurably higher than you."

"I humbly beg pardon, my lord. I shall watch my tongue in the future."

"You had better. A good public flogging would quench any remaining rumors. As it was, Talitha seemed to be recovering from her ordeal at last when the burden of the monarchy was literally thrust upon her shoulders. A few days ago she summoned me in considerable distress and asked me to cooperate in this shameful deception. I consented out of my fondness for her as a lifelong friend and my duty to her as my queen. Otherwise, I would never have supported such a deceit."

"Your kindness does you great honor, my lord."

"I just hope that you appreciate your good fortune. And never forget that—by the terms of my agreement with Her Majesty—if the least hint of this conspiracy leaks out, it's the Dark Cells for you, boy." Elgomaisa stood up, as if to leave.

"I do pride myself," Rigel said, "that Her Majesty seems somewhat more serene since I began the treatment."

"Insolent savage!" Elegy ran out into the water and plunged beneath the surface. In a few minutes he came up for air and a mermaid appeared beside him to lead him down to the palace.

"I can't see any whales," Ukdah said.

"I 'spect they're merfolk I saw," Izar muttered, his mind racing over what he had just learned. He felt somewhat uneasy thinking about Rigel bouncing Mom around at nights, but she *had* been happier since they came to Segin. But Rigel . . . Rigel, Izar decided, had been happier at times, but moodier at others, up and down. Like sitting staring at the sea! Halflings were weird.

Chapter 18

A few days later, while Izar was still in bed but enjoying a 'vigorating wrestle with Slinky, the pet squid the merkids had given him, in walked Tyl the Horribly Hairy.

"Hail, most noble Izar, lord of the heavens."

Izar just grunted, his face being much occupied by tentacles.

"I'm supposed to take you to court to watch Halfling Avior being granted status. I thought we might go early and pick up some toasted goat eyes in the bazaar for breakfast?"

He was joking about the goat eyes, but there were lots of toothsome treats in the bazaar.

"Where's Rigel?" It was still early; Izar had a very good idea where Rigel might be.

"He's coming."

Exactly. "Well, I'm sort of tied up right now, Tyl, but if you'll help get this mollusk off of me . . ."

Breakfast sitting on the harbor wall was great. The court, when they got there, was deserted.

Izar shouted, "Come on, Fatty! Race you to the end and back." He tore off.

Predictably Tyl, who had eaten half a roast ibis, made a very disrespectful retort and stayed where he was. So Izar abandoned his run and trotted across to one of the great statues and pretended to read the inscription on its plinth. This little strategy paid off very well when Thabit arrived with Avior. The three of them said a lot of things they would never, never, never have said had they known that Izar was listening. It was all he could do not to stare along the court at them with his mouth open. Wow! They not only did those awful things, they talked about them afterward. *Just wait till Dschubba hears about this!*

Rigel and Mom appeared with a starborn recorder in tow, but Izar didn't bother returning to the group. He'd watched status ceremonies before, and there was nothing special about this one except that Mom was the sponsor. Besides, the loyalty oath was basically meaningless—it didn't stop you changing your mind later. He listened to it all, anyway. The recorder departed, and Izar wandered along to another statue.

"Now," Mom said, "let's hear this mysterious plan you have in mind."

"I'd like to show Avior around Kraz first," Rigel said. "That's the place we picked out for your studio," he told the halfling.

Mom laughed oddly. "Are you implying that you don't trust me?"

"Of course I do. I trust you implicitly. But what you don't know, you can deny on the Star. That's the Vildiar technique, and we know it works. If what I'm going to ask her to do isn't possible, I'll tell you about it later. If it is, you'll find out soon enough. All right?"

"Of course," Mom said. "Carry on, er, halfling. What about the terror?"

"Tyl's going to take him fishing this morning," Rigel said. "At least that was the plan. To what do you attribute his sudden interest in epigraphy?"

"Guess!" Mom said. "Some of those old stories are very racy. I remember sniggering over them when I was about his age."

Oh? Izar took a harder look at what he was studying, but it was all about someone building a library. Then Rigel called him, so he went running like a good little imp should. Just this once, to show that he could.

"You're going fishing," Rigel said.

"I want to come with you."

Rigel smiled and shrugged. "Very well. Halfling," he told Tyl, "you have the rest of the day off."

Later, Izar realized that he should have foreseen trouble in that suspiciously easy victory.

Kraz was just a portal step away. Though it was part of the royal domain, Izar hadn't seen it before. It was a normal sort of private home: a group of stone cottages with thatched roofs set beside a promising-looking swimming hole with a small waterfall, and the usual trees, animal paddocks, and flowering shrubs. There was no view and the surrounding forest didn't look very real, but the unicorns in the yard were real enough. So were the two overmuscled, mother-naked, hairy mudlings who were grooming them. They gaped in dismay when they caught sight of the visitors and rushed off to find proper coverings.

Rigel ignored the cottages and led Avior and Izar straight to a slightly larger building set apart from the others on a knoll. "Whichever long-ago starborn imagined this place was probably a mage or an artist, because this looks to me like a perfect studio—roomy, bright, and very secure."

"Who else lives here?" Avior asked as they climbed the path.

"No one. Just you and whatever servants or friends you want. Those two mudlings we just saw are called Nusakan—they're a special gladiator line, bred for fighting. They're illegal, but they didn't ask to be born, so it's not their fault. No Nusakan will ever harm a starborn or a halfling, but they fight one another when ordered to do so. Humanoid pit bulls. Like all mudlings, they're very eager to please."

Avior said, "I see," in an odd tone, and nothing more. Izar wondered if she was thinking what he was thinking about what Rigel might be thinking.

The studio building was just a big shed to Izar, a barn, although it smelled of dust rather than unicorn poop. Avior enthused politely. So now Rigel was probably going to explain the secret plan, and Izar would have to figure out how to listen if he was sent outside and they stayed inside. The pink amulet didn't work through walls.

But Rigel led the way out again, bringing Avior to a bench under the eaves.

"Think I'll go down and 'spect the unicorns," Izar told him.

"Good idea. Oh, by the way, little buddy." Rigel sat down and leaned back against the wall with his long legs stretched out as if he were completely relaxed, but his all-white eyes held a gleaming brightness that Izar knew and had learned to distrust.

"Yes, halfling?"

"I could have sworn that you had thirteen ear studs. Now I see fourteen."

Izar realized that his ears had folded back defensively. He forced them to spread out as usual. "Dschubba gave me this blue one."

"Oh? And what does it do?"

"It doesn't seem to do anything, but it's supposed to help me with my magic lessons."

The halfling nodded. "You're required to ask your mother about anything to do with magic, aren't you? Never mind now. Go see the unicorns."

Whew! Narrow escape—Izar ran off down the slope. The mudlings had returned, now completely swathed in leather work garments and hats. He ignored them and leaned on the fence to gawk at the unicorns like an innocent imp.

And listen.

"What was all that about?" Avior asked.

"I can't take my eyes off that little devil for a moment. But let's talk about his father."

"My father too."

"Right. How do you feel about that?"

"I thought he looked like a reptile, and what Tyl and Thabit have told me about the Family makes him sound like one."

"Either I will kill him or he will kill me, eventually."

"I'll help you. You want me to swear to it on the Star?"

"I might," Rigel said quietly. "Later. The problem is how. As I told you, he's both Naos and a mage of the highest rank. Grenades and machine guns aren't available in the Starlands, and nothing magical will work against him, not even Saiph."

"No? But I thought—"

"Saiph's a defensive amulet, although when I was about to be attacked by Halfling Tarf and some other members of the Family, Saiph attacked them first. Frankly, I'm not sure there is any way of killing Vildiar. If there is, it will certainly require taking him by surprise. The first step must be to distract that halfling gang of his, and you can help me there, with a bit of luck."

"I don't see how, but keep talking."

"I have an idea, but the first thing we'll need to do is get rid of Hadar, who's his adjutant and the brains of the assassins. Without Hadar, he'll be crippled. And what Hadar wants more than anything is this."

Just in time, Izar stopped himself from turning around to look, but Rigel obviously meant Saiph.

"A bracelet?" Avior said with a laugh.

"Yes. He can't get it off my wrist without killing me first. When I saw your work, and how realistically you could model dead bodies, I wondered if you could make a dead Rigel good enough to fool people."

"Easy, if you get me the materials. You'd have to model in the nude."

"No. You've seen as much of me as Hadar has. Make up the details."

Izar thought that was pretty funny but managed not to laugh.

Avior did laugh. "No, that wouldn't do. You can't do this with magic?"

"I could, but it wouldn't fool Vildiar, or even his thugs, if they're wearing the right amulets. I have a ring, this one, that squeezes my finger if I point at anything that isn't what it seems. Of course your creations won't pass close inspection either, but they're incredibly realistic and most people only see what they expect to see. What materials would you need?"

"I don't suppose you can do plastics here, but plaster is about the right specific gravity, depending on how much sand I add . . . We'll have to suppose rigor mortis, of course. Paper and paste for papier-mâché. Wax and colorings. Wire, bones, or wood for stiffening. Hair."

"As long as there's nothing industrial in the list, everything should be available here. How long will it take you?"

"A month or so once you've collected the stuff for me. A barrel or two of hard wax—you're not exactly a miniature subject, you know! And how do you plan to die?"

"That's going to be a problem. It won't be very convincing if you fake a cut throat and they try poison. Hadar favors archery so that he can stay out of range of my sword, and we saved a couple of the arrows he used against me in his last-but-one attempt, so plant a few arrows in 'my' chest and hope for the best. I haven't worked out all the details yet. But why don't you take a look around Kraz here and think over what you'll need. I'll send an aide who can furnish the place with everything you want, from paintbrushes to sofas. I'll have her here in an hour or so. She'll show you how to go by portal to the markets. You can charge everything to the royal account, just on your own say-so, because nobody lies or steals here."

"And what are you going to do with your doppelganger?"

That was very much what Izar wanted to hear. Whatever Rigel was planning sounded dangerous, and Mom didn't know about it. Izar might have to warn her, even though that would mean giving up his eavesdropping amulet.

Rigel said, "Doppelgangers walk. What I need is a dead ringer."

"All right, smarty. What are you going to do with your dead ringer?"

"I'm going to pick a fight with a couple of the Family. Two would be best, but I can handle three as long as one of them isn't Hadar—he has an amulet called Sulaphat that's almost as deadly as Saiph. I'll kill them both. I won't feel guilty about that, because every single one of them is a killer.

"Then I'll leave one body and remove the other. The fake Rigel corpse won't be wearing Saiph, of course. When the Family finds the evidence, they'll assume that the missing brother has stolen Saiph and scarpered. While they're running in circles trying to find him, I hope they'll lower their guard enough to let me get at Vildiar."

Izar didn't think much of that plan.

Neither did Avior. "That's the weakest, stupidest idea I ever heard!"

"Improbability is one of its strengths," Rigel said. "It'll need a lot of luck, of course, but they may fetch Vildiar to see the evidence. They may take it to show him, although I realize that your creation will feel less like a corpse than it looks. Either way, there will be a brief interval when the Family is distracted and isn't expecting me and Saiph to turn up. Think of it this way: What am I risking? A lot of work by you, of course, but I can set up the trap so that I won't be in much danger. Who knows, I might even catch Hadar himself, and without him Vildiar will be greatly weakened. Starling, come here. You want to go down and inspect the living quarters, Avior?"

Izar had turned and taken about three steps before he realized how he had been tricked. *Simon says, you idiot!* He was so mad that he stalked past Avior on the path without even looking at her and came to a halt in front of Rigel, glowering.

Rigel held out a hand. At least he wasn't smirking.

"What?"

"The pink one, I think."

Grumpily, Izar removed the stud and dropped it onto Rigel's palm.

"It eavesdrops?"

Izar nodded.

"From Dschubba?"

Nod.

"That day you ran away? What did you give him in exchange?"

"Ride on a hippogriff."

That rattled him. "*What?* Stars above, Izar, if you'd run into a male one, it would have bitten your head off!"

"It . . . we, I mean, didn't."

Rigel sighed. "I got suspicious in court this morning. The magical acoustics weren't turned on, but I was pretty sure you were eavesdropping on us. Your mother trusts me with your life, Izar."

"So?" It was humiliating for a starborn to be outsmarted by a mere tweenling who was barely older than he was, just more grown-up.

"So . . . do you? Do you really trust me, imp? You think I'd come to your rescue no matter what?"

"Of course! You did, remember, when Hadar had me locked up at Giauzar?"

Rigel nodded. "And just now I let you overhear my secret plans. So I'm trusting you with *my* life, Izar."

Izar gulped, then said, "I won't tell anyone, Rigel."

"No one at all? Not Dschubba or Salm or Ukdah? Not Tyl or Thabit?"

"I swear!"

"Not even your mother?"

Shocked, Izar shook his head.

"Unless she asks you, I mean. Then tell her.You should never lie to her, but don't offer the information otherwise. You know that I never tell you lies, right, Izar?"

"I know, Rigel."

"I got mad at you last week for telling Avior that your mother and I were lovers."

"Yes, Rigel. I don't say that any more."

"Just as well, because now it would be true."

Izar's stupid face gave him away by grinning.

"You knew that too?" Rigel asked.

Izar nodded. "I'm glad."

Rigel's smile was less convincing. "So are we, but now it's even more important that you don't tell anyone. If I get asked now, I can't deny it on the Star any more."

"No." Izar shivered.

"So be careful." Rigel held out the pink stone amulet. "Here."

Izar grabbed. "You mean I can wear it?" he asked in disbelief.

The halfling shrugged. "If you want to. Personally, I think that spying on your friends and family is pretty *schmoory* behavior. I wouldn't do that, but it's up to you." He rose and strode off down the path.

Izar clipped the gem on the waistband of his wrap and hurried after.

"Rigel?"

"Mm?"

"I know you don't lie to me, but did you tell the truth to Halfling Avior?"

Rigel muttered something toxic under his breath. "I never tell you lies, imp. But sometimes I don't tell everybody all the truth."

Chapter 19

"Can you tell me anything about Vindemiatrix?" Rigel said. "The queen wants to move the court to Vindemiatrix soon, and even Saidak doesn't know where that is. Not in the royal domain, obviously."

One of the great blessings of the Starlands was the absence of committees, but Vildiar's criminal conspiracy was a completely exceptional circumstance calling for extreme countermeasures, and thus Rigel had invented the Royal Security Committee. So far it had worked better in theory than in practice.

For one thing, it had to meet outside, because centaurs were never welcome indoors. For another, standard patio seats were shaped like earthly deck chairs, being roughly N-shaped, and the sitter had to lean back with knees raised, an awkward posture for those dressed in meager wraps. Moreover, providing a boardroom table for paws and talons would have been ridiculous. So here he was, on a terrace of the palace in Canopus, trying to do business in the heat of a sleepy afternoon. At least the palm trees drooping motionless overhead were date palms, which provided shade without dropping coconut bombs. The ambience would have been quite soporific without the raucous swarms of gulls, parrots, doves, cuckoos, kookaburras, and harpies.

Soporific did not mean that there was no tension. Recorder Matar, in the other chair, was making no effort to disguise her disgust at having to consort with a half-breed and a pack of animals. Commander Zozma and Squadron Leader Gianfar, crouching opposite each other with front paws and talons outstretched, were barely managing to cooperate professionally in the queen's service, for sphinxes and griffins traditionally despised each other as freaks.

The fifth member of the group was Inspector Bellatrix, a centaur mare—huge and black and Menkent's mother. She preferred to stand, so she towered over all the others, sometimes clumping a hoof on the marble and frequently swishing her tail, although flies were as rare as committees in the Starlands.

Matar pouted at Rigel's question and fumbled with her collection of bracelets. "There are at least fifty starborn by that name." She would get the answer eventually, for her amulets were the magical equivalent of search engines.

"I got the impression that it was more a place than a person," Rigel said.

"I know of a mountain range called Vindemiatrix," Gianfar said, in her usual harsh screech. "Very narrow passes. Bad headwinds."

"The third raven turned up with its neck wrung," Zozma growled. He was a free-range creature who sniffed the wind, and could never understand the idea of following a linear agenda like a tracking dog. "Want to send more?"

"No." Rigel wondered if he should ask about compensating the dead ravens' mates and fledglings and decided to wait until he could discuss it with the commander in private. His scheme of sending talking ravens to spy on Prince Vildiar had never sounded promising. Rigel doubted that anyone could spy on a Naos mage undetected, except possibly another, like Prince Kurhah, who had shown no interest in joining the security committee or assisting in its work. Fomalhaut was a mage, but not Naos. Talitha was Naos but not a mage.

Vildiar and Hadar were terrorists, and the peaceful folk of the Starlands had no idea how to deal with terrorism. Rigel himself didn't either, but at least he knew that mere wishful thinking would not make the problem go away.

"I've gone back a thousand years, halfling," Matar grumbled. "Do you want me to continue?"

"Please do, my lady."

"I have an appointment with the farrier," Bellatrix remarked impatiently, "to pick out some new shoes."

"I'm going hunting with my wives this afternoon," said Zozma. "There's nothing quite like a fresh haunch of ostrich still dripping blood."

"I prefer cat, myself," Gianfar countered, although her rear half was lion.

Rigel's campaign against Vildiar was not going well. In fact, it was not going anywhere. Fortunately, the opposition had not been doing much either. The Hadar gang had been at least temporarily balked by the return of Naos Kurhah, whom the starfolk in general must have seen as a much more acceptable candidate for the throne than either Vildiar or Talitha. The terror would start up again when the enemy had adjusted to the new circumstances, but Rigel wanted to take advantage of the lull and strike first.

The trouble was that he still had no acceptable campaign plan. He had ideas, but they would not come together to form a strategy. Avior was still at Kraz, working on her sham Rigel corpse. The month she had requested had come and gone, and the last time he had gone to visit, she had still been assembling boiled pig bones to make the skeleton.

Fomalhaut had previously belonged to a secret lodge of mages that called itself Red Justice, formed to oppose Vildiar. He refused to discuss it, but it seemed to have fallen apart since Hadar murdered its leader, Starborn Cheleb.

Yesterday, Counselor Pleione had provided Rigel with a very interesting answer to a legal question he had posed, but he had not yet figured out how to apply it in practice. That was so often the problem with ideas: good ones were rarely practical and practical ones not much good.

The Hadar gang's next move would very likely be an attempt on Kurhah's life. Everybody knew that. Rigel would dearly love to set up a trap for the killers, using the Naos as bait, but Kurhah had rudely spurned all Talitha's offers to provide him with sphinx or centaur bodyguards. Nor did he seem interested in joining forces against the common foe.

Apart from the frustrating stalemate, though, life was sweet. Elgomaisa escorted Talitha to social or political functions by day and tactfully vanished at night, leaving her free to enjoy her frantically passionate affair with Rigel. Even Izar had been behaving himself so perfectly that Rigel would have suspected he was sickening for something if elves ever got sick.

"Found it!" Matar announced triumphantly. "Vindemiatrix! Domain imagined by Starborn Ascella during the first decade of the reign of King Procyon. That would be about seventeen hundred and forty years ago."

"Marvelous!" Rigel enthused. "I don't know what we'd do without you. Do you know anything more about it, or about Starborn Ascella?"

"She's Starborn Elgomaisa's mother."

"Good grief!" Elgomaisa was not yet sixty, Talitha had said, barely adult by elfin standards. But Rigel's own mother had been almost two thousand years old when he was born, so why be surprised? "Does she still live there, or just lend it to him for parties?"

"You will have to ask her," Matar said sourly. "Or him. I have no other information about the domain, except a comment that it's of earthly mythic design and is notable for a dramatic entryway across a rainbow bridge."

"Oh, sh . . . shinbones! Any mention of giant wolves or eight-legged horses?"

The others' reactions varied from amusement, in the case of Zozma, to disgust from Bellatrix. The griffin merely opened her beak to display a long black tongue.

The centaur snorted. "Eight-legged horses? That's absurd!"

"Probably a late addition based on a misunderstanding of artistic perspective," Rigel agreed. His haphazard education in the School of Library Dumpsters paid curious dividends sometimes. If Vindemiatrix was older than both the prose and poetic *Edda*s—let alone Richard Wagner's operas—it should provide an interesting insight into early Nordic myths, and specifically those featuring Valhalla, the home of the gods. This wasn't the kind of information he needed, however.

"I'd like someone to inspect it from a security point of view." He looked meaningfully at the griffin.

Gianfar nodded her great raptor head. "We can take care of that. What's the address?"

Matar consulted her bracelets again. "Ascella's overlord is Starborn Menkalinan, whose overlord is . . ." Addresses were personal. After ten or so names, she reached Naos Vildiar, underling of the queen.

That was no great surprise. Vildiar had inherited almost as many domains and underlings as the monarch herself, so no one but Rigel would see anything sinister in the relationship between Vildiar and Elgomaisa. Before he could comment, he heard himself called.

"Half-breed! Hey, by-blow! Bucket-head!"

He turned his head to scowl at the harpy perched on the marble balustrade. "Well?"

"Fomalhaut wants you right away. It's urgent, he says. I think he stepped in something nasty and wants to wipe his feet on you."

"Very likely. Go away." Rigel heaved himself to his feet. "Committee adjourned! Please do check on Vindemiatrix for me, Squadron Leader."

He ran for the nearest portal. Talitha was visiting a thousand-year-old cousin somewhere in the royal domain, so *Saidak* should still be anchored at Segin—unless Elgomaisa had borrowed the barge for his own purposes. The starborn had many flying vehicles, but all required more magic than Rigel could muster. His best bet was to portal to Mabsuthat and ask Kitalphar for a ride.

The Time of Life continued its endless swing, while around it pools bubbled and tendrils writhed. The mage's workshop was just as before, except that Rigel's friend Achird was waiting to greet him as he stooped in through the low doorway. He was the only adult male starborn who ever welcomed Rigel with a smile, usually a wry grin that did not show too many shark teeth. Also his sandy hair and eyes made him seem closer to human than the customary poster-paint coloring.

"Guess what? You were right," he said. "There is treason brewing at Alathfar."

The mage strode off across the great courtyard at a pace Rigel was hard put to match.

"So seancing within the Starlands is possible after all?"

The grin grew wryer. "It is much harder than seancing Earth, though. On Earth they have no portals and have to move their fat asses around on wheels. When subjects portal, you can't follow them. You have to guess where they've gone."

Their shadows raced over the bright floor, under midnight stars above. A bronze tiger bared its teeth at them when they went too close, but they arrived safely at the seance court, where Mizar stood with hands and forehead against the great crystal ball. Fomalhaut was there too, one hand on the other mage's shoulder.

"Any change?" Achird asked.

Fomalhaut opened his eyes. "Chancellor Celaeno just walked in," he said glumly. "They've closed the door, so that must be everybody."

By that time Rigel was there to grab hold of Mizar's arm and join in the seance. Instantly he found himself back in the big hunting lodge at Alathfar, and a moment's reflection told him he was seeing it from the corner that held the grand piano. He recognized blue-haired Shaula standing by the fireplace, seemingly acting as hostess. Several mudlings in turbans and eastern robes were passing among the guests, offering trays of refreshment, but it was the guests who interested Rigel.

And appalled him. About thirty starfolk, males and females, were sitting or standing around the big room, chatting quietly in small groups. Chancellor Celaeno was there, and so were at least half a dozen other members of the queen's council. Rigel recognized few of the rest. There was no way to judge elves' age from their appearance, and wealth was a meaningless concept in the Starlands, but judging from the few he recognized, he could guess that the rest were also respected, senior people. He did not need a mage to tell him that there was a conspiracy brewing.

The latest arrival had been shown to a seat. Shaula was scanning the assembly, counting heads. Then she nodded a signal to nowhere in particular.

An interior door opened to admit the host, Naos Kurhah. Silence closed in around him like a fog. Smiling, nodding to friends, he began winding his way through the crowd to the fireplace. Then a green-haired female rose, a couple of males copied her, and soon almost everyone was standing. It was a royal tribute, although in this case it might be dismissed as an appropriate welcome for a long-lost friend—not quite treasonable but close. With some relief, Rigel noted that the chancellor and several others had remained seated.

The prince reached the fireplace and turned to smile at the company at large, holding his hands out in greeting.

"Friends, my friends! Please be seated. My thanks to all of you for coming on such short notice. I will get directly to the point so that those of you with other commitments can leave."

And so that so many absences would not be noticed, if the Naos's intent was as treasonable as Rigel suspected . . .

"My purpose in inviting you here was twofold. First, it has been far too long since I saw you all, and I hope many of you will stay on so that we can dine and rummage over old times together. Secondly, I want to draw your attention to the serious political situation here—"

A male with flaming scarlet hair sprang up and shouted, "Naos!"

"Yes, Starborn Yildun?"

"I will not be part of any seditious conspiracy!"

"I should hope not, starborn. You are free to leave at any time. Or you may remain and hear what I have to say and then go straight to the queen and report it to her. And perhaps her 'head of security'?" He smirked to invite a laugh. "The distinguished marshal of Canopus, I mean."

Yildun sat down, frowning. Kurhah went back to his speech.

"Now, let us not mince words, my friends. We all know the source of the pestilence. Naos Vildiar has created and trained a private army of halflings and encouraged them to assassinate any starborn with a claim to the throne, meaning all the Naos in the realm. Had Queen Electra tended to her duties as she should, she would have stopped him after the first three or four deaths, but instead she extroverted. Either she was hiding from Vildiar's killers or—as she later claimed—hunting for a lost child she had borne to a mudling. I honestly don't know which excuse I would find more repugnant. Whatever the truth, the regent she left in charge was incompetent, and his dereliction of duty gave the villain free rein."

Kurhah paused to peer around at the gathered crowd. He was an effective speaker. Rigel was already seething at this insult to his lover and his martyred mother, but he saw many nods of agreement.

"Regent-heir Kornephoros was a weakling and a coward," Kurhah continued. "And Vildiar bullied the poor thing into giving up his daughter. Have you realized that even that was part of the villain's plan, twenty years ago? The Starlands cannot be stolen. They must be freely given by the retiring monarch to a chosen successor. Vildiar foresaw that his crimes would become public knowledge. He knew that the last legitimate ruler would never voluntarily abdicate in his favor, so he sired a child with Talitha to open a way for him. Electra chose to give the realm to her, as he no doubt foresaw, but she remains fearfully vulnerable, just as he planned. Sooner or later that fiend will get hold of the imp and demand the Starlands as ransom. What mother could refuse such a threat?"

He shrugged. "Had the rest of the Naos had the common sense to band together in time, this need not have happened. No, please do not argue at this point. It is too late to attach blame."

"Is it?" someone shouted. "What were you doing during all this?"

"Fading." Kurhah sighed. "Drifting among the stars. We all return there in the end, and I assure you it is a sublime experience, infinitely rewarding, offering peace and closure. On what I expected to be my last visit home—I came to greet a new greatchild and say farewell to one whole branch of my descendants—I was told of the queen's disappearance and what was happening to the Naos. The knowledge disturbed me so much that I returned to reality one more time, a few years later, only to learn that the situation had become even worse, that only three or four Naos remained."

Only a starborn could ever confuse the Starlands with reality.

"Very much—very, very much—against my will, I decided that I must postpone my final exit and resume corporeal existence. My friends, it was like battling with dragons, a reawakening of pain and sorrow, a return to tumult and mundane cares. I would wish such an ordeal on no one, even the despicable Vildiar himself. But I persisted, and eventually reclaimed my physical presence. Dear Shaula bade me welcome here in Alathfar, and offered me protection.

"You do see that I was a crab without its shell? In grave danger of violence and murder? I had given away all my amulets, and if Vildiar's assassins had learned of my return too soon, they would have crushed me like an egg." With a tinkle of many bracelets, he raised his gem-laden hands. "I needed several months to create a new set, including defenses such as I had never felt a need for before. Then came word that Electra had returned and promptly expired from the guilt curse when she realized the massacre that her neglect had made possible. I had waited a few days too long to reveal my renewed existence. Does my explanation satisfy you? For if it does not, then I shall cheerfully return to the peace of the stars and leave you as you were, ruled by a willful child and threatened by a monster."

Heads were nodding. A low murmur of agreement filled the great room.

It did not satisfy one onlooker. If the magic of seancing made it possible, Rigel would storm into the Alathfar lodge that very second and charge Naos Kurhah with sedition and high treason.

Again the red-haired Yildun sprang to his feet. "Just what are you planning to do, prince? And what do you want of us?"

Smiling catlike, Kurhah surveyed the assembly, neither answering the question nor even glancing at the questioner until he had sat down again.

"First, Starborn Yildun, I propose to deal with Naos Vildiar, a mass murderer such as the Starlands have never seen before. Second, I propose to ask Queen Talitha to step aside and let me rule for a few centuries. I will swear on the Star to abdicate in her favor when I depart—or possibly her son's. They are very nearly the same age, you know, or at least they seem so to my old eyes." He waited for the chuckles to fade. "And there will be no Naos more senior."

"That is treason!" someone shouted.

"No, my friends. Talitha is a wonderful person. My only complaints against her are youth and immaturity. Her obvious infatuation with a halfling was a folly of youth, no more, and now that she has paired respectably with a starborn, it may be forgiven—although he, too, is very young. Had she chosen a more mature partner, one who could have tempered her flightiness, I would have gratefully gone on my way and let her be, as soon as I had dealt with the murderous Vildiar.

"But she did not. Elgomaisa is a mere adolescent by my standards. I am old, old. I will appoint Talitha regent-heir, and will happily return the royal burden to her when she is ready for it. If she refuses to see reason, then I think that you will have to insist. Yes, *you*. I chose you all very carefully as the best, the eldest, and magically the strongest of our time. Many of you are members of her council. I did not choose you in the hope that you would betray your oaths; I chose you for the same reasons she did—wisdom and character. She cannot rule alone; she needs you. She needs me."

A woman by the door rose. "Just how do you intend to dispose of Vildiar?"

"I shall not announce that at the present," Kurhah said, glancing down at his left hand. "I spent the last few days preparing an amulet to detect when I am under surveillance. It indicates that some ill-mannered mage is spying on us at this very—"

A roar of outrage shook the hall.

He waved a hand for silence. "It may be Vildiar's assassins, or it may be some of the queen's helpers, in which case that tweenling pretty boy of hers is most likely behind it. Only halfling perverts could engage in such behavior. Or it may be both parties, I cannot tell.

"But let us now adjourn for a repast. Think over what I have said. Discuss it with your companions, by all means. And then make your decision. In a couple of hours, those of you who wish to leave may do so, and no hard feelings; those who wish to assist me may remain. At that time we shall discuss tactics. And if you are spying on us, Naos Vildiar, then I bid you to join this meeting at that time. The same goes for you, if you are also snooping, Rigel Halfling, *marshal of Canopus*.

"But I offer neither of you safe conduct."

Chapter 20

Rigel jumped back, breaking out of the seance. "He's found a way around the guilt curse!"

The mage and his apprentices disengaged also. Fomalhaut was scowling. "No. Absolutely inconceivable! The maximum achievement to which they could aspire would be to overwhelm Naos Vildiar and denude him of his sorcerous accoutrements. He is trammeled by the same limitations as they are, remember."

"Hadar will never allow it!" Rigel shuddered at the thought of naive elves going against the well-seasoned halfling storm troopers.

"That may be the underlying strategy," the mage said. "If Kurhah Naos and his confederates can exterminate the mongrel assassins, Vildiar will be rendered impotent."

"No, they're the ones who will be slaughtered! According to Tyl and Thabit, Vildiar has two hundred trained killers in his service."

Mizar said, "That many?" and Achird, "Including females?"

"Two hundred and three as of a couple of months ago. I need a ride back to Canopus, please." Kitalphar would not have waited around for him. Hippogriffs were too proud to be servants.

Rigel could see a clear way at last. Pieces were starting to fall into place.

Fomalhaut just continued to scowl at him. "What are you planning to do? Expediate to Alathfar and apprehend the entire multitude?"

"Rush to Alathfar, yes, but I'm going to offer to help them. We earthlings have a saying: 'The enemy of my enemy is my friend.' But I must see the queen first. Please?"

Still the mage balked, while Mizar and Achird watched in the background, Mizar with a faint sneer, Achird chewing his lip. However eager the sandy-haired elf might be to help Rigel, he could not oppose his teacher.

"Do you comprehend the predicament into which your importunities have placed me?" Fomalhaut insisted. "I could be confined in the Dark Cells for spying on starborn."

"You uncovered treason," Rigel said, as patiently as he could. "So Queen Talitha will never convict you. King Kurhah might, though."

Achird hastily scratched his nose to hide a grin.

As if he could see out the back of his head, Fomalhaut swung around to glare at him. "Take this 'breed back to Canopus. And come right back here! I won't have you involved in any of this."

"Yes, my lord! This way, halfling!" The apprentice took off across the great courtyard like an Olympic sprinter.

Rigel raced after him. Achird was youthful, just past his first century. Ignoring the doors, he crossed under the Time of Life, which was currently high overhead, and came to a sudden stop at what looked like a collection of brightly colored planks leaning against a low wall. He threw the closest pair flat and Rigel saw that each bore two straps, positioned like the stirrups on a snowboard. Achird was already slipping his feet into the loops on one of them.

"Skyboards," he said with a bloodcurdling grin. The one he was standing on rose a few centimeters into the air. "If you lie underneath this one and wrap your arms and legs around, I'll fly you to Canopus faster than a speeding arrow."

Elf humor was rare and often malicious, but Achird had a genuine sense of fun. Disregarding the invitation, Rigel put his feet into the stirrups on the other board. "You can control two?"

Achird shrugged. "Dunno. Never tried."

Both boards shot up vertically, banked in unison, and soared past the endless rod of the great pendulum, off into the midnight sky above the crater outside. Rigel windmilled his arms frantically until he caught his balance.

"This is the fastest way to go," Achird yelled.

Although Rigel had inherited the imps' love of low temperatures, he thought the gale force rush of air was likely to freeze him solid very shortly. But he knew when he was being hazed.

"The faster the better."

"Right." The skyboards rocketed forward, turning the wind into a screaming hurricane.

"These must be new?" Rigel yelled, clutching his helmet firmly to his head. Fortunately moon-cloth wraps were held in place by magic.

Achird bellowed, "What?" and moved his skyboard closer, although Rigel could not see how he was controlling it.

"These must be new?" Obviously skyboards were copied from earthly snowboards, and snowboarding as a sport wasn't much older than he was.

"Yup. Mizar and I dreamed them up a couple of days ago. They still worked the next morning, when we were sober."

Rigel hoped that he was still being hazed, but before he could inquire further, both boards and riders went into a steep dive. Ahead of them now, and lower, a huge horizontal wheel of cloud was slowly turning and glowing brightly in the night, more like the mouth of a tornado than the eye of a hurricane. He knew it for a highway, presumably the link between Fornacis and the royal domain.

"Can Kurhah really tell when he's being seanced?"

"If there was no way of knowing, it wouldn't be illegal, would it?"

"I have to get royal permission first, but I do want to go to Alathfar and speak with Kurhah. Assuming your boss keeps on seancing, would you ask him to break off for a few minutes when I appear on stage? That way we might find out if the Phegda gang is spying as well. It could matter a lot."

"I can ask," Achird said. The two riders were lying almost flat, their boards practically vertical as they plunged toward the whirlpool. "If we get separated in that vortex—"

"Yes?"

"You're dead." Grinning, Achird held out an arm.

Rigel grabbed his wrist, felt his own grabbed in return, and then they were in . . .

And out, and it was blinding daylight, with Canopus spread out along the shore beneath them.

"Wow! This is some ride! How much magic do you need to control these things?"

"At least orange," Achird said sympathetically. He grinned again. "And about twenty years' practice."

"Please don't let Izar find out about them!"

As the skyboards swooped down toward the palace, he saw *Saidak* floating in the Sirius pool and guessed that Talitha must be in Miaplacidus, the royal treasury. He directed his pilot to the doorway, thanked him, and watched enviously as he soared away, the spare board now tucked under his arm.

Rigel ran inside, heading for the secret door.

"Six!" said the guardian Anubis beyond it.

That meant that Izar and the twins were also present. Sure enough, he saw them rollicking in the pool, which meant that even the imp was out of earshot. Talitha was sitting on the sand with Wasat, and the old man could be trusted not to gossip.

Chapter 21

For weeks Saidak had been promising Izar that she would show him an active volcano, the highest waterfall in the Starlands, and various other wonders, so he insisted that Talitha use the royal barge for the long-promised visit to Starborn Azelfafage. She agreed readily, because she never seemed to have enough time with her son now that her days were filled with ruling and her nights with loving.

The sightseeing was a success, the family reunion was not. The relationship was quite distant, involving a great-great-great-great-great-grandmother on Azelfafage's side and four more greats on Talitha's. Azelfafage herself was truly ancient, even by starfolk standards, and would normally regard Talitha as too young to be of interest. At the same time the old relic was a terrible snob who felt that everyone must grovel before royalty. The fact that none of her innumerable descendants had ever developed Naos magic was another sore spot. There were no imps present to keep Izar amused; the escort of armed halflings who accompanied him was an outrageous insult to a noble hostess, although it could not be mentioned . . . and so on.

It was a great relief to plead urgent state business, escape back to the barge, and head home.

"Mom," Izar muttered as they went up the gangplank. "I got something I gotta show you."

Any mother would recognize a fire alarm in that reluctant confession, especially since Izar normally preferred to ride out in front with Saidak. At the hatch Talitha flashed Thabit a Gioconda smile that told him that he and his twin were not welcome below deck, and then followed Izar down the companionway. Tyl closed the hatch behind them.

She made herself comfortable on the bench and waited. Izar walked over to stare out a window at the far end. Worse!

Once they were truly airborne, she said, "Well, what is it you have to show me?"

Looking alarmingly guilty, he came over and held out an ear stud with a pink jewel. The moment he dropped it onto her palm she felt the power of it. Whatever it was, it was no child's plaything.

She said, *"Screeps!"* which was his latest exclamation. "What is it?"

"I'm scared I'll lose it . . . and I don't think I oughta wear it."

"Oh?" That was worrisome. "But what does it do?"

"It eavesdrops," he mumbled, staring at her toes. "Lets you listen to what people are saying."

"Sit down, for stars' sake. It *does*? How far away?"

"Far."

A few more delicate questions established that it had been a present from Dschubba, and that Rigel had noticed Izar using it, and had disapproved. In Izar's universe, the stars revolved around Rigel. Anything he disliked was anathema.

"I agree with Rigel. This is probably an illegal use of magic. It's sneaky to eavesdrop on people."

"Friends," he agreed, staring longingly at the gem she was holding. "How about enemies?"

At that point most mothers would ask what enemies, but the hard fact was that Izar did have enemies. To confiscate it outright would be a negative reward for his honesty.

"It might have a use there," she agreed. "Why don't we ask Halfling Wasat to hold onto it in case you need it to spy on your enemies someday."

He brightened. "And we could have a swim!" He had been dry for all of half an hour.

"We could indeed."

Needing no further encouragement, Izar ran to the bow to open the window and tell Saidak to take them to the Sirius pool.

He came back looking much more cheerful. "Maybe the old man will have some other starry amulets for me?" He bounced down on the bench and stretched out his legs to admire his toes. Wasat Halfling had given him his beloved dragon.

"Any more and your ears will fall off. Did you spy on me with this thing?"

Izar said, "Um," and turned pinkish. "Not much."

Rephrase the question. "What did you overhear that you weren't supposed to hear?"

Mutter. "Heard Rigel tell his secret plan to Avior Halfling, 'cept he knew I was listening, so that wasn't really eavesdropping. He said I wasn't to tell you it unless you asked me."

"Then you mustn't." Talitha had guessed enough of what Rigel was planning to know that she definitely did not want to know more. "That all?"

Redness flowed up all the way to the tips of Izar's considerable ears. "Listened to Elegy hectoring Rigel."

Oh, so that was it! "And?"

"He isn't really your consort," Izar whispered, not looking at her. "Not really, er, really."

"Do you have any idea of the trouble you would cause me if you told anyone that?"

He nodded vigorously. "Haven't told anyone! Won't. Promise." But then he did dare a glance. "I'm glad."

"I trust you." She hugged him. "So am I—glad, I mean."

"You love Rigel?"

"I adore him. He's a wonderful person, a fitting son of a queen and lover of a queen."

Toothy grin. "Is he good?"

She had long ago learned that she couldn't raise Izar by pulling from above. She had to go down to his level and push.

"He's terrific; very gentle and patient."

"Oh." Not what Izar had expected to hear.

"If you ever tell *anyone* I said this, especially him, I will tear your ears off, I swear, but I would give up the throne rather than give up Rigel. Not because he's great in bed, but because he's brave and kind and honest and fun, and so it wouldn't matter if he couldn't get it up more than once a year, understand?"

Impressed at sharing such grown-up talk with his mother, Izar nodded emphatically. "I love him too." He considered for a moment and then said solemnly, "I've 'dopted him as my big brother. You'd better not tell him that."

"Of course I won't," she said, never doubting that Rigel had known it for a lot longer than Izar had.

The Sirius pool was one of many pools in the palace large enough for *Saidak*, but it was the closest to the royal treasury of Miaplacidus. Since Tyl and Thabit had never seen the treasury before, Izar thought it funny to prattle to them about all the wonderful stuff in it as he led the way to the anteroom. When they arrived, he laughed at their puzzled expressions. The room was small, with an unglazed window overlooking the harbor. Its doorway was unenclosed, the walls were covered with images and inscriptions, and the only furnishings were a small rug and a low table.

Then Talitha joined them. She laid her hand on the key symbols, the magic recognized her royal authority, and a section of wall faded away.

"And watch this!" Izar crowed, pushing through first.

"Two!" said the Anubis statue.

Then "One," as he backed out again. "Two, one . . ."

"Out of the way," Talitha said.

"Two, three, four, five, four, five . . ."

"Close the door, Anubis," Izar commanded. "Come on, you two!" He took off over the sand, heading directly for the pool.

Miaplacidus was an oasis, complete with swimmable water, palm trees, various whitewashed buildings that housed the royal collection, and sand extending forever in all directions. Wasat Halfling was sitting cross-legged in the sunlight, wrapped up against the elfin chill, sorting through a heap of bracelets laid out on a rug. Steadying himself by leaning one hand against a palm tree, he struggled to his feet, making it just in time to bow to the queen when she reached him.

By then Izar was already foaming his way through the water and his guards were stripping off their robes to join him. Talitha felt safe, therefore, in giving the old man a buss on the forehead. He gaped up at her in astonishment, then smiled toothlessly.

"He told you?"

She smiled. "No, Electra did. You must be very proud of your fine son."

"Indeed, indeed, Your Majesty. Very proud . . ." For a moment sadness darkened his ancient face, for Rigel's birth had brought his parents more trouble than joy. Then he began babbling about fetching a chair.

"The sand is fine," she said, dropping to her knees. "Tell me what you make of this," she said, holding out the pink amulet.

He settled down awkwardly, and much more slowly, then accepted the earring. As a halfling, he could have very little magic of his own, but after a century or more as royal curator he knew more about amulets than anyone else in the Starlands. After a few moments, he lifted his head cloth to fix the device in his puny human ear and turned toward the pool, where Tyl and Thabit were currently throwing Izar back and forth like a beach ball. His screams of gleeful outrage were perfectly audible to Talitha, and Wasat winced at the amplification. He removed the hearing aid quickly.

"Illegal for any of Your Majesty's subjects to possess, of course," he said. "Very probably stolen, but old enough to be unusually powerful. Any provenance?"

"My son got it from a friend, probably by dubious means. The friend probably stole it. Rigel caught Izar with it and talked him out of it, or talked it off of him. Now you're supposed to keep it safe until he needs it."

The old man nodded doubtfully. "As Your Majesty commands."

Wasat's appearance was deceptive. He had been Electra's chosen lover for a hundred years, trusted by her to keep watch over the priceless royal collection of amulets.

"What are you thinking?" Talitha said. "Tell me."

"It can be turned off, you know. Maybe Izar doesn't know that? If you turn the stone, like this . . ."

"You think I should let him keep it?"

"An ordinary boy, of course not. But your son is not an ordinary boy, ma'am, if I may say so. It might make a big difference—if he thought he was being followed, for example. Could you trust him to use it only in emergencies?"

Talitha nodded. "Yes, I can trust him now. He's grown up a lot over the past few months, and your son has done wonders for him. Thank you." She held out a hand and took back the amulet. "Has Rigel told you we are lovers?"

His sudden blush was answer enough. "No, Your Majesty! In fact he strongly denies it. Vicious lies, he said."

She laughed. "They were lies until a few weeks ago. One night our dreams suddenly came true. I love him very much."

Tears glistened in the halfling's eyes. "From his expression whenever your name is mentioned, I am sure Your Majesty has no more devoted servant."

Before he could comment further, the Anubis statue proclaimed, "Six!"

Talitha turned to see the subject of their conversation stalking across the sand toward them. Watching him in broad daylight—a luxury she rarely dared indulge in now—she realized how intense her infatuation was. He was tall and skinny for a mudling, short and muscular by elfin standards, but he moved like a dream, sinews flexing under his skin. She loved the feel of that skin, his scent, his taste—there were very few parts of Rigel she had not licked, sucked, and nibbled by now. His white eyes and hair made him seem like an overgrown imp, but that he was certainly not. "Madly" in love was not just an expression. She dreamed of him whenever they were apart and could barely keep her hands off him when he was within reach.

She had expected to be safe from interruptions here in Miaplacidus. Only four people in the Starlands could open the way to it, but Rigel was one of them.

His expression was grim.

There were witnesses—Izar was shouting for him—so he bowed formally to her and waited for her command before he sat. He smiled cryptically at his father.

"What's wrong?" Talitha said. "Bad tidings?"

He shrugged. "Kurhah's trying to raise a palace revolt against you. But that may not be a bad thing. I need a favor, Your Majesty."

"What?"

His eyes gleamed. "A royal warrant for the arrest of Vildiar Naos."

Chapter 22

As Rigel quickly told his news, he caught the old man smirking at the pair of them and guessed that he had been told of their romance. He must be both proud and amused that his son had taken over the family business of being the queen's lover. May the new love affair last as long as the old one had!

"Not a bad thing?" Talitha exclaimed. "He's planning to depose me and you say that's not a bad thing?"

Rigel explained. "He's planning to bell the cat."

"What cat?"

"To attack Vildiar, I mean. He hopes to muster an army of starfolk to back him up, so he must have worked out some way around the guilt curse, although even Fomalhaut doesn't know what that can be. Dad?"

Wasat shook his head. "No idea, lad . . . Wait!" He frowned, all hideous wrinkles. "There is a record from ancient times, back before the Dark Cells were invented, likely . . . As I recall, a group of starborn tried to put a powerful mage to death. They used poisoned throwing darts, designed so that it would take at least two hits to kill. They hoped that when their victim died after taking six or seven hits from a dozen or so darts, the guilt would be so equally divided among them that no one could know which ones did the deed."

Talitha made a vulgar, un-queenly noise. "Did it work?"

"No, my lady. They all died. I think more of them died than actually managed to hit their victim, so even the intent to harm was enough to create a fatal dose of guilt."

Rigel said, "I hope Kurhah has a better idea. The guilt curse works both ways, of course: they can't kill Vildiar and he can't kill them. Fomalhaut thinks they may try to overpower him and strip him of his amulets. That would cause Hadar and his pack to intervene, of course, but Kurhah could be counting on the fact that they, at least, could be killed without activating the guilt curse. Without his goons, Vildiar will be helpless."

Talitha said, "Hah!"

"I agree. I think Hadar and company will make rat bait out of them. Kurhah himself is fiery enough, but the rest are good musicians and dancers. Unless the old boy has something tremendous up his sleeve, it will be a massacre."

"I still don't see this as anything but a bad thing," Talitha said firmly. "An extremely bad thing! We must stop it." She was a very typical elf, nauseated by talk of violence.

"But if you were to help?" Rigel persisted.

"Help? He wants to depose me and you say I should help him?"

"Yes, I do. If you stand back and let them all be killed, you'll look weak and uncaring. If you stay out of it and yet they win, then you'll certainly be deposed. You have to lend your support and hope to share in the glory. That way, even if Kurhah fails, you will at least have tried."

She sulked for a moment, then asked warily, "Help how?"

"Send along a troop of centaurs, a couple prides of sphinxes, and some griffins. They'll smash Hadar and his gang. Bellatrix has been wanting to do it for years, but of course she wouldn't have a chance against Vildiar. With a Naos and a couple dozen starfolk to take care of him, she'll kick his halflings' teeth in easily."

Talitha shied away from both him and the idea. "Rigel! I am sworn to uphold the laws and the queen's peace. What you're proposing is civil war."

He played what he hoped was his trump card. "Not if we go in with a warrant for Vildiar's arrest!"

Unexpectedly, she flared up in a sudden rage. "Oh, it's 'we' now, is it? *You* are not going to Phegda, you hear? I absolutely forbid you to go to Phegda, today, tomorrow, or at any time in the next century."

"But—"

"No buts. That is final."

This he had not foreseen. Never let the boss fall in love with you! They all understood that Vildiar, if he could kidnap Izar again, could then coerce the queen into giving up the throne to him. Now the same was true of Rigel. More so, perhaps. Even Vildiar might hesitate to harm his own son, if only because of the public disgust it would create, but he would take great pleasure in sending Talitha some pieces of Rigel to reinforce his demands. And Talitha would yield to save her lover.

Before he could say more, she spoke even more forcefully. "Besides, I cannot issue a warrant for Vildiar's arrest. A Naos can only be tried after a charge has been sworn on the Star. Vildiar himself said so in court last month and the counselor agreed. We have no proof that he has done anything wrong, so no one can make that charge."

She was wrong, of course, but only Rigel had seen the correct answer. Even Pleione, who was the Starlands equivalent of a lawyer and had done his research for him, had argued for about an hour before agreeing that what he proposed was legal and would work. Talitha would very likely take longer to convince, and he had no time to waste.

"Fine," he said. "I won't go, I promise. That doesn't matter! You say you don't want a civil war? Well, Kurhah is going to start one very shortly. But if you give him a warrant to deliver, he'll be acting legally as your agent, which means that the Vildiar goons will be in rebellion if they resist. Vildiar will be in the wrong! And then we've got him!"

"A warrant on what grounds?" Talitha asked, pouting more sourly than ever.

Rigel shrugged. "Doesn't matter. The charge can be completely trivial. If he refuses it, he's in rebellion."

"And if he doesn't? If he turns up in court? He'll make fools of us all again."

"Oh no, he won't! This time we'll be ready for him. Oh, darling! How many times over the last month have you told me you love me? How many times have you *shown* me how much you love me?"

She blushed furiously, because Wasat was listening. "That has nothing to do with—"

"Yes, it does! If you love me, how can you not trust me? Now trust me! Kurhah is presently wining and dining his guests, softening them up. At the end of the meal, he'll launch his rebellion. I haven't got time to explain, so you will have to trust me."

She glowered at him. Even when Talitha knew she was beaten, she would never admit it. "You are not going to Phegda!"

Chapter 23

Kitalphar banked steeply over Alathfar. Rigel, fingers knotted in the ridge of hair along her back, was astonished by the extent of the valley and its battlements of mountains. Kurhah had to be an exceptionally powerful mage to have imagined a domain on such an impressive scale. Far below him a herd of large animals was grazing. He failed to appreciate their size until he noticed the familiar stone tower blind, which was a tiny dot next to their massive bodies. He was fairly sure that elephants did not eat grass, but rhinos? Hippos? Or were these mythical monsters?

As the hippogriff sailed lower, the mudling village came into view, set among taro paddies and fenced pastures. Beyond it, nestled in several clearings in the forest, lay the sprawling buildings of the station, covering much more ground than he had realized on his previous visit, with livestock corrals and the inevitable swimming pond, which in this case was a small lake. At the moment, a dozen or so air cars of various sorts were parked near the main house and at least as many watercraft were moored in the lake, which also contained two gigantic passenger swans. There were four hippogriffs and a pegasus in the paddocks, and an even larger group of air cars off in the trees, probably transport for the cooks and waiters who were catering the banquet.

The meeting was still in progress, and soon he saw the guests themselves, dining outdoors at white-draped tables tended by many servants. No doubt his approach would have been noted already, but he could not be recognized at such a height. At a quick count, he estimated about fifty starfolk, more than he had initially thought.

"As near the front door of the main building as you can, please," he told his mount.

Kitalphar turned steeply and whirled him down in a dizzying helix. By then sunlight flashing off Meissa would have given him away, for no one but the marshal of Canopus strutted around in a bronze helmet. He hoped that Kurhah would grant him a hearing before blasting him out of the sky, but even magic might fail to hit a moving target moving at that speed. The hippogriff set down gracefully right at the base of the veranda steps.

He slipped off, his head still spinning, and bowed to her. "I am much in your debt for this favor, great one. I am on very urgent business for Her Majesty. I humbly beg you to wait here for a few minutes, until I see if I am made welcome."

To his relief, Kitalphar dipped her ferocious head in acknowledgment. Rigel turned to the steps and discovered his host standing at the top of them, fists on hips, glaring at him.

"I promised you no safe conduct, mongrel."

Rigel raised his right hand to show the silver bracelet on his wrist. "I brought my own, my lord. But I come in peace." He climbed up three steps, and halted one step lower than Kurhah.

"What do you want?"

"I came to help."

The opalescent eyes narrowed. The old man had not expected that, or perhaps he just did not want it. "Help how? Did she send you?"

Diners at the tables behind Rigel were watching, whispering like bees.

"Are you still being observed?"

Kurhah glanced at his left hand. "Yes."

"That is Phegda's doing. My friends were, but agreed to stop seancing when I arrived here." Achird had agreed; Fomalhaut might have overruled him, but it was safe to assume that Hadar, with his hundreds of helpers, was keeping Naos Kurhah under surveillance. He had probably been doing so ever since the old man's reappearance.

"Am I supposed to be frightened of Vildiar's dogs?" the mage barked. "I am not, nor am I frightened of you, boy, not even when you threaten me with your Lesath. It is time somebody restored order and respect for the law to the Starlands, and since that slip of a girl is clearly not up to the task, I shall do it myself, with the assistance of some of the noble lords and ladies gathered here today. You are neither wanted nor required, and you may depart."

Rigel stood almost two meters tall on his bare feet, but Kurhah, like most male starfolk, was handily taller. He was also perched one elfin step up, thirty centimeters higher, and yet somehow he seemed *small*. By earthly standards he would be a very well-preserved forty, likely a retired basketball player, and he had no wrinkles or age spots to betray his many centuries. His voice was strong and steady, but the way he used it gave him away. His words—and probably his thinking—were those of a testy, cantankerous old man, rooted in ancient ways.

Rigel said, "Hadar and the rest of that pack have murdered three dozen Naos, several of them trained mages, my lord. Were all their victims blind fools? No one except me has ever killed any of them." That was not strictly true, because Izar's Lesaths, first Turais and now Edasich, had slain more than he had, but it was true in terms of personal combat. "Will you not at least listen to the advice I bring, and hear the support that Her Majesty offers?"

"I will give you five minutes, no more." The Naos turned and stalked indoors. Rigel hurried after him. They crossed the big room, and strode along the corridor to the kitchen area, where mudling servants hastily stepped out of their way. Kurhah turned into a tiny storeroom, hardly more than a closet, its walls lined by high shelves. Rigel followed, pulling the door shut behind him. In a faint light from a ventilator grill, he was nose-to-neck with the elf.

The Saiph bracelet was quivering faintly. He was in some danger; not much yet, but some.

Kurhah barked, "This space is shielded from observation. Speak up."

"We did spy on you earlier, obviously. You didn't reveal your plans, but I assume that you think you can overpower Vildiar—one Naos against another—and that you'll take along a dozen or so mages to hold off the Family?"

"Assume any accursed thing you want, boy. I don't answer to you."

"First, of course, you will have to find him, and he has all of Phegda to hide in."

"Let me worry about that."

Rigel quoted again the numbers he had spouted at Fornacis. "Are you aware, my lord, that Naos Vildiar still has at least two hundred and three trained halfling assassins at his command?"

Kurhah's reaction was barely more than a twitch, but he clearly had not known. "I don't believe it. He told you this?"

"No. I had it on the Star from two of his halfling sons who have sworn allegiance to Her Majesty."

"Traitors to their sponsor, then!"

"Who is also their father, yes. Personally, I honor them for their courage and ethics in changing sides. Each one of those two hundred has killed at least one earthling with his or her bare hands. It's part of their training. There may be even more of them now, because that was months ago, and it included only adults; there were a few dozen cubs coming along as well, eager and vicious. Of course the starfolk helpers you hope to enlist need not fear Vildiar himself, but they know how deadly his halflings are. Most of your dinner guests will vanish into the sky the moment you get around to asking for volunteers."

The elf laughed scornfully. "You think I have not prepared suitable defenses for them? You think they'll be braver if you're there to help?"

"I am not offering to accompany you myself, my lord." Rigel did not care to explain that the queen loved him so much that she kept him tied to her apron strings. "But Her Majesty is willing to provide you with battle-trained centaurs, sphinxes, and griffins."

"Oh, rubbish! I do not need her circus animals. They would be worse than useless, because they would get in my way. If that's the best you can do, boy, you're wasting my time. Obviously your mistress realizes how negligent she's been and wants to share in the glory after I've done all the work for her. Well, I have no intention of letting her have any of the credit. Open that door."

The stupid ancient would listen to no one's advice, and Rigel could smell disaster in the making. He produced the scroll he had brought tucked in his waistband. He did not offer it or unroll it, but it caught the old elf's attention.

"My lord, may I ask, because it is vital, just what you propose to do with Prince Vildiar himself—if you can find him and if his thugs do not kill you all before you can get near him?"

"Pull his fangs and clip his talons. Now go back to your—"

"Impossible."

Kurhah glared, and Saiph shivered a warning on Rigel's wrist.

"You're going to create a bloodbath, my lord."

"Have you ever heard of a cockatrice, boy?"

"I've ridden one. The queen and I went to Tarazed with Starborn Cheleb the day before Hadar killed her."

"Did you really?" The mage made no effort to hide his disbelief of this fantastic claim. "Then you know what one glance of a cockatrice will do."

"It petrifies people."

"Correct. Cockatrices are imaginary, of course. What one starborn can imagine, so can another, and I have imagined amulets that act like a cockatrice's gaze, except on starborn. Us they merely blind, and I have other amulets to cure that blindness. So unless our beloved queen wants to decorate her palace with statues of centaurs, sphinxes, and griffins, she had best keep them out of my way. When Naos Vildiar has sworn on the Star that all his trained killers have been accounted for and he will create no more in future, I will restore his sight. But every year from then on, I will summon him to my court in Canopus and have him swear that he has bred no more halflings. Now open that door and get out of my way."

"I hope your cockatrice spell has a longer range than Hadar's bows. He cannot miss at three hundred paces. And I hope he hasn't equipped his troops with basilisk masks."

"I told you to get out of my way."

Rigel offered the scroll. "Here's a better way."

Kurhah made no effort to take the paper. "What is it?"

"It's a royal warrant, authorizing Prince Kurhah and a posse of his choosing to arrest Prince Vildiar and convey him to the Dark Cells at Dziban."

Kurhah's face flamed red. "On what grounds?"

"To await trial on charges still to be specified."

"Get out of here!" The mage was almost spluttering. "How dare she treat me like a servant? How dare she menace Naos Vildiar that way, her senior by more than four centuries?" He shoved Rigel. *"Move, boy!"*

Sadly Rigel opened the door and went out. Kurhah pushed past him and strode back the way they had come, muttering furiously to himself. The kitchen staff continued their clean-up work, carefully not looking at the halfling in the shiny helmet. Rigel sighed and followed his host.

Of course it was good news that the starfolk were starting to fight back against Vildiar, although their timing was only barely better than never. They should have done it two dozen deaths ago. But Kurhah was not hearing anything he did not want to hear; very likely this myopic, pigheaded fossil was going to make matters much worse than they already were. Dare one hope that so many of his guests would have the sense to stay out of it that he would have to give up and try something else?

The great room was already almost full, as the guests returned from their meal to hear the rest of the plan. Judging by the babble, wine had flowed generously, probably much too generously. Discretion would be more valuable than Dutch courage if Kurhah was planning to start his campaign right away.

Meanwhile, there was no reason for Rigel Tweenling to stay around at Alathfar. Rather than jostling his way through the incoming stream of jabbering starfolk, he turned and retraced his steps to the kitchen area. The root portal he had used the last time he was in Alathfar had disappeared—as had its other side, in Canopus, where the camel yard had metamorphosed into a copra warehouse several months ago. Unless Kitalphar had waited for him, he would have to wait and beg a ride home from one of the starborn. He left through the kitchen door.

This was where most of the air cars had been parked, on a wide lawn enclosed by even more cabins, with forest spreading out on all sides. He headed for the corner of the main building. Just as he reached it, Saiph began vibrating fiercely on his wrist and a bright light flashed from a point almost straight ahead of him, between two cabins. He thought it must be the sun reflecting off a mirror, but then he saw another like it, two cabins over, below a rising swirl of pale smoke. He thought, *Oh God, why didn't I foresee this?* and started to run.

Chapter 24

Of course Hadar would strike first!

Hadar was a terrorist and here his next target was laid out on a slab, waiting for him.

The other air cars he'd seen, the ones hidden away in the trees, which he had assumed were transport for servants, belonged to the Family. No doubt they had completely encircled the station now and were starting to close in with whatever those bright weapons were.

As he sprinted alongside the building, heading for the front lawn with the banquet tables, the servants clearing away dishes began to scream. More curls of smoke were rising from the ground. A pillar of white fire, far too bright to look at directly but roughly elf-sized, came sweeping into view from between two cottages and leaped into an open air car. The vehicle exploded in red and yellow flames. The white shape passed through the flames, descending to the ground on the near side. It kept coming, moving as quickly and steadily as if it were a person running.

Rigel turned the second corner and raced for the front door. A male starborn, probably the last guest left outside, stood on the veranda screaming, "Salamanders!" at the starfolk in the building. "Flee!" he yelled. "Salamanders! Run for your lives!"

That was no way to organize a defense, but what defense was there against moving pillars of fire?

At the far side, another of the salamanders had almost reached the house, zigzagging across the lawn between the parked air cars, swatting at them with its hands as it passed, setting every one ablaze. Even the grass was erupting in flame and smoke wherever the creature's feet touched, and it left a trail of black ash behind it. *Oh, for a set of welder's goggles!* As near as Rigel could make out through almost-closed eyes, the salamander was a biped, somewhere between human- and elf-sized. He had no doubt by then that it must be a halfling, one of the Family somehow raised to white heat. He thought it was probably naked, but the incandescent white glow around it made the point immaterial. More and more of them were emerging from the forest, and now most of the outlying cabins were in flames.

The closest salamander plowed into the banquet tables like a jet of molten iron, and carried straight on through them as they exploded into flame. Rigel changed direction to intercept it, or maybe her; something about the way this one was running made him suspect it might be a woman. Smoke stung at his eyes and throat, obscuring the scene.

Saiph had become a sword and gauntlet, but the gauntlet extended almost to Rigel's elbow and the sword was longer and thinner than usual. He recalled that the last person to wear Saiph had slain a dragon with it.

Later he had died of burns.

The heat from the salamander forced him to turn his face away and shield it with his left arm, but Saiph needed no guidance from him. He felt the blade penetrate flesh, and risked a quick glimpse. There, impaled on the end of his sword, he saw for a brief instant Alkes, the halfling who had driven the getaway car from Calgary. She was indeed naked, her hair awry, her eyes wide with horror, skewered below her left breast by Saiph's deadly point. But then she vanished in a blaze of flame, consumed by her own magic.

Hearing turmoil behind him, Rigel spun around. Through a haze of yellow afterimages, he saw the windows at the front of the house explode, showering the veranda with shattered glass and timber. Crowds of screaming elves started tumbling out. A salamander coming to intercept them leaped up on the veranda, cutting through the railing as if it were butter, but promptly vanishing into the floorboards in a gout of flame. The air was full of eye-nipping, choking smoke.

A mob of servant mudlings, halflings, and elves had escaped from the main house only to run into a band of seven or eight unapproachable salamanders, who were now relentlessly herding them back. Rigel was trapped between them and the blazing veranda. The entire settlement seemed to be on fire now—buildings, air cars, even people. A screaming pegasus galloped past him with wings ablaze and vanished again into the fog. He lunged and cut at the attackers, Saiph slaying flaming halfling after flaming halfing, but his success attracted more attackers, and others began closing in on him. He was convulsed by coughing and could barely see what he was doing in the smoke and blinding light, but he sensed a shadow sweep over him. He felt his upper arms gripped in twin vises. The salamanders roared in fiery rage as he was swept up into the smoke, far out of their reach.

Kitalphar had waited for him. Squinting up at her great beak and plumaged breast against the sky, he tried to thank her, but his lips were burned and his mouth too dry for speech.

Below him, Alathfar was an inferno, every roof aflame. He closed his eyes and savored the cool rush of air on his scorched skin. He suspected that his moon-cloth wrap had burned away and did not care. He had a healing amulet on his left ankle, or was it the right? Didn't matter. Kitalphar had rescued him. This time he would live and his burns could be healed.

He wondered if Kurhah had managed to escape.

Chapter 25

Rigel's amulets were strong enough to keep him alive until he returned to Canopus, where more potent magic restored him to health, but he was the only survivor of the Alathfar massacre. The toll of murdered starborn was tentatively set at fifty-five, although many of the elderly might have faded from the shock. How many mudlings and halflings had died could never be known. Two-thirds of Talitha's council had perished, and it was a week before she managed to patch together enough of a government to hold a state funeral.

The great court was packed with thousands of mourners, but no secondary thrones stood on the great steps. Izar was being kept in maximum security at Segin, driving his guards crazy. Standing on the sidelines with other government officials, mostly senior halflings and junior starborn, Rigel scanned as much of the crowd as he could see, wondering if the prince was present but dissembling. Was Hadar here somewhere? Had he brought any of his killers along to gloat? Naos Vildiar had been summoned to attend, but had not appeared when the funeral began.

Officially the funeral was the only item on the agenda. Only three people knew that there might be a showdown right afterwards. The previous night, Rigel had persuaded Talitha to slip away with him by portal to her palace at Dziban—hoping to evade any seancing watchers that way—and had spent most of the night talking her into letting him make a public denunciation of Vildiar. This morning he had told the plan to Aspidiske, the new chancellor, but nobody else could possibly know what was about to happen. Hadar might very well guess that something would, though, and might have some sort of diversion or retaliation prepared.

There was a strange mood in the great courtyard, almost an odor. The thousands gathered were sharing their sorrow, their fury, and their fear. Vildiar's terrorism had focused the starfolk's attention on politics as nothing else had ever done. For the first time something had distracted them from their frenetic pursuit of pleasure, their sex and sports and scandal. They were outraged, but they had no idea what to do about it.

A Starlands state funeral was no novelty for Rigel, who had attended the rites for Regent-heir Kornephoros, but this one was different because it honored so many. The great court was filled with muffled sounds of grief. Talitha's eulogy for the dead laid no blame. She did not denounce the Alathfar gathering as a treasonous conspiracy, but rather implied that it had been a celebration of Prince Kurhah's return. The deaths she attributed to "foulest sorcery" without even hinting who might have been behind it. Everyone knew.

Ever since the queen entered, the sun had been growing fainter, the air cooler. When she finished speaking and sat down again, mournful horns wailed. The last thin slice of sun vanished behind the darkness of the moon, and night replaced noon below the corona's ghostly flames of glory.

Only three biers commemorated the dead because officially only three bodies had been recovered, all burned beyond identification. That way every mourning family could hope that one of the three coffins held their dear one, but Rigel knew that the caskets contained nothing more than timber for ballast and a few charred teeth and bone fragments, some of which were probably not even elfin. The destruction at Alathfar had been total. The domain itself had followed its owner into the void, fortunately fading slowly enough for the spear-carrying mudlings of the theme park village to be rescued.

With the sun snuffed out, and the black moon crowned in pearl, a myriad stars arrived to accept the spirits of the departed. The biers ignited in the usual upward roar of white fire. Were there more than the usual number of sparks ascending? Chancellor Aspidiske might have arranged something appropriate. All too soon daylight came rushing back, seemingly much faster than it had gone. And the crowd's strange, all-pervading mood was now a dirge of despair. Who would be next and who could put a stop to this slaughter?

Now Halfling Rigel must stiffen his backbone, square his shoulders, and prepare to risk a ghastly death on the Star of Truth. Cowardice whispered in his ear that the gamble was not worth it; that even if he survived, he would gain very little. Vildiar was too strong now. His terrorists ruled the Starlands in all but name. Who dared oppose him?

A tweenling? If no elf stepped forward to support him today, then the cause was lost and so was he.

Talitha sat hunched, almost crouching, on the great throne, with her arms folded and her radiance reduced to a faint bluish glow. Rigel dared not meet her eye in case she signaled that she had changed her mind yet again, and he was not to proceed. For hours in the night he had argued, cajoled, persuaded, and even threatened. He was convinced, and had eventually persuaded her, that if she were to let Vildiar commit such an atrocity without so much as sticking her tongue out at him, her credibility as a ruler would plummet well below zero. That would leave Vildiar as the only possible alternative. It had been close to dawn before she had reluctantly agreed. By then they had both been too exhausted to do anything more romantic than fall asleep in each other's arms.

The odious Elgomaisa stood beside the throne, arms folded, permanent sneer in place. Even the two crouching sphinxes were wrinkling their noses, but they were probably reacting to the smell of fear from the crowd.

Chancellor Aspidiske was an elf of the very oldest school, having served as King Procyon's chancellor, back before the time of Christ. His hair was still deep scarlet and his backbone as straight as a laser beam. He had very little use for halflings in coal-scuttle helmets, but his opinion of mass murderers, Naos or not, was even lower. He had grudgingly spared Rigel "half a minute, no more" before the funeral service began, glaring at him with ever-increasing fury as he relayed the queen's new instructions.

A denunciation at a funeral? Shameful! A halfling accusing a Naos? Worse!

"Not only will your complaint have absolutely no standing in law, but the prince will be within his rights if he insists that you be turned over to him for punishment. You can't be stupid enough not to know what that will mean."

It would mean as much as Saiph let it mean, but all Rigel said was, "All I plan to demonstrate is that the accusation is true by making it on the Star. Then some starborn will take my place and repeat it."

Aspidiske glowered. His eyes and hair were the color of fresh blood. "Such as whom?"

"Such as Court Mage Fomalhaut, my lord. I plan to quote his report on the Front Street massacre. Prince Vildiar never denied that the dead halflings were his retainers. Fomalhaut will certainly be willing to confirm his own conclusions."

"Fomalhaut? Oh, him." The old starborn spoke as if Fomalhaut was an upstart child. "Well, I wish you luck. You'll probably just make things worse."

"I don't think they can get much worse, my lord."

Aspidiske lowered his bloody eyebrows like window shades. "You may be right," he conceded. Rigel took that as progress, a major concession.

Now the time had come, but Talitha seemed paralyzed on her throne. Things had already gotten worse, because while Court Mage Fomalhaut ought to be standing where Rigel was, with the royal officials, he was nowhere to be seen. He was tall, even by elfin standards, and had distinctive golden hair; he ought to stand out if he was anywhere near the front of the main crowd, but there was no sign of him. Who would follow up Rigel's lead? It would take two to draw Vildiar's fangs.

Was that why Talitha was hesitating? Had she noticed the mage's absence? Rigel had no idea whether she was going to give him his cue or just dismiss the assembly. Elgomaisa whispered to her impatiently. Mourners were already starting to slip out the many exits from the court, not waiting for royal permission. Rigel had just decided that she was not going to follow through with the plan—which, he realized, would be a huge personal relief—when she straightened up and said, "Chancellor. We commanded Vildiar Naos to come before us today. Is he in the court?"

Aspidiske ordered the heralds to summon Prince Vildiar. Trumpets blared. A magically enhanced voice shouted for Naos Vildiar to come forth. The court went quieter than Rigel would have believed possible, as if everyone had stopped breathing. He strained to detect the new mood: more fear? Or could it be the first twinge of hope?

Suddenly the giant Vildiar was there, striding up the wide steps. Where he had come from, Rigel had no idea, and nobody else seemed to either, for the front rows of the congregation uttered simultaneous yelps of alarm. At the edges of the court, more people continued to trickle away.

One step down from the throne and slightly to the queen's right, the tall elf halted and spread his great arms in an elfin bow. Then he straightened up and insolently put his fists on his hips.

"How may I please Your Majesty?"

"We have honored our dead," Talitha said. Her voice was soft, but everyone could hear it. "Now we must investigate their deaths."

"I'm afraid I cannot help you, my dear. I wasn't there. I was kite riding with some starborn friends, over at . . ." He stopped and turned to watch Rigel heading for the Star of Truth.

Rigel took his time, scanning the crowd again as he walked. Still no Fomalhaut! He tucked his helmet under his arm, stepped onto the Star, turned to face the throne, and knelt.

"Your Majesty, I call for justice."

This was how it was done.

The chancellor strode forward to stand nearer the throne, on the opposite side from Vildiar. Aspidiske looked thousands of years younger than he truly was. He might be even older than Kurhah had been, but he didn't speak with the same surly geriatric certainty.

"Identify yourself and state your complaint."

Counselor Pleione should be conducting this case, for she had done the legal research on which it would be based, but Pleione had died with the rest at Alathfar.

Vildiar was watching warily, no doubt wondering what venom had been brewed up in the queen's kitchens. Beside the throne, Elgomaisa stood glaring, furious that he had been left out of the secret.

"I am Rigel Halfling, retainer of Queen Talitha, and I accuse Vildiar Naos." Here it came. Deep breath. *"Several of his halfling retainers have been supplied with, and have used, amulets of Lesath grade."*

Rigel's tongue did not become a burning coal in his mouth.

He must not say, because he did not know for certain, that Vildiar had provided the weapons. That sort of inference was reserved for the queen. There was no need to say it, because the law was known to everyone present: A starborn who sponsored halfling retainers was responsible for their behavior. No other starborn would give them amulets of any sort.

Vildiar snorted and seemed to relax. The charge was petty, about equivalent to accusing an earthbound homeowner of disturbing his neighbors by holding loud parties or letting a dog bark. The audience knew that too, and sounds of befuddlement and irritation rumbled throughout the courtyard.

"What evidence do you offer?" the chancellor demanded.

This was where Starlands court procedure deviated from an earthly court of law. Any eyewitness evidence Rigel managed to give would be treated as fact.

"About six months ago, while on Queen Electra's business, I entered a building on Front Street which I had been informed belonged to Naos Vildiar. I was accosted by four halflings, who indicated to me that they were his retainers. They were armed with Lesath amulets, which they used against me. One of them, Halfling Hadar, escaped through the portal. My amulet, Saiph, slew the others: the female halfling Adhil, and the male halflings Tarf and Muscida."

Details of the fight on Front Street were not generally known, and the crowd immediately broke into speculative chatter. Chancellor Aspidiske had to call for order. He asked a question that Rigel had given him beforehand.

"You faced odds of four to one and yet killed three of them? Your amulet obviously has massacre potential, but it does not sound as if theirs did."

The audience sniggered, but it was a sound of nervousness, not mirth. Vildiar shrugged, looking bored.

Rigel continued. "In calling their amulets Lesaths, my lord, I was quoting the report that Court Mage Fomalhaut later made to Her Majesty." Rigel noticed that Talitha was frowning. Clearly she did not like the way things were unfolding, and if she, sitting higher than anyone else, could not see Fomalhaut in court, then he probably wasn't. The old elf had not been informed that his presence would be required, because the queen had insisted on total secrecy, but he had always claimed to be prescient. *Ominous!*

"The court mage," Rigel continued, "was especially offended by amulets worn by both male corpses, which had made their blood a deadly topical poison. In trying to heal their wounds, Regent-heir Kornephoros got their blood on his hands. That was what killed him."

Uproar. Horror. Calls for order.

The chancellor was starting to look much happier than he had just a few minutes ago. By tying in the death of Kornephoros, Rigel had raised his case to a much higher level.

Vildiar was frowning again and glancing over the crowd, as if seeking out supporters. Talitha's greatest fear had been that this confrontation could end in another massacre, or even civil war. She might be right yet.

"Does that complete your complaint, halfling?"

"Not quite, my lord. Eight days ago, I was the only person who escaped from the disaster at Alathfar—other than the killers, of course. I did manage, or my amulet managed, to kill some of those attackers. One I identified as Halfling Alkes, known to me as one of Prince Vildiar's retainers. She and the other attackers were wearing amulets that clothed them in fire. When my sword pierced her, just for an instant, she was visible to me."

Still his tongue did not burst into flames.

"That is all?"

"That is all, my lord." Rigel had survived. His ordeal was almost over, leaving him sweating and shaking. But he had done it.

"Naos Vildiar, have you any questions to ask this witness?"

"I never talk to halflings when I can help it. Talitha, my dear, this is both ridiculous and absurd. I certainly do not have to answer to such slanders unless they are pressed by a starborn. Bring forth your court mage if he thinks this nonsense is worthy of his time."

The queen nodded to the chancellor and he to a herald on the sidelines. Trumpets blared.

"Come forward, Court Mage Fomalhaut!"

Silence.

Rigel rose and stepped aside from the Star. He replaced his helmet.

Still, silence. Again the court mage was summoned.

Vildiar was smiling shark teeth at Rigel. Had he foreseen or been forewarned of this accusation in spite of all Rigel's precautions? If so, then Fomalhaut was very probably dead.

Fomalhaut was paged a third, and final, time.

By law, a halfling who falsely accused a starborn must be turned over to him or punished as he decreed. Rigel did not think Talitha would abandon him that way, but to avoid doing so she would have to use her royal authority to overrule the law, which would further weaken her position.

The mood of the court had now sunk to rank despair. If even the queen's favorite could not threaten Vildiar, who could?

But then the chancellor glanced over Rigel's head and frowned. A murmur of surprise passed through the assembly like a breath of wind in a forest. Rigel spun around and saw salvation zooming in on a red and gold skyboard. It was probably a gross breach of court etiquette to arrive that way, but the sandy hair and eyes of Starborn Achird were the most welcome sight Rigel had seen in a very long time.

Chapter 26

Achird made a perfect landing alongside the Star and bowed to the queen.

"You are not Starborn Fomalhaut!" the chancellor barked, for the benefit of everyone not close enough to read the newcomer's name.

Achird shot Rigel a you-owe-me-for-this look and stepped onto the Star of Truth. He was not required to kneel.

Another bow. "I am Starborn Achird, mage of the second grade, pupil of Starborn Fomalhaut. I assisted the mage in his investigations of the events at Front Street. I am familiar with the report the mage gave to the queen. I also know this halfling personally and would believe anything he said."

Give the old sourpuss his due: Aspidiske looked relieved. "You support the halfling's accusation against Vildiar Naos ?"

"I did not arrive in time to hear the exact words used, my lord."

"Then the halfling will have to repeat it."

So Rigel returned to the Star for just long enough to repeat his charges.

Achird took his place. "I support him absolutely, Your Majesty. Mage Fomalhaut characterized the poisoned-blood amulets as the most evil devices he had ever encountered. They killed two sphinxes as well as Regent-heir Kornephoros. Between them, the three dead halflings bore forty-seven amulets, seventeen of which Court Mage Fomalhaut classified as Lesaths."

The chancellor was actually smiling now. "Prince Vildiar, have you any questions to put to this witness?"

Vildiar still looked bored. "How do you define a Lesath, mage?"

"My master taught me that a Lesath is defined by two factors: It is capable of causing grievous bodily harm or death to a starborn, and is therefore forbidden to anyone other than a starborn."

"And how many are you wearing, sonny?"

"Four, Your Highness."

"Would you call this a Lesath?" Vildiar hurled a ball of purple fire at him. About nine hundred people screamed in alarm. The missile struck Achird on the chest and vanished. He staggered, though, and his face twisted in sudden pain. The threat was blatant.

"Yes, Your Highness, I would."

"But you wear a defense against it?"

"Obviously, or I would be a smoldering ember."

"Did you ever hear of a starborn who didn't?"

"The question is disallowed as too vague," the chancellor ruled.

"No more questions." Vildiar yawned.

Rigel raised a hand.

Aspidiske frowned and then reluctantly said, "We will allow the plaintiff one question."

Rigel turned to face Achird, who flickered him a wink that almost made him laugh aloud. Rigel hoped the chancellor had not seen it—and that Vildiar had.

"My lord, how many of the seventeen amulets recovered from Front Street could be blocked by the sort of defensive amulet that just saved your life from the defendant's attack?"

Achird's frown was almost as menacing as Vildiar's balls of fire. "My master did not include any such estimate in his report. He did mention that nine of them were new to him, which I interpreted to mean that he knew of no defense against them."

"Vildiar Naos," said the chancellor. "You have heard the charge that you gave Lesaths to your halfling retainers. Do you wish to refute it?"

Vildiar strolled down to the Star, glanced with distaste at Achird, and took his place. The court was as quiet as . . . er, a tomb.

"Your *Majesty*." His tone turned the honorific into a sneer as he turned toward Talitha. "My domain roots more than seventeen hundred other domains, most of which have many subdomains. The population, of all species, crossbreeds, and imaginings, numbers billions. I am responsible for maintaining the law and order within it. For that I rely on halflings, *as we all do*, whether or not we care to admit it. They are necessary *servants*." Another sneer there. "A few of those I trust most, I arm with Lesaths. *As we all do.* Who are you to judge me? You sent this half-breed of yours onto my property, where he slew three of mine. Are you claiming he did that with his bare hands? *If I am guilty, then so are you.*"

Which was all very logical. The audience groaned.

But Talitha was smiling. She had her foe on the Star of Truth, where she had never hoped to get him. "Halflings can wield Lesaths, but they certainly cannot make them. Only a mage of orange or red rank can do that. *Naos Vildiar, have you ever fashioned an amulet that would turn the wearer's blood into a topical poison that is deadly to starborn?*"

Silence. The giant folded his arms and considered the question carefully. Then he said, "Yes."

A flurry of shouts and whispers broke out in the crowd, and the chancellor called for order in the court.

"It was an interesting problem in applied magic," the witness said. "High-rank mages take—"

The queen cut him off. "Have you made more than one of these horrors?"

"Yes."

"And did you ever give any of them to halflings?"

"May I qualify my answer before I give it?" Vildiar's mood had changed. He sensed a trap somewhere.

"Briefly."

"The Lesath in question is purely defensive. It presents no danger to anyone else unless the wearer is made to bleed. As I said earlier, I rely on halflings to keep order within my domain and sometimes they may have to resort to violence. So the answer to your question is, yes. I have given Lesaths to halflings, including that one."

"Then you plead guilty?" Talitha said.

The giant shrugged his shoulders, higher than Rigel's head. "Of that? Certainly. If you want to make a mockery of your justice system by fining me a couple of subdomains, then go ahead. Of course you will have to do the same to every domain owner in this court. I wish you luck trying! Please, can we all go home and get on with our lives?"

To the elves this would make perfect sense. Normally the Starlands had no violence, no embezzlement, almost no theft;

Vildiar was a pathological exception. Starfolk had never learned how to deal with major criminals who carefully hid behind underlings. They had never heard of Al Capone or mafiosi. To explain mail fraud or income tax evasion to an elf would take weeks. Even Talitha had found it hard to understand how criminals who covered their tracks in great crimes might be ensnared by the minor infractions they could not avoid committing in the process.

But now she knew. "Chancellor, what is the law that Naos Vildiar has admitted to breaking?"

Yesterday old Aspidiske would have looked totally blank if asked that question; this morning Rigel had showed him Pleione's notes. "One of our most ancestral and honored laws, Your Majesty—Statute Sixty-five of King Heze. Although proclaimed eons ago, it has never been amended or repealed."

As near as Rigel had been able to discover, King Heze had reigned about the time earthlings had thought of bows and arrows as high tech.

Vildiar unfolded his tentacle-like arms. It was a fair bet that he had never heard of this law either, but he could guess that he had been snared somehow. Saiph began to vibrate on Rigel's wrist.

"And what is the maximum sentence decreed in this law?"

"No maximum is set."

Gasp from a thousand throats . . .

"Naos Vildiar," Talitha said, and now she had a joyful look of victory in her pearl-colored eyes. "The Lesaths wielded by your halflings were used to commit major crimes, including the murder of numerous starborn. *I sentence you to two thousand years in the Dark Cells.*"

Vildiar knew his enemy. He glanced down at Rigel with a look of intense hatred—and vanished.

Rigel leaped sideways, Saiph glittering in his hand. A ball of violet fire came hissing out of nowhere, and the sword swiped it aside in an eye-dazzling flash. More followed, with the same result, Rigel leaping like a ballet dancer, his feet and arm moving without any direction from him. All around him starborn were screaming and trying to flee. The action stopped as suddenly as it had begun and Rigel was left with his arm extended, the shining bracelet back on his wrist.

The rest of the crowd began to cheer insanely. The queen and chancellor did not join them, and even Elgomaisa was frowning, knowing that the problem had not gone away—it had only changed. Achird, who had moved out of reach of the onslaught, came wandering back.

Rigel said, "Thanks."

The mage could produce a very convincing sardonic smile. "If your saliva has curative properties, you may lick my hide after my master finishes tearing strips off of it."

"That bad? Why? And why did your master not attend in person?"

Shrug. "He foresaw a revolution starting if Vildiar appeared. The monster came incognito, so that didn't happen. When you headed for the Star, I insisted on coming to back you up."

"I'm very grateful." Rigel stared up at the elf's face for a moment, and then said, "But?"

"Fomalhaut said the best I could do would be to extend your life by three weeks. Maximum."

"My people!" the queen said. The magic acoustics made her voice audible everywhere and suppressed everyone else's. The court fell silent. Here it came, the stroke of the ax.

"Vildiar Naos has fled from our justice. We proclaim him outlaw! His domain is forfeit to the crown, and his underlings are released from their oaths of loyalty. Wealth beyond dreams will be bestowed on whoever delivers up his head. Death awaits any who aid or shelter him."

"Big words," Achird murmured.

Empty words, of course. No power in the Starlands could throw Vildiar into the Dark Cells, a form of solitary confinement so dire that it forced its otherwise immortal inmates to commit suicide.

"Traditional words," Rigel said. "I wonder what happens now?"

His mage friend sighed. "My guess would be a revolution."

Chapter 27

There was nothing exciting about making a corpse; Avior had created dozens in her career, whole or partial, although never one as large as a life-size Rigel. Despite his best efforts to help, or at least find her people who could help, setting up a studio in the Starlands had brought endless frustration. All sorts of things taken for granted in the real world were unobtainable here, even something as pedestrian as an ordinary measuring tape. She knew Rigel's height by comparison with her own, but how broad were his shoulders? How wide was his chest? What were his upper arm measurements? Having to work by eye, she soon discovered that his height disguised unexpected brawn. She ordered six more tubs of wax, and cattle bones as well as pig bones.

She'd tried to get some *closer* estimates whenever he dropped by Kraz, but she got nowhere with him now—once bitten, twice shy. Thabit admitted that his boss seemed to be finding what a man needs somewhere now, although he didn't know who the lucky lady was, or he *said* he didn't. Definitely not Queen Talitha, who now had an official partner.

Boring, boring work! Avior liked her corpses to expose the agony and horror of death. Planting the arrows in this one would be fun—she was looking forward to that—but she had to produce an unmarked corpse first. His features were so perfect that she wanted to scream and at least break his nose. By the time she was down to his hips, though, she had come to see this figure as a possible Prometheus, chained to the rock, writhing in agony as Zeus's eagle ripped out his liver yet again. She would ask for the piece back when Rigel was done with it. Meanwhile she ordered a stuffed eagle and some chains.

The rest of her life, what there was of it, was equally boring. Not that she missed neighbors or friends, because she had never bothered with either, but her sex life needed boosting. Tyl and Thabit were losing interest, having exhausted the opportunities offered by their threesome. The two Nusakan mudlings were less the pit bulls that Rigel had called them than lapdogs, disgustingly eager to please. They would fight each other for the right to entertain her, but even their fighting failed to provoke the testosterone rush it did in earthling males. Back in middle school Avior had learned how to set two boys at each other's throats by offering herself as the prize. Often she would pretend to back off when the winner got her stripped, just to incite him more—but even that trick failed to arouse any initiative in Mutt and Jeff.

She had no use for unicorns, either; smelly brutes. The best that could be said of them was that they gave Mutt and Jeff something to do, the unthinking in charge of the inedible.

One stuffy afternoon, while she was wrestling with Rigel's left kneecap, someone rapped on the studio door. It was open, and a woman walked in without waiting for an invitation. *Oh, crap! There went security.*

Wiping her hands on her apron, Avior hurried over to greet the intruder before she could come too close. "Can I help you?"

Her name was Botein, which sounded familiar. Someone had mentioned a Botein. She was too short and buxom for a starborn, but otherwise she seemed elfin, with cat ears, pale brown irises, and matching scalp fur. Rings, anklets, and bracelets galore glittered and jingled. She had darkened her lashes and rouged her nipples and her smile would terrify a polar bear.

"Ask, rather, how I may help you, dear! I'm Botein, your sister."

Oh . . . One of the Family, come to spy.

"You mean that Prince Vildiar raped your mother also?"

"Correct." Botein's eyes were busily scanning the studio. "Daddy would like to meet you."

"I have absolutely no desire to meet him." Avior noticed that her visitor did not *seem* to be looking past her, toward her worktable with the corpse on it. That was almost proof that she had done her real prying before she even knocked.

Botein sighed and turned away to stare out the open door. "Understandable, but of course the accident was not Daddy's fault. I remember how furious he was when the watchers lost track of her—your mother, I mean, Maria Evangelina Leandra Stornelli. Hadar had the two boys who were responsible strung up by the wrists and flogged, but even that wasn't enough to satisfy Daddy."

"He should have been strung up by the balls and left to rot," Avior said, furious at having her mother's maiden name thrown in her face. "Now, if there is nothing else, Ms. Botein . . . ?" Avior edged forward and Botein went like a lamb, speaking over her shoulder.

"He will do anything he can to make amends. Remember he is a Naos mage, the most powerful sorcerer in the Starlands. He could grant any wish you put to him."

Could he, now? Avior was trying to remember what Tyl had said a few days ago, when he dropped by to see if there was anything she needed. Anything *else*, of course, because the twins always tried for a quickie when they came calling. Tyl had babbled happily about Rigel trapping Vildiar somehow and the queen outlawing him.

Now, with Botein scoping out Kraz and Avior's workshop, Rigel's plans to use the dead ringer as Hadar bait must be even deader than all that bone and plaster on the table. But information on where the outlaw was hiding out might be extremely valuable to him. Could Avior help the Sheriff of Nottingham by making a quick visit to Sherwood Forest? Anything to get out of working on that boring corpse.

They emerged, blinking in the sunshine. Botein curled her pretty lip at the view. "Frankly, my dear, I don't think much of your quarters. Rigel Halfling hasn't exactly been generous with his sweetie pie's money, has he?"

"They are quite adequate . . . for my work."

Botein picked up the hint almost before Avior realized she had dropped it. "Stars above! Aren't those two apes Nusakan? What in heaven do you use them for?"

"Muscle definition, mostly. Good models. They'll stand for hours if I tell them to."

"Not good for much else, though?" Botein offered an all-girls-together smile.

Avior matched it. "The flesh is willing but the spirit is nonexistent."

"No improvement over Thabit and Tyl, you mean?"

That was a fairly open admission that the Family had been keeping watch on Kraz and prying into Avior's affairs.

"Orang and Utan? They're pretty good, I'd say."

"Imaginative, but short on stamina."

That was like calling the Pacific Ocean short on damp.

"You must have very high standards." Not to mention the endurance of an alley cat.

Botein laughed. "Oh, I do! And since we're admitting to incest, I'll confess that once, a few years ago now, I set out to try a brother a night. They varied a lot, of course, but several performed much better than those two turncoat apes."

"How long before you ran out of brothers?"

"Almost four months," Botein said with a shrug. "By then I was scraping the bottom of the cradle and they weren't much good for anything yet. Look, are you sure I can't persuade you to come and say hi to Daddy? He'd love to meet you, and he really can be your fairy godfather and grant you three wishes. I'll see you back here within the hour, I promise."

Only a suicidal zombie would trust any promise from a member of the Family. Avior knew that. But she did need a break, and this might give her an excuse to stop work on the Rigel-corpse altogether. In that case, it would be nice to help the lad somehow. He'd done his best for her, despite what Botein said. And if the corpse scam was blown, then the opposition had no motive to harm Avior—had nothing to gain by locking her up or killing her. A chance to see more of the Starlands and meet the Monster Himself was very tempting, too. She glanced where Botein was looking and her decision was made instantly.

"My god! Is that what you came in?"

Parked on the shady side of the studio building stood a golden chariot, a Ben Hur–style, two-wheeled racing chariot.

It balanced on its wheels, leaning forward with the single shaft extending out in front of it to keep it from falling over. That it was magic was obvious from the way it was powered. One shaft would normally imply either two or four horses, but this one had no provision for horses. Four short crosspieces along the shaft served as perches, and on each crouched an enormous eagle. Avior thought they looked miserable at being so close to the ground.

"Isn't it bully? Oh, damn! That's out of date now, isn't it? Groovy? Is that still the in word? Come along, dear. I'll give you a ride."

Avior went with her, fascinated by the prospect of such an adventure. "I thought only elves could work magic?"

"Never call them that, dear. They're liable to burn your nose off, or worse. Some halflings have magic up into the green. About a quarter of the Family can fly something like this. Hadar's better than I am. In you get."

Botein offered a hand. Unwilling to be touched, Avior scrambled up unaided. The chariot rocked, steadied, and rocked again as her chunky guide joined her. Botein gripped the rail with both hands. There was something odd about her right wrist, as if it had been broken and badly set. Avior tried hard not to stare, but disfigurements were her speciality, and this was the first one she had seen in the Starlands.

"Hang on, darling. Giddyup, chickens! Lean back, dear."

As the passengers shifted their weight, the shaft started to rise. The birds extended their wings, displaying a wingspan of at least three meters, and then began to flap them, starting with the closest, because it was highest. The others soon joined in, gently at first, then with longer, stronger strokes. Dust swirled and the shaft tilted upward. Wheels turned, the chariot ran forward, and in seconds they were airborne, with all four eagles working in a rhythmic flow. Studio and other buildings slid away beneath them. The unicorns galloped wildly around their pen, and the two foreshortened Nusakan gaped up stupidly. No noise, no vibration, just effortless flight.

Avior didn't even have to raise her voice to converse with her half sister. "How do you *do* this?"

"With an amulet," Botein admitted. "But it needs personal magic, too, and a lot of training. Many of us can work air cars, and this is just a fancy air car. That's a pretty skimpy little domain your tin-hatted boss gave you."

The whole of Kraz was visible now, a sizable sprawling farm to Avior's eyes. Its surroundings were hidden by clouds that she did not recall noticing from the ground. The chariot continued to soar upward and soon Kraz had disappeared altogether.

"What did you mean, it was skimpy?"

"I mean what we saw from up here is all there is of it. That's hardly a planet you're living on, Sister. Don't go for any long walks. Here's the highway to Phegda."

The chariot shot down through a hole in the cloud cover and Avior's ears popped. Here the sky was blue and cloudless again. Below her lay a sprawl of fields and buildings, apparently all one gigantic ranch. She saw white horses, or possibly unicorns, several rows of parked vehicles, and lakes with huge white swans on them. Then Botein told her to lean back and do as she did.

The chariot glided in low over some rooftops, the eagles' wings outstretched. The wheels touched down on the grass in a perfect two-point landing, and the car coasted over to a barn door before it came to a halt. Botein shifted her weight forward to lower the shaft. *Just like magic!* The eagles folded their wings and turned fierce glares on their passengers. They didn't seem to be chained to their perches, but something had to be holding them there. A couple of mudling boys came running out to assist.

"Daddy told me several places he might be," Botein said as she led the way over to the barn. "But I've had a wonderful idea, dear."

"Do tell, *dear*." Avior still hated that idiotic form of address.

"Let's go and call on Sterope while we're here—not that 'here' or 'there' matter when you're in the Starlands, just as long as you're staying in one domain. Phegda is big enough that you could spend your whole life exploring it. Daddy's told me that he hasn't even seen everything yet . . ."

Botein continued her empty chatter until they were inside the barn, where dozens of chariots and other wheeled vehicles were stored, and hammering noises suggested repair work underway. At once she turned toward a smaller door, set just inside the big one but in the same exterior wall. It hadn't been visible from the outside, so it had to be a portal.

Botein threw it open. About to go through, Avior recoiled from the ammoniacal stench of confined livestock.

"Sorry," said her guide. "Should have warned you. It does get stinky in here on warm days. Try not to notice. They're naturally a bit sensitive. You'll love Sterope, though."

This second barn was even larger than the first, but was it a barn or a jail? A wide corridor ran off for at least thirty meters straight ahead, which was far from being the end of the enclosed space. Smaller passages led off from it on either hand, but all the walls and dividers were made of steel bars. The stalls were large enough for horses, yet they seemed more like cells, and most of the doors were closed. Sweating mudlings were scrubbing the paving of the corridors with buckets and long brooms, or tramping around, pushing barrows of straw, clean or soiled.

Just inside the portal stood a long wooden bench heaped with miscellaneous baskets and stacks of cloth, perhaps towels. A woman was sitting there, suckling a baby. Her name was Sterope and she had short vertical horns between her elfin ears. Even without those, she was much too ugly to be a starborn: her teeth were square, not pointed, and her nose was almost nonexistent. She wore the usual simple loincloth wrap, but below that her legs were thickly furred, and they ended in black hooves. She looked up, her oversized mouth open in a winsome smile.

"Botein Halfling! Been a long time."

"Yes it has. Nanny Sterope, this is Halfling Avior. She's Family."

Nanny? Or nanny goat?

Both!

Another animal smile. "Pleased to meet you." Sterope looked down at the baby, whose tiny, fuzzy legs were hooved. "You finished on that one? Try a burp." She transferred the load to her shoulder, and patted its diaper. "What can I do for you, halflings?"

"Avior might have a job for a young buck, if you have one available?"

Avior had worked out what species she was dealing with now and was torn between revulsion and raging curiosity. The stench was bad, but it wasn't straight pig farm or feedlot. There were interesting odors mixed in there too.

Sterope had pursed her thick lips doubtfully. "We're a little short just now, dear. There's Scheddi. But he blotted his copybook on his first rut and was sent home."

"What'd he do?"

"Got a little too enthusiastic."

Botein laughed coarsely. "I thought that was the whole idea! Let's have a word with this Scheddi."

Still looking dubious, Sterope heaved herself to her, um, hooves, and led the way along the wide passage. With a chorus of shrill squeals and screams, a dozen or so youngsters came streaming past, little hooves pattering on the flagstones. They seemed to be both boys and girls . . . billies and nannies . . . bucks and does? They were playing chase and the ones in front were certainly female.

"Kids, kids!" Sterope shouted reprovingly, but no one paid any attention and the herd vanished around a corner. She turned into the passage the stampede had come from. Most of the cells, or stalls, were empty, but a couple of them had straw in them. The one she stopped at was in use.

The occupant was a male satyr, asleep on his straw; face-down, because his horns were enormous compared to Sterope's, rising straight up from his head and then curving back, and sleeping in any other position would be almost impossible for him. Apart from that he looked human above the waist, but he was thickly furred from there to his black hooves.

"You keep him locked up?" Avior asked nervously.

"It's his first rut," Sterope said, as if that explained everything.

Scheddi hit the cage door with a clang, and all three woman jumped. He had moved faster than a startled cat, from prone to operational in nothing flat. Massive fists clutched the bars, and he thrust his snout through them, sniffing. That wasn't all that was thrust through the bars. Avior had never seen junk like that on a biped. His eyes fixed unerringly on her.

"Lady want fukfuk?" he said eagerly.

His smell was rank, but it was rank male. She was suddenly certain that Scheddi would make the twins look like celibates.

"You need fukfuk, Scheddi always ready."

"Talk properly, lout!" Sterope barked. She positioned the baby at her other teat and adjusted it to suck.

The satyr pouted, then said primly, "If my lady wishes discourse on philosophy or the literary arts, then I regret to confess that I am unable to oblige. When it comes to copulation, though, I am in my métier and can keep going indefinitely." He showed his teeth again. "Come on in for a free sample."

"What do you think, Avior?" Botein asked, looking doubtful. "We'd have to ask him, but I'm sure Daddy will let you borrow Scheddi if you fancy his type of service."

"I service very well," Scheddi said. "One hour? Two? Just set my timer."

"And how would I explain him to Rigel?"

"You could tell him you tired of the Nusakan and traded them for Scheddi at the market in Canopus. I'll have to remove them anyway, because Scheddi will get possessive. Let's go and see what Daddy says. Let him out, Sterope."

The nanny hesitated. "You promise to behave this time, buck?"

Scheddi's elfin ears drooped in submission. "Yes, Mommy. Lady says stop, I stop."

There was no key in sight, but the gate opened at Sterope's touch. Scheddi emerged and went straight for Avior. He was not quite as tall as she, but his ears and the enormous horns made him much taller overall. Moreover, a Nusakan would have very little over him when it came to Hunk of the Year. He slid one arm around her and leered. At close quarters his smell made her eyes water, but it was not repellent. Far from it, in fact. He sensed her interest. Golden eyes gleaming, he licked his lips, and then his nose, with an enormous pink tongue.

"Fukfuk soon?" he whispered.

"Don't you have to put some clothes on?"

"No. Fukfuk soon?" Scheddi was nothing if not single-minded, and a moon-cloth wrap would not hide much of his grotesque anatomy anyway.

"Let's see what the prince says." Avior had no doubt that Vildiar would agree to the arrangement. This whole thing had been set up in advance. The Family had analyzed Avior well enough to know that a satyr would be the perfect bribe. How fortunate that they happened to have one available!

Botein led the way back to the portal. Scheddi's one-arm hug grew so tight that Avior was almost lifted off her feet. His large, rough hand had closed on her breast. She tried to pull his arm away and nothing happened. It felt like a steel girder.

"Let me go!"

"Why? You not care for Scheddi?"

"I haven't decided."

He clearly did not believe her. His grip grew tighter.

This time the portal led them to fresh air, very fresh. Freezing, in fact, for Avior lacked the starfolk's preference for low temperatures. The room was large and bare, more of a gym than anything else. Unglazed windows looked out on towering ice-clad mountains, range after range below a wintery-pale sky. About fifty starlings, from toddlers to Izar-type preadolescents, were exercising, playing games, shouting, and laughing, just like earthling children.

Four or five adult starfolk were supervising, and one of them was Prince Vildiar, recognizable by his startling height. The fact that Botein had known exactly where to find him merely confirmed Avior's suspicion that her afternoon had been scripted in advance. She recalled Tyl mentioning a Family crèche at somewhere called Unukalhai. Now all she needed was some way to get word to Rigel that the outlaw might be hiding at Unukalhai. But Vildiar was planning to use her against Rigel, and perhaps against the queen to whom she had sworn loyalty. She resented the assumption that her allegiance was so fragile.

But she could not deny that the bribe was tempting.

Vildiar was supervising a bare-knuckle fight. Two imps much younger than Izar were slugging away at each other with more ferocity than science. The ring was exactly that: a circle painted on the floor, with the spectators standing around the edge, ready to push the contenders back in if they put a foot over the mark. The smaller boy was obviously getting the worst of it, and the spectators were jeering at him.

Vildiar frowned at the new arrivals, especially at Scheddi. He pointed a long arm at the door.

"You! Go and stand over there, facing the wall."

Scheddi reluctantly released Avior and stalked away. Even a satyr could not defy Vildiar Naos.

Vildiar turned back to the fight. The bigger boy had managed to make his opponent's nose bleed. "Oh, good one, Pherkad! Don't stop now! Keep after him. Hit! Hit! Hit!" The smaller boy was obviously hurting, and now had to endure a renewed assault.

Avior was furious. Did they think she enjoyed watching children being hurt? She had her faults, but she never descended to that. Or was there a double bluff involved? If Vildiar was hoping to persuade her that he was a kind, loving, law-abiding father, then he would never let himself be seen tormenting baby halflings, would he? Unless he wanted her to think that he hadn't planned this meeting. She didn't believe that.

"Fight back, Wazn!" the prince shouted. The smaller boy's eyes were now so full of tears that he was having trouble even seeing Pherkad, let alone defending himself against his opponent's fusillade of punches. Soon his lip was bleeding, too. Eventually Vildiar seemed to decide that he had been punished enough, and he called a halt. Gasping and puffing, the combatants stopped fighting.

"Pherkad won," the referee announced. "So Wazn gets a free punch. Hands behind your back, Pherkad. Wazn? Are you brave enough to hurt him now?"

"Yes, Father."

"Not too scared of him now that he's beaten you?"

Wazn shook his head.

"Then go ahead."

Revealing bloody teeth in a smile, the smaller boy hauled back and smashed his fist into Pherkad's nose as hard as he could. Blood spurted and the victim reeled back with a cry. Everyone else cheered. Vildiar laughed and said well done, then sent them all off to the swimming hole.

He turned to look down at Avior. She bowed, not too low. She was afraid that he might try to embrace her, but he didn't. She sensed a calculating, predatory mind behind the opalescent eyes.

"Daughter!"

"Your Highness."

He shook his head as if he could read her thoughts. "The boys all have healing amulets. They'll be good as new by bedtime."

She hadn't thought of that.

Vildiar pressed his advantage. "I am truly sorry about what happened to you. Had we been able to find your mother, we would have rescued her and brought her to the Starlands, to bear her child in peace. The woman who was supposed to keep track of her was severely punished."

After being transformed from being the two boys in Botein's version? And if they *had* found her mother? Would Avior have grown up here at Unukalhai, learning to box, learning to be an assassin? She had no answer to that, either. Silence was the best defense.

It didn't faze the giant elf, though. He seemed amused. "Whatever I can do to make redress, you have only to ask." Fairy godfather, three wishes.

She pulled off her head cloth. "Can you heal my ears?" Rigel had suggested that it might be possible, but he had never followed through.

Vildiar frowned and took a closer look, right then left.

"Yes. I'll send you some ointment. One application will be enough, but they'll need a year or so to grow back fully. What else?"

Despite herself, Avior glanced across to where Scheddi was obediently staring at the wall, hiding his grotesque genitalia from the children.

"Scheddi?" Botein suggested.

"Certainly. If you want that satyr, Avior, I'll gladly give him to you."

She gathered her courage to talk back. "That's very kind of Your Highness, but may I ask what my side of the bargain will be?"

"Nothing at all!" he said at once. "I know Halfling Rigel has set you up with a studio, so I assume that's what you want. He may have asked you to do something for him. I don't know whether he has or not. I don't want to know either way, and I won't stop you doing it, whatever it is. The ointment is a free gift and the same for that animated dildo over there. And anything else you may think of later." He smiled. "All free, no strings attached. It's not nearly enough to make amends."

Damn him, he had charm when he wanted!

Scheddi greeted his new owner with a predictable, "Go fukfuk now?," squeezing her in another one-armed hug all the way back to the air car barn. The chariot was very crowded with three in it, even without any airspace between Avior's back and the satyr's hairy chest. She was glad that he needed one arm to hold them both in, or else he probably would have had her wrap off before the brief flight ended.

But they weren't back at Kraz. Not in Sherwood Forest, either. The chariot stood in front of a shabby cottage in a little clearing surrounded by giant beech trees. On the other side was an overgrown swimming hole that might have come from a Monet painting. Scheddi jumped down and lifted Avior out of the car. Instead of setting her down, he just cradled her in his arms. He tried to kiss her, but she turned her face away. Not yet!

"This is home?"

Botein jumped down also. "No. This is the Hermitage. I told you I'd need to remove the two Nusakan. You don't want to have to groom the unicorns yourself, do you? Scheddi won't do that sort of work."

"Not my purpose in life," Scheddi said, very nearly managing to steal a kiss when she looked up at him. *Oh, that tongue!*

"And I can't carry unicorns in my chariot," Botein finished triumphantly, "but we can drive them here through the portal." And she looked at Scheddi.

Scheddi said, "Right." Carrying Avior as if she weighed nothing, he followed Botein over to the tumbledown little cottage.

Avior had been a resident in the Starlands for long enough to know a bit about portals. She knew they worked only within a single domain and its subdomains, so this Hermitage must be in the royal domain, like Kraz. Botein was trespassing here. From this bridgehead the Family goons could access anywhere in the royal domain, except specially guarded places such as Castle Escher.

Vildiar had told her she need not tell him what Rigel was up to, but Scheddi was certainly smarter than he pretended, and Scheddi was going to be the Family's spy in Kraz. He wouldn't need an air car, and probably couldn't drive those contraptions anyway. But he could step through the portal to the Hermitage to report and be back before Avior even missed him.

"Been lovely meeting you, sister," Botein said. "It'll only take a minute to get the Nusakan to drive the unicorns through, and then I'll get out of your hair and let you go on with your painting or whatever you were doing."

I was modeling Halfling Rigel's left knee, and you bloody well know it, lady.

Scheddi said, "Then we'll be alone?"

"Yes," Avior sighed, leaning her head on his shoulder. Even the scent of his skin was exciting. "Will we have time for a drink first?"

"Certainly not," said Scheddi.

Chapter 28

"What happens now?" Izar demanded angrily. "If I have to stay one more day in this aquarium, I will turn into a *shark*!"

"Could only be an improvement," his bodyguard said.

"A halfling-eating shark!"

"Oh, not so good. And your mother wouldn't approve. What do you have in mind?"

It was early morning. They were gathered around a table on the royal patio in Segin. Izar and his visiting friend Ukdah had just eaten their usual breakfasts, about two thousand calories apiece. Their plates were being cleaned by a school of shrimps. Thabit, his eyes even redder than usual, was sipping black coffee and growling in response to suggestive questioning from his twin, who had been on duty the previous night and had thus missed whatever party or orgy was now exacting its toll.

Rigel was preoccupied too. It was one day short of three weeks since Vildiar had been outlawed, so Fomalhaut's latest prophecy of Rigel's death, as relayed by Achird, should be fulfilled the next day—unless, of course, it had been greatly exaggerated, like rumors of Mark Twain's death. Nothing had happened since, except that the queen's popularity had soared, as measured by people willing to join her council or be seen around court. The starfolk were assuming that the Vildiar problem had been solved. It hadn't.

No one had seen any trace of "V" or the Family killers. No additional members of the queen's council had died. Her officials had moved into Phegda and started taking oaths of loyalty from Vildiar's most senior underlings, just a few dozen starfolk out of the hundreds whose domains were directly rooted in his. None had refused to change allegiance and none had suffered unexpected death as a result.

So the monster had vanished? Being essentially immortal, he could easily afford to take a twenty-year vacation, and the waiting would be much harder on his potential victims than on him. It was especially hard on Izar, who was being held in virtual house arrest in Segin. Rigel sympathized, knowing how soon the blue-green light and breathable water palled. The imp still missed Turais, too.

"What would you like to do?" he asked again.

"A hippogriff ride!" Izar said at once. "Down into that volcano, Whasisname, where the dragons nest. And some whitewater barrel riding." His standard technique was to ask first for something totally suicidal, in the hope of winning his second choice, which would be only slightly suicidal.

"Hippogriff possible. I need to head over to Kraz first. Do you want to come with me?"

Izar opened his mouth, then his opalescent eyes flickered to Ukdah as he remembered that Kraz was where Tweenling Avior had her studio and there were secrets there that he had sworn never to tell *anyone*. So Ukdah couldn't go with them. "Can't take more than two on a hippogriff, though, can you?"

The kid was faster than a shyster lawyer on booster rockets.

"'Fraid not. But Thabit can see Ukdah home. Have you chosen a gift for him?"

"Not yet." Being royalty, Izar had to give every visitor a going-away present. He loved it. "What'ch fancy this time, Uk?"

Ukdah's hair and eyes were turning from childish white to pale green. He was slightly older than Izar, and thus could usually manage to hold his own without being browbeaten into utter submission. "A couple of those electric slugs!"

"That all? Just two?"

"How many does it take to *kill* somebody?"

Rigel and Tyl rolled their eyes in unison. Just one electric slug left in a person's bed or a clothes drawer could deliver a very memorable shock. Fortunately starfolk were rarely subject to cardiac arrest.

The outer door flew open and in strode Starborn Elgomaisa. The queen was still in bed. Rigel was quite certain that the royal consort had not slept here in Segin the previous night, but other people were not supposed to know. He noticed the two starlings exchanging meaningful glances.

So, he thought, did Elgomaisa.

Everyone rose and bowed—except Izar. A month or so ago he had announced that he was Naos now and did not have to kowtow to anyone except his mother. Rigel had put the matter to the queen, and she had agreed, much to everyone else's astonishment. Elgomaisa had not been pleased.

"Halfling," he said, addressing Rigel. "My mother is grievously insulted by your continued refusal to certify her home as a safe place for the queen to visit. I will go over the arrangements with you one last time. Be there in about an hour."

Rigel bowed again as the consort crossed the patio and disappeared into his official bedroom.

"Halfling," Izar told Thabit, "help Ukdah Starling collect as many slugs as he needs before you take him home. Good of you to come, Uk. We'd better move our buns, huh, Rigel?"

Meaning he wanted to be included in the visit to Vindemiatrix, which he hadn't seen yet. It was still scheduled to become the next royal residence, but Rigel kept postponing the move because of his doubts about security.

"How could I refuse a request so graciously worded, Izar Naos?"

Izar laughed. "Smart-ass halfling!" He faked a punch, man-to-man style. Grown-up guys did that.

Kraz was within the royal domain and thus on the other side of any portal, but Rigel had not been there for weeks. At first Tyl and Thabit had kept him informed of the sculptor's progress, but lately whatever there had been between her and the twins—the details of which Rigel would much rather not know—had apparently cooled. Yesterday he had received a note passed on by the Palace Guard in Canopus to say that she wanted to see him. It was early to go calling, but he and Izar could always pass the time with a unicorn ride.

So he thought, but the portal at Kraz was set in the outside wall of the barn, so when he stepped out into the yard, the first thing he noticed was that the paddock was empty. Rigel glanced around the little cluster of buildings and decided the whole place had an air of neglect, almost abandonment: weeds were starting to sprout, and the shutters had been closed on many of the windows. Either the two Nusakan mudlings had been neglecting their duties, or they were no longer working there. His first instinct was to grab Izar and drag him back through the portal to somewhere safe, like Castle Escher. Izar, too, had sensed something wrong and edged closer to Rigel. But Saiph was not indicating any danger.

"What is that appalling stink?" Izar demanded.

"Me," said a voice at his elbow.

Starling and bodyguard simultaneously leapt about two meters sideways and spun around to view the speaker. He was short by starborn standards, about Rigel's height, but he did have elfin ears flanking huge upright horns. His face was incredibly ugly, a protruding muzzle whose smile displayed a graveyard of marble tombstones, not elfin spikes. From the neck to the waist he was a burly, hairy youth, but below that he was all goat—furry pelt, two cloven hooves and . . . and everything else. He was also naked.

His name was Scheddi.

"What is that?" Izar squealed.

"I'm a satyr," Scheddi said, his voice seeming to fight its way through those great teeth. "What're you?"

"I'm not a *what*, I'm a *who*!"

"Scheddi means that he's a who, too." Rigel tried not to smile.

Izar wrinkled his nose. "Why don't you go and bathe?"

"I just did," Scheddi said, and indeed his fur was damp. "I'm told the perfume is part of my appeal, although I can't smell it myself. Did you come to see my mistress?" He grinned in a blaze of ivory.

"Is she awake?" Rigel asked.

"Probably not, but I was just going to wake her. I'll tell her you're here." He trotted up the slope to the studio, hooves drumming on the hard ground and short tail twitching from side to side. The visitors followed more slowly.

"You suppose he goes around all day like that?" Izar whispered.

"You ask him. I don't want to know."

After a moment the imp added, "You suppose the twins gave up because they couldn't match the new competition?" So he had noticed that estrangement, and yet his smile was not his usual leer.

Izar was growing up. Although he still played the enfant terrible most of the time, glimpses of maturity showed through when he forgot to hide them. At times now it was even possible for Rigel to accept that they were almost the same age. Rigel wondered if he could claim any credit for the change, but he had no idea how starborn youths normally developed. When he met Izar's friends, they were always on their best behavior, which was very rarely true of Izar. Besides, the imp had survived an attempted murder and two kidnappings. That sort of childhood would make anyone streetwise.

As they neared the studio, Scheddi appeared in the doorway. He leaned against the jamb and grinned. "She says you can come in. Some people have no shame."

"Do satyrs?" Izar asked innocently.

Scheddi looked indignant. "Of course not!"

The inside of the big shed was dim and the reek of satyr made Rigel's eyes water. Avior came forward to meet them, looking bleary and sleepy, but she was respectably dressed by Starlands standards, wearing a moon-cloth wrap and a bandana over her hair. She had learned local ways well enough to bow to the starling and express the wish that the stars might shine on him forever. Izar acknowledged her greeting politely, but his gaze was darting to and fro as he assessed the chaos.

Scheddi was opening shutters, gradually illuminating a muck heap that would not have shamed a major hurricane. The floor was carpeted with an ankle-deep layer of rags, liquor bottles, dirty dishes, and many pots and boxes of plaster, pigments, and other art materials, resting on a mixture of trodden clay and sharp chips of stone. Fortunately much of the mess was hidden from view by canvases on easels, clay models on pedestals, and partly chipped blocks of marble. A bed in one corner held a rumpled blanket but no pillows. It seemed as though Avior worked, ate, and slept in this one room. And so did Scheddi.

How could anything close to beauty ever emerge from such a midden?

"Hi!" Rigel said. "How do the Starlands compare to Saskatchewan so far?"

She smiled. "Closer to heaven."

"Getting everything you need?" Rigel asked. He must be catching Izar's style of humor, but Avior's ran along much the same lines.

She laughed. "As much as I can handle."

And that was at least as much as was good for her health. She sported several multicolored bruises, a badly split lip, and a puffy eye, while the marks on her breasts and arms looked suspiciously like bites. All her injuries must date from the last few hours, because Rigel had supplied her with healing amulets from the royal treasury.

"You sent word that . . ." He stopped in front of an easel, struck dumb by the portrait on it. The setting was a green jungle, with every fleshy leaf gleaming wet, every raindrop shining. This dark but detailed background set off a three-quarters portrait of Scheddi, lit by a shaft of sunlight and depicted in harsh, crude strokes of brilliant color. Yet the likeness was perfect, from the tips of his horns down to his grotesquely oversized genitals. He stared out from the canvas with sadistic mockery, the ultimate in male lust and dominance. The image was even more repellent than the original—possessive, menacing, brutish.

Rigel had privately dismissed Avior as a skilled, if skewed, craftsperson. But if this was not a work of genius, it had to be close.

"That's magnificent!"

"He likes posing," she said dismissively. "It's the only way to make him keep still. I call it *Man*."

"Is that how you see us?"

She flipped a cloth over the picture to hide it. "An artist's mission is to teach other people to see more clearly."

Before Rigel could think up a believable rebuttal, he heard a cry of horror from Izar, who had gone buzzing off like a bluebottle.

It took a lot to shock him. Rigel quickly dodged around the easel and found the problem. On a long worktable in the back of the room lay the body of a halfling, faceup, arms by its sides. It was corpse pale, with white hair and barely visible scars where it had been clawed by a bear in the spring. The mouth hung open in a corpse's gape, the lips streaked with dried blood. No navel, no nipples. He had known he would have to face this sometime, but he hadn't expected the head to be turned his way or the dead white eyes to be open and staring at him.

And he had certainly not expected to see the wounds—four black arrow punctures, the shafts broken off a few centimeters above the flesh, barbed heads left in place. They were gruesomely realistic, ringed by caked blood. No two were exactly alike; some had been cut off closer, some had bled more than others. But the worst horror was that there were four, placed about as he had seen them in the Time of Life vision: right elbow, left shoulder, abdomen, and lower chest. *How had she known there would be four and where to put them?*

"That's incredible!" he said hoarsely, instinctively reaching out a hand.

"Don't touch!" she snapped. "Some of the wax hasn't quite hardened yet. It *looks* perfect, but it's never going to feel *exactly* right."

"It's *schmoory*!" Izar said disapprovingly. Apparently he lost his taste for the macabre when it involved his friends.

"You can say that again." Rigel's mouth was dry. He felt sick. "How did you know . . . I mean, how did you decide how to kill me . . . him?"

She shrugged. "You suggested the arrows. The ones in your right arm and left shoulder so you couldn't wield your sword, and two in the belly to kill you." She smiled mockingly. "Why? Do you *know* how they should be?"

He hadn't quite believed he did, not until now. Only Fomalhaut could know what the Time of Life had prophesied. *Not that it mattered where the arrows were put. The purpose of this imitation was to balk the prophecy, and it would never be needed if the prophecy had already been fulfilled.*

"I hope I never do, lady! How soon can it be moved?"

"Tomorrow."

"Then I'll come for it tomorrow morning at about this time." One more corpse ought to fit Vindemiatrix very well, because it was the abode of the slain.

"I'd like to come along and watch over it on the trip to make sure it's displayed properly."

Rigel shook his head. "I'm afraid that won't be possible. Security, you know. But I am extremely grateful for all the work you have put into this. Is there anything you want or need?"

"Nothing I can't supply," said Scheddi, who was standing right behind Avior. He slid a brawny arm around her waist and clasped her breast with his other hand. She sighed happily and leaned back against him.

Rigel ignored that. "You've certainly done everything I asked. You're quite sure there is nothing more you want? How about another satyr to help Scheddi with his duties?"

"No, no! Scheddi would kill it." Her gaze was defiant, intended to show that Avior Halfling had survived the transition to the Starlands.

"I certainly would," Scheddi said, lowering his horns menacingly.

"Then I'll see you tomorrow. Come along, Naos. I need to find a swimming hole."

Izar was out the door in a flash, but he lingered on the path to let Rigel catch up.

"Where," the imp asked, "do you find . . . What was that?"

That had been a cry of pain from the studio.

Rigel didn't break his stride. "Scheddi at work, I think. Pay no attention. We were meant to hear it. Some people have very strange ideas of fun. What were you going to say?"

"I was going to ask where you got satyrs? I've never heard of them before!"

"I don't know. Ask Tyl or Thabit. They ought to know. They probably went to the same school as Scheddi."

Chapter 29

Rigel insisted on going first through the portal to Mabsuthat, as he always did, telling Izar to stay close, as he always did. Izar hadn't visited the glade of the hippogriffs since that day with Dschubba. He was fairly sure that some of big standing stones had moved since then, but the pearly mist never stopped shifting around, making the landscape oddly variable. The trees were more golden than he remembered, and the rocks' humming song had changed to a more disturbing tone. There were notes in there he knew he couldn't make on his lute.

"Rigel?"

"Yes, Izar?"

"You suppose four unicorns and two Nusakan mudlings would be a fair trade for one satyr?"

The halfling put on his taking-Izar-seriously face. "I have no idea. Why do you ask?"

"I just wondered if you think Scheddi could have been given to Avior as a bribe."

"Starlings of your age shouldn't have to worry about things like that."

"But this one has to, don't I?"

Rigel sighed. "I'm afraid you do, and I'm very glad you take it seriously." He scanned the mist, hunting for hippogriffs, or anything worse that might approach. "Yes, the satyr could have been a bribe. Very few people would want to own one, but Avior is a strange lady."

"So you think she might have been bought by Hadar?"

"It's possible."

Izar nodded grimly. Any mention of Hadar gave him squiggly-worm feelings in his belly. "You didn't tell her where the fake body's going to be moved. You don't trust her!"

"Vindemiatrix is supposed to be a secret. You know that."

The portal at Mabsuthat was set in a big slab of white stone, probably made to match the big menhirs. The back of the slab was blank, as Izar knew because he'd looked at it the first time he was in this subdomain. Now Rigel moved to the rear corner, so he could make sure nothing was creeping up on them from that direction. There were supposed to be hydras, chimeras, and even manticores here.

Izar stayed at the front, to watch that way. "And you're not happy about Mom moving the court there anyway."

"No, I'm not. It's too old, too tricky, and it has too many secrets. My palimpsest amulet tells me a lot of things there aren't what they seem to be, but it can't tell me what they really do."

"Here comes our ride."

A huge flying shape zoomed into view overhead and circled down to land.

"That's not Kitalphar! Let's go!" Rigel ran back to the portal.

"No, wait!" Izar knew this hippogriff.

"It's a male, Izar! They're deadly."

"This one isn't!"

Rigel had the door open. *"Starling, come now!"*

"No, we'd offend him terribly. You know how proud they are." Although he wasn't sure of that and his heart was beating awesomely fast, Izar took three steps forward and bowed to the approaching monster. "Our eyes are honored to behold Your Magnificence, noble Torcularis Septentrionalis."

The great eagle beak could bite his head off. The huge talons on the front legs could crush him. But the fearsome head dipped graciously, just as it had the last time.

"Would Your Splendor consent to transport my humble self and my servant to Vindemiatrix?"

Torcularis nodded again, then turned around and lowered his horse rear so that Izar could mount, which wasn't easy, and he appreciated a hefty boost from Rigel, and even Rigel had some trouble mounting on that huge back. The great feathered wings spread and the hippogriff soared upward.

"This was how you got that amulet from Dschubba?" Rigel whispered in Izar's ear. "You told me you didn't run into a male!"

"Well, it's safer for us Naos," Izar said, because he couldn't think of a better retort. "They honor us." That wasn't a lie because he didn't know for certain that it wasn't true.

"Remind me to wring your neck after lunch."

The nice thing about riding a hippogriff was that it kept its head down like a real eagle, so you could look straight ahead. Centaurs were bad that way. All you saw was a sweaty back.

Mabsuthat had vanished into the mists below, so there was no land to see, only blue sky. Now that Vildiar had been outlawed and Mom had confiscated Phegda and all its subdomains, she could open the root portal on Front Street in Canopus to the royal domain, if she wanted. Then any portal would work between Phegda and the royal domain, and they wouldn't need hippogriffs or *Saidak* to go to places like Vindemiatrix. She'd told him she wasn't planning on it, though, because both domains were too big already and she'd rather divide Phegda among V's heirs. His heirs hadn't been identified yet.

The hippogriff was climbing over mountains of puffy cloud, evidently heading for a very high highway. Izar turned side-saddle, hanging both feet down on the left and gripping Torky's spinal fringe with both hands; that way he could talk to Rigel better. Rigel hung onto his arm, but he wasn't much more securely seated than Izar was.

"Is Avior still loyal, Rigel?"

"She never sees anyone except Scheddi, apparently, and he's only interested in one thing."

"Which he does very well?" He was certainly built for it. Whoof!

"I'm sure he does."

"So Tyl and Thabit don't go there anymore. I think that's really supsishus! You think she's gone over to the Family?"

"Mm . . ." Rigel didn't often seem unsure of himself, but he wasn't answering.

"You told me you'd never lie to me!"

"And I never do. If the Family knows what Avior's been doing for us, then my plan won't work, will it?"

"You don't lie, you just ask more questions instead of answering mine." Suddenly Izar had a brainwave. Smart imp! *"Was it ever meant to?"*

Rigel shot him an irritated look. "Was whatever ever meant to do what?"

"The plan. It was always a *schmoory,* stupid plan! I never thought much of it, and today Avior told us that the dead ringer still won't feel like a real corpse. So that isn't the real plan at all . . . Never was. You were careful not to mention Vindemiatrix by name." *Yes, this made more sense.* "You knew what sort of things Avior made before we even extroverted to fetch her: corpses and bits of bodies and stuff. Hadar must'a known too!"

"Go on."

"You didn't mention Vindemiatrix to Avior, but you promised to go back to Kraz tomorrow morning. So what happens tonight?"

"Why should anything happen tonight?" Rigel asked warily.

"Because you expect Hadar to try and ambush you tomorrow morning at Kraz. So you'll have a counterambush waiting!"

"Yuck! That is the most disgusting, twisted, deceitful thinking I ever heard of! Did you always have a messed-up mind like that, or did you pick it up from me?"

Izar crowed in triumph. "I was a *nice* imp till you came along."

They both laughed. It was good to see the halfling happy. He'd been mopey lately. "So what does happen tonight?"

"Tonight, my young friend, we load up Kraz with centaurs, sphinxes, griffins, cyclops, and minotaurs galore, all armed with swords and bloodthirstily delighted by the prospect of getting a fair fight for once. If Hadar and the Family take the bait tomorrow, they will be slaughtered down to the last man or woman. No quarter given. And no, you can't be there."

"How will you get all your troops through the portal?" That would be suicide. Hadar would be waiting to pick them off, one by one.

"I won't," Rigel said. "The portal will be locked. We'll come at them from every other direction."

"And what will you do about Avior?"

"Avior?" Rigel said. "Why should I do anything about Avior?"

"You just admitted that she's betraying you to Vildiar!"

"Ah." For a moment the halfling seemed to study the scenery, but then he sighed and smiled sadly. "I knew she would, Izar. See, Avior had a terrible, terrible childhood. It wasn't only what Vildiar did to her mother; her own mother and stepfather were even worse. She's been damaged and warped in a way normal people like you and me can never understand. Hadar's gang found her and then used her as bait for me, right? And now I'm using her as bait for Hadar. Am I any better than he is?"

What? "Of course you are! Hadar's a great horrible monster!"

"Then I must be a little horrible monster. Hadar knew that you and I had rescued her and he would naturally watch to see what use we made of her. I was sure he'd manage to turn her somehow. So I don't blame her, and I won't *do*, as you call it, anything about Avior. She enjoys solitude, and she's got it at Kraz. She likes making those nightmare works of art, and she can do it all day long now, without ever having to worry about paying the grocery bills. And she has Scheddi to give her whatever else she wants from life, Heaven help her. Avior's as close to Heaven now as she can ever be, Izar, and your mother and I plan to let her enjoy it."

Izar said, "Oh!" and put that little talk away to think about later.

A highway came into view, a wheel of cloud beneath them, and Torcularis swooped down *wickedly* fast. *Oo! Cool!* That was a Rigel word, meaning "doggy!" The other starlings had laughed at it at first, but now they were using it too. The 'griff shot through the link and leveled out, soaring low over a landscape of drab black rock, under a gray and drizzling sky.

Izar looked around, wondering why anyone would bother to imagine a domain so depressing. It pretended it was a very wide mountain valley, which ought to be walled in by very high peaks, but the clouds hid everything above the lowest slopes. That was cheating, probably; there wouldn't be any mountains behind most of the clouds. When he was old enough to imagine his own domain, it was going to be all *real*, no cheating! And the animals would all be *really* dangerous. Here he couldn't see any animals, or any chance of any. Not even rabbits or marmots or ground squirrels. The landscape was nothing but rock: slabs, boulders, cobbles, pebbles, and shingle. Streams of disgusting milky water wandered through it all, joining and dividing. Perhaps that much water put all together would count as a big river, but it wouldn't be any use for anything, not swimming, boating, or even drinking.

"*Schmoory!*" he said. "It's ugly. Who committed this atrocity?"

"Vindemiatrix was imagined by Elgomaisa Starborn's mother around seventeen hundred years ago. She still lives there, but I haven't met her—she doesn't receive halflings."

"Does it ever stop raining here?"

Rigel was grinning. "Never when I've come here. But it's meant to be ugly, I think. Look up ahead."

Ahead there was just more barren valley, no grass, no flowers, no trees. A patch of sunshine in the distance, under a gap in the clouds, looked hopeful. As Torky flew closer, the view resolved itself into a great snow-capped peak, towering over the valley. And a rainbow.

"Pretty," Izar conceded. Almost impressive, maybe. "But that's all? They live in tents here?"

"Over there, to the left."

Ah, yes. Now he saw a house of some sort perched on a rocky shelf about a third of the way up the mountain. The rainbow seemed to start from it, leaping upward to frame the valley in its great poly-colored arch, from red to ultraviolet, which he knew that Rigel, like many other halflings, couldn't see.

A golden house. Nothing elaborate about its shape, just four walls and a gable roof, but all of gold, and soon he began to realize that it must be *doggy huge* up there, so high above the valley floor.

Yes! Wow! "Vindemiatrix?"

"That's it. The foreground is ugly, but the ugliness outside emphasizes the beauty of the interior. It's symbolic: beyond death lies the abode of the gods. And then there's the bridge."

Izar couldn't see any bridge. He was distracted by a wicked itch on his wrist. He was just about to scratch it when he realized that it was coming from his warning bracelet. Rigel would notice if he scratched that, because Rigel never missed anything. And if Vindemiatrix meant danger for Izar, then Rigel would send him home.

Rigel was frowning. He looked down and caught Izar's eye. "All right?"

Izar shook his head. "Warning bracelet." Heroes didn't waste words.

"Saiph too," Rigel said softly.

Neither spoke again for a few minutes. Izar watched as the gorgeous golden building grew larger. He wondered why Torky was continuing to glide close to the ground rather than gaining height. And that splendid rainbow? Was it possible that the rainbow was growing nearer, too? That had to be cretinous imagery, because rainbows didn't do that! But this one was, or rather it wasn't running away as it should. As they approached it, it was also growing bigger and bigger, huger and huger, and soon it was clear that the hippogriff was heading for the base of the rainbow on the far side of the river from Vindemiatrix.

Rain stopped; the sun came out. Better!

"Izar? How well can you control this steed of yours?"

Izar looked up at Rigel and shrugged. "Dunno."

"When we land, ask him politely if he'll take us back to the royal domain. Very politely! You know how touchy they are."

The warning bracelet was itching enough to drive him crazy. He reached down to touch Saiph on Rigel's wrist, and felt it vibrating. Imp and halfling exchanged concerned glances.

The base of the rainbow stood on the riverbank, where a stretch of sward offered the only patch of color in the dreary valley. Two unicorns and a pegasus were grazing, but as Torky approached, they trotted to the far end of the tiny meadow and stood there, eyeing him nervously. The hippogriff set down his talons and hooves and waited for his passengers to dismount, folding his great wings.

"Most royal Torcularis Septentrionalis," Izar said, "mightiest of hippogriffs, it seems that danger awaits here for my humble self and my churl. Would you most graciously consent to return us quickly to—"

The answer was in the negative. Torcularis reared, sending Izar and Rigel hurtling to the ground. For a moment Izar was winded, lying flat on the pebbly grass, staring up in horror at the nightmare towering over him, bigger by far than any horse. Balanced on his hind hooves, mighty wings spread, Torky's great front talons appeared ready to seize and crush him.

Then Rigel was standing over him, his sword streaked with sunlight.

"Back, hippogriff!" he roared. "This is ancestral Saiph, the King of Swords. Add not your name to its grisly necrology!"

Torcularis clacked his beak a few times in frustration, then leaped into the sky. Rigel stood back and watched him soar away. By the time he had dismissed his sword, Izar was on his feet again.

"All right?" Rigel asked.

"Think so." He hadn't wet himself, although he'd come awful close.

"Well done, hero! I think both of us had better stay well away from Mabsuthat in future. What's your warning amulet doing now?"

"Nothing."

"Honest?"

"Of course honest!"

"Interesting," Rigel said. "So we were only in danger from the hippogriff."

That didn't sound right! Torky had only become dangerous when they asked him to take them home, and the only reason they'd done that was because of the warning signals. Still, Izar's bracelet wasn't itching anymore.

"What's Saiph say?"

Rigel gave him an exasperated why-did-you-have-to-ask-that scowl. "Shivering like a bird in a net."

Izar nodded solemnly, pleased that his bodyguard hadn't lied to him. He looked around at the minute stretch of grass, and all the barren rock around it. There was nowhere to go, no way out, except perhaps on the pegasus, and they were one-owner pets. "Now what?"

Rigel smiled and looked up at the rainbow, which filled the sky. "Fortunately I don't think that little hassle was visible from Vindemiatrix. It seems we have to visit there whether we want to or not."

That "hassle" had nearly killed them both, and it was all Izar's fault for taking Dschubba to Mabsuthat without permission and getting himself adopted by a male hippogriff. But Rigel knew he knew that and so wasn't going to reproach him for it, or punish him more. Which made him feel worse, of course, and Rigel probably knew that, too.

"You'll love the place," Rigel said, heading across the grass toward the rainbow. "So would Avior. It's her dream world."

"Why?" Izar distrusted that innocent tone.

"It's full of corpses."

"Real corpses?"

"They look real. But they dance and fight and sing songs, so perhaps not."

He jumped over a murky, earthy-smelling pool of dark brown water. Izar took a run at it and followed. He'd never seen a rainbow from the side before. At this angle it was a wall of red light almost too bright to look upon. It was at least twenty starborn paces wide—meaning that rainbows were that *thick*—hanging from the sky like an enormous curtain with fuzzy edges. He could see into it a pace or two, but beyond that everything faded into the red mist. The other colors were hidden behind the red.

"Now we walk up this?" he demanded.

"Of course. Better hold my hand if you want us to stay together. I think you'll go faster than I will."

Guys did not hold other guys' hands! Izar grabbed Rigel's wrist instead, and they stepped into the red fog together. His feet left the ground, which quickly faded out of sight, but that was the only sensation of movement. At first he just seemed to be floating in the red mist, but soon the rainbow began to curve and his head emerged enough for him to see. The light hung around his neck, like water, just below the level of Rigel's shoulders. Rigel was watching his reaction and grinning, so he grinned back.

Had he suggested holding hands in case Izar was frightened? No, the bridge really was trying to pull them apart, dragging Izar forward.

"Does this work at night?"

"It's never night here. Always sunshine, always a rainbow."

"Cool! How do we come back?"

"Just jump aboard and it brings you automatically." Rigel grinned again. "It's kind of fun, isn't it!"

"Yeah. Then why's Saiph shivering?"

Rigel sighed. "It's a warning. Not really close danger, not yet. It was tearing my hand off when you started talking to that hippogriff again. This is just a 'Be Careful!' sign."

"Stop babying me!"

"Sorry. You remember how I told you that Vindemiatrix has too many secrets? Well, this bridge is supposed to be the only way in. There's some sort of magical defense against air cars. I had Achird try it out and he agreed, said he couldn't get near enough to land, even on his skyboard. Squadron Leader Gianfar admits that her griffins can't land there either."

They were rapidly approaching the crest of the bow, with the red light down around their knees. Ahead loomed the sunlit mountain, glorious against looming storm clouds.

"But?" Izar prompted. Why did danger always make a guy want to pee?

"But this was Starborn Elgomaisa's childhood home," Rigel said. "He was born here and grew up here."

"Explains a lot." All this gloomy rock and cloud—no wonder he had black hair!

"Then listen. The palace can only be entered through the corpse hall. Everyone must enter by the main door and walk the length of the hall. In ancient earthling mythology, Valhalla was a feasting hall for dead heroes waiting to fight for the gods in the final battle at the end of the world. It's where they would spend centuries carousing and having a great time. They won't pay any attention to you as long as you leave them alone. I don't like this, because Hadar could hide the entire Family in that mob and you'd never notice. Starborn Elgomaisa says I shouldn't worry about that, because the warriors would notice and make a fuss. But Saiph has never warned me like this before, not here at Vindemiatrix, so something's wrong."

Rigel was in danger but Izar wasn't? That sounded more like Elegy than Hadar.

"If," Rigel added, "there's something nasty waiting for me up ahead, I'll trust Saiph to come through as usual. You're quite certain your alarm bracelet isn't itching? I must have the truth, starling."

"Not a twitch, Rigel, honest."

"Good. Then I want you to scamper! Get out of the way so that I don't have to worry about you, just me. I must be able to concentrate. All right, hero?"

"Scamper how?" If Hadar and his killers were waiting at the far end of the rainbow, then jumping back on it would do no good. They would follow, and there was nowhere to hide down in the meadow.

"There are two ways. If you go to the far end of the corpse hall, you'll find a corridor leading through into what feels like it ought to be the middle of the mountain, but it opens into a sunny garden with a lake and fruit trees, and all sorts of villas, cottages, pleasure gardens, and so on."

Izar nodded, trying to ignore his bursting bladder.

"The moment we land," Rigel said, "I want you to run to the far end of the hall, along the corridor—you can't miss it—and into the main palace. And there you must insist on being taken to Starborn Ascella, Elgomaisa's mother. Your Naos hair will get you past any arguments. I told you she won't have anything to do with halflings like me, but her son is paired with the queen at the moment, so she's very unlikely to turn you over to Hadar. Ask her to see you back home."

No! Izar would warn her that his bodyguard was in danger and if anything happened to the marshal of Canopus in Vindemiatrix, the queen would feed Ascella Starborn to the palace dogs. "Yes, Rigel. You remember how Naos Kurhah planned to attack the Family, but Hadar struck first? And tomorrow you're planning to ambush Hadar at Kraz? Isn't that a worrisome simil'rarity?"

They were right at the crest of the rainbow now, looking down on the golden hall ahead.

"Stars!" Rigel said. "That isn't imp thinking. You're growing up awful fast, Naos Izar."

Izar was pleased, but not about to be distracted. "Answer my question!"

"Yes, my lord. Hadar may not be the problem here. Elgomaisa has his own reasons to hate me."

Yes, there was that. And what Rigel didn't know was that just last night Izar had stupidly let Ukdah into the fake-consort secret and when Elegy had turned up this morning, he'd noticed Ukdah's silly smirk at Izar, so he knew they knew. Still, Elegy must know how dangerous it would be to challenge Saiph. "What's the second way to scamper?"

They were sliding swiftly down the great arch now.

"There's a throne at the far end of the corpse hall. In the legends, that was where Odin sat, the chief god, so I suppose the lord of Vindemiatrix can sit there and pretend he's Odin. There's a shield hanging on the back of the throne. If you push it aside, you'll find a secret portal behind it. At first Lord Elgomaisa said he didn't know it was there."

Izar stared up at him in disbelief. "You mean Elegy told you there was no other way in or out 'cept the rainbow? And he *grew up* here? Grew up here and didn't discover a concealed portal?" What sort of a thud-brained starling had he been?

Rigel nodded. "Then he changed his story and said it was the root portal, sealed up."

"That could be."

"Except my amulet says it's still active. It doesn't work for me, but that may be because it only leads to other portals in Starborn Ascella's domain, and I don't know any of them. Or it may open to portals in Phegda that you don't want to visit, like Unukalhai. So I think Starborn Ascella would be a safer bet."

So Izar and Rigel probably couldn't escape through that portal, but Hadar might be able to bring the whole Family in from somewhere. Then Izar looked up at Vindemiatrix straight ahead and said, "Oh, wow!"

From this angle all he saw was the gable end, with no windows, only a big central door, but both the logs of the walls and the thatch of the roof were gold. Because the ledge on which the hall stood was so much higher than the river, the rainbow hardly started to bend downward before it ended, not far in front of the door.

Rigel said, "The living quarters are all in back. This is just the theme-park part."

"What's a theme park?"

Before Rigel could explain, they arrived at the end of the rainbow. The red light was still barely up to their knees, but they felt rock under their feet and stopped moving. When Izar let go of Rigel's wrist, Saiph was hammering like a ravenous woodpecker, while his own warning bracelet was still doing nothing.

Chapter 30

Izar saw Starborn Elgomaisa waiting for them, and wished he didn't. But just the sight of him in the doorway emphasized how enormous the hall was. Built of tree trunks two or more paces thick, set directly in the ground, it really was god-sized. And, judging by the appalling racket, there was a major war going on inside.

Nobody bowed to anybody. Rigel had already greeted Elegy that day and Izar honored only Mom now, except sometimes when he forgot. The next step would be to insist that adult starborn bow to him, but he was going to wait awhile before announcing that.

"Welcome to Vindemiatrix, starling," Elegy told him with a piggish smile. "I'm sure you're grown up enough not to let the dead heroes in here frighten you. As long as you just look and don't touch, they won't even notice you. Even then, all they'll do is shout at you. Run in and have a look! As for you, halfling, you're late! You've kept me waiting."

"I didn't realize, my lord," Rigel said. "We had to wait for a hippogriff. Naos Izar wanted to come by car, but the queen still forbids him to fly one without a qualified driver along."

Oh? Izar had never mentioned air cars, and Rigel never called him Naos Izar in public. That pig dung must mean that Rigel was trying to tell him something. Was the message that there had been no air car or other vehicle parked at the far end of the rainbow? How had Elgomaisa himself gotten here?

"That's a beautiful pegasus down by the river, starborn," Izar said, to show that he understood. "Who owns him?"

"My mother does. Now why don't you run around, starling? Have a look while I put the halfling's mind at rest about some of his concerns."

At that moment a dead mudling came staggering out of the hall. He was corpse-pale, dressed in blood-soaked rags, and had lost half his left forearm. Jagged bone showed through the stump. He fell on his knees in front of Izar and vomited violently.

"I told you you'd feel right at home here," Rigel said. "That's the way they welcome all first-time visitors."

Izar detoured around the still-vomiting corpse. Another one, with half his head cut away, was peeing on one of the doorposts. That reminded Izar of his own problem, so he went to stand beside him—or it—to relieve himself of his own troubles. The monster looked down at him with half a smile and said something with half a jaw and half a tongue.

"It sure does," Izar agreed. He hadn't understood a word, but guys' usual remark when meeting under such circumstances was that it felt good, didn't it?

Meanwhile, what was he going to do? A guy couldn't desert his friend, even if his friend had asked him to! Izar's amulet still wasn't sending him warnings, but Saiph had certainly been signaling danger to Rigel. And while Izar himself wasn't built like a warrior yet, he did own a Lesath that crisped nasty people for him. As soon as he had finished what he was doing to the doorpost, and sure he was far enough away from Elegy and Rigel that they wouldn't hear him—the din from the hall was loud enough to drown out a thunderstorm anyway—he stamped his left foot twice and said, "Edasich! Edasich!" He only had to say it once more for his friendly halfling-eating pet to appear and start cleaning up any Family trash that might be prowling around.

He also turned on his eavesdropping ear clip. The result was a most enormous roar of sound. The corpses seemed to be doing all their yelling in some unfamiliar language, or perhaps it was just invented babble. As he moved his head, he picked out snatches of individual voices, but he understood none of them.

At the entrance to the great hall stood two enormous piles of ever-shiny swords and axes, left there by the guests. It really was doggy! There had to be about a thousand dead warriors feasting, but it didn't seem cramped at all. Somewhere far ahead, probably in the middle, a huge fire was blazing, billowing smoke up in a cloud that hid the tops of the huge carved and gilded pillars.

Most of the warriors were grouped around long plank tables, which seemed to be placed at random, but others were walking about, or standing up and singing, carousing, or speechifying. Some were just fighting—rolling on the floor, punching, strangling, and doing their damnedest to kill other corpses that were already as dead as themselves.

In fact, Vindemiatrix looked like a lot of fun, but it would be a lot more fun if Dschubba or Ukdah was there to share it. And a lot less fun if any of his murderous half brothers and half sisters were skulking in among all that scenery. As Rigel had said, it would be easy to hide in the crowd.

Yes, Avior would love this place! It was her sculptures come to life . . . or at least action. All the corpses were earthlings, most of them very large, as tall as starfolk males, but thicker and broader. They had wimpy little human ears and masses of hair everywhere. Most wore armor of either leather or metal, in many different styles, and almost all of them displayed hideous wounds. They were all corpse-pale, with blue lips and unblinking eyes, but there was no stench of decay, or blood, or even male sweat; just wood smoke and beer fumes.

Slaves in rags and metal collars were hurrying around, refilling drinking horns from buckets. Buxom maidens were assisting the entertainment along in various ways. None of those were corpse-colored, but they still weren't *real*. If this were a real feast, or if Izar had designed it—and he was already planning the magnificent battlefield he was going to include when he imagined his own domain—then the floor would be covered with scraps of meat and bones and puke and scavenging dogs. Instead it was just smooth, clean gravel—sharp underfoot and shiny clean. The air ought to stink more, too. Small details could ruin a domain.

Meanwhile, how could he help Rigel? Well, Rigel was being distracted by Starborn Elgomaisa, so Izar should look around to see who might have joined the party without being dead yet but should be. If he found any, he would loose Edasich, and she would liven up the party.

Two men crashed to the floor right in front of him. The one on top was huge and stark naked, all covered in blond hair. The one underneath was quite young and much slighter, wearing bloodstained furs and handicapped by the absence of his right hand and left foot. With both hands around the other corpse's throat, the big man started beating his victim's head up and down on the gravel, splattering blood and systematically caving in the youngster's skull.

Inspired by a sense of fair play, Izar kicked the attacker in the ribs. His foot didn't go right through, as he expected. It hit something hard—as hard as . . . as the side of a bull, maybe.

"Cut that out!" he said. "You can't make him any deader."

The big corpse roared in fury and sprang to his feet. He had been disemboweled and had shiny entrails dangling. He shook a truly enormous fist in Izar's face and bellowed at him in a tongue so guttural that Izar could not even tell whether it was proper language or not.

The victim scrambled up to join in the abuse, as if he had been enjoying the match. His head gradually resumed its former shape, spitting out embedded rock chips, which turned from red to white when they hit the floor. Then the younger corpse stopped shouting long enough to resume the fight by trying to stamp on the naked man's trailing viscera with his one good foot. He overbalanced on his stump and fell hard. Instantly he was underneath and getting his head flattened again. He had probably been doing this for seventeen hundred years.

Izar left them to it and wandered off through the mob. He saw Rigel's shiny helmet and Elgomaisa's black hair moving along the wall, so there had to be a clearer passage for the living on that side of the room. He paused to gape at what seemed to be an orgy of four dead warriors and a couple of the buxom maidens, until he remembered that it had been in progress for centuries and nothing more was going to happen. He resumed his journey. This was all very showy and must have taken years of work, but it wasn't all that convincing. If the same things happened over and over again, and there was no progress or genuine life, then the corpse who greeted visitors would have drowned the whole mountain in puke long ago.

Izar's battlefield, now—when he got around to imagining it—was going to have real dragons, dragons that mated and laid eggs and grew up and got killed. He was going to start with the dragon nest and once he had gotten that right, he would go on to imagine the castle where the heroes lived, and they would grow up and mate and die, too. He might even let real starborn joust with his dragons, making it real enough that some of them would get scorched to cinders. Real sport, like that chimera at Alrisha that had eaten chunks of Starborn Sadatoni!

The noise of this place was making his head throb.

He was tempted to turn off his eavesdropping amulet, since all it was giving him was meaningless jabber. These corpses weren't speaking any language he had ever heard. What could be putting Rigel in danger? Hadar, of course, but how could he have known that Rigel would be coming here today? Vindemiatrix had been kept very secret. Even Avior . . .

Oh, piss! Elegy, of course! Elgomaisa had *ordered* Rigel to come, and no doubt because he'd set up the trap with Hadar days ago. Traitor! The threat wasn't Hadar *or* Elegy, but the two of them in cahoots.

". . . coming directly from Alsafi, so be prepared to . . ."

Izar stopped dead. He knew that voice! It belonged to one of his odious half brothers—Sadalbari, maybe? Izar carefully turned his head to and fro a few times, trying to pick up more, but the thread of conversation had disappeared. All the same, he was sure he had heard those few words correctly. He knew Alsafi, because it was a subdomain in Phegda; he had used the swimming hole there many times as a young imp. It was where he had met Mom after Rigel rescued him from Giauzar. And "coming directly" almost certainly meant coming by portal. Vindemiatrix might have other portals, of course, but maybe the one Rigel had described had been opened, at least to a portal in Alsafi. If the two of them could escape to Alsafi, they'd be safe!

He hurried past the fire, which was obviously fake, just a great heap of flaming logs that gave off flames and sound but no heat. He could see the throne Rigel had mentioned—just a giant-sized timber chair, nowhere near as impressive as Mom's throne. A warrior to his right was the same sort of healthy color as the buxom maidens. Of course he was, because he was still alive. He was Almaak, one of the Family. He was wearing a wig and a fake helmet disguise that made his starfolk ears look like birds' wings attached to the helmet.

Almaak was vicious, one of the worst. A sudden spasm of terror almost made Izar upchuck like the hero at the door. Almaak was leering at another orgy in progress and didn't seem to have seen him. Izar put his head down and ran like a hare, weaving in and out through the crowd, feet going *crunch, crunch* on the gravel. Members of the Family were already here! No wonder Saiph had been screaming warnings to Rigel.

Did Rigel know this yet? Izar had to warn him. For the first time in his life he regretted his ears. Big ears were much admired among the starborn, and people often complimented him on his, but they did make him conspicuous in this company.

Oh, stars! There was Botein straight ahead! He dodged behind one of the great carved pillars and struggled to catch his breath. Botein was Hadar's deputy and was just as evil. It had been she who had led the raid on Spica, when Albireo and Baham and so many others had been killed. Turais, Izar's first

Lesath, had killed three of the Family and almost bitten Botein's hand off. He peered cautiously around the pillar. She had her back to him, because she was heading in the direction Rigel and Elgomaisa had gone.

He couldn't do anything about his ears now, but he could avoid drawing any more attention to himself by running. He must *walk*, not *run*. He stepped out from behind the pillar and headed for the throne to see if the portal was open. Rigel had been heading for the back of the hall, and the throne marked the end of the heroes' feast.

Izar had that bladder problem again already. He wondered if the corpses did. They seemed to be quaffing beer from drinking horns all the time, but it was probably no more real than they were. There was an open space in front of the throne and Izar decided to make a dash for it. He sprinted forward, dodged between two arguing heroes and a bard playing a harp, jumped over a comatose berserker, raced around the throne, and ran straight into Hadar's arms.

Chapter 31

Hadar was not just the leader of the Family, he was also the biggest and meanest. He liked to maintain discipline by battering his half siblings senseless with fists and boots. His ears were as big as any starborn's, but his face was uglier than a pig's, made all the uglier by a heavy beard shadow, even when he'd just shaved. He usually dressed in black earthling clothes decorated with braid and medals. Rigel called this the uniform of a Nazi storm trooper, whatever that was, and couldn't say enough bad things about anyone who would wear it.

Hadar also stank. Izar would have known him in pitch darkness.

For a moment he *was* in pitch darkness, because he was being crushed hard against that massive, bemedaled chest. When all the breath had been squeezed out of him, he was lifted clear of the floor, and heard that hateful voice say, "Gotcha! Strip him, lads!"

Busy hands grabbed his ankles and wrists and began pulling off his rings, bracelets, anklets, and ear clips. When he tried to resist, his fingers were roughly pried open. He had no chance to call Edasich.

After that, he was turned around and a stinking hand clamped over his mouth. He tried to bite those great smelly fingers. Hadar retaliated by jerking his hand up against Izar's nose so hard that he would have cried out, had he been able. Then he pinched it, so Izar couldn't breathe.

"Any trouble from you, brat, and I'll rip your ears off."

Hadar's helpers were Maaz and Diphda, both of whom could pass for mudlings. Maaz was one of the youngest of the Family graduates. He was garbed in a fanciful warrior costume and was using his helmet to hold Izar's amulets. Diphda was posing as one of the buxom maidens, wearing a blonde wig and not much else.

Suffocating, Izar struggled and tried to kick Maaz. His half brother punched him in the chest instead, and for a moment the world went black.

Even when Izar could breathe again, Hadar still kept one hand firmly clamped over his mouth and held him aloft with his other arm, so that Izar's feet didn't touch the floor. The brute could probably walk around like that all day without noticing the weight.

"Do we have to gag you and tie you up?" the giant growled. "We don't mean you any harm, starling. We're going to return you to your daddy, and we're going to kill that halfling flunky of yours, but we shan't hurt you."

That was why his warning bracelet hadn't warned him.

This was disaster! Without his amulets, Izar was helpless. Now Vildiar had what he wanted and could force Mom to give him the throne. Everything was lost. Izar would be sent to Hadar's goon training school at Unukalhai and turned into a monster. Or perhaps both he and Mom would be sent to the Dark Cells, so there wouldn't be any other claimants to the throne.

Then another half brother appeared, Tegmine. "We've got him!" he told Hadar jubilantly. "Walked right into it."

"Good. Go and tell V. He wants to see it done." Hadar gave Izar a playful but agonizing squeeze. "Like to go and say good-bye to your pet, hmm?"

He led the way, with the other Family members following, and they emerged from the dead heroes' feast, what Rigel had called the theme park, into one of the rear corners of the great hall. There was the nightmare Izar had expected: Rigel held at bay, with Saiph in his hand. The empty corner was as big as a whole hall might be anywhere else. The cordon of six archers fencing Rigel in were standing seven or eight paces back, too far away for him to rush them, but close enough for them to be sure of hitting him. He didn't look at all frightened, more sort of mildly annoyed, as if he were being kept from attending to some important business. When he saw Izar clutched to Hadar's friendly bosom, his eyes narrowed, but he didn't say anything.

Hadar did. He could never resist any chance to jeer. "Hey, look what I found! Your master!"

"Why don't you pick on someone your own size?" Rigel asked scornfully.

"Want to fight me for him?"

Rigel shrugged. "Sure. I beat you last time, when you had Tarf and Muscida and Adhil to help you. How many helpers will you need this time?"

Hadar didn't answer that, although Izar felt a sort of silent grunt of anger pass through him. Izar peered around at as much of the group as he could see. The dead heroes were still roaring and carousing behind them, as they had done for centuries and would go on doing for as long as the Starlands continued. Another six or eight members of the Family had collected behind the archers to enjoy the coming execution, and among them was one starborn.

Hadar said, "My lord, we are very grateful for your aid. We'll try not to make too much mess here." He set Izar's feet on the ground and reduced his grip to a hand around his upper arm.

Elgomaisa said, "Make as much mess as you want. Take all day. This gravel is self-cleaning."

"You have a strange way of treating guests, starborn," Rigel said.

"Guests?" the royal consort shouted. "Halflings are never guests! Servants, never more. Flunkies. You forgot your place. You have only yourself to blame for the mess you are in now."

"You swore loyalty on the Star."

Elegy was turning purple with fury. "I don't have to listen to this filth. Halfling Hadar, you promised me you would kill him. Do it now!"

"He's frightened I'll tell tales," Rigel said. "He likes to preen around as the queen's lover, but in fact—"

"Kill him!" Elegy shrieked.

Hadar had taken his hand off Izar's mouth, so the imp could join in the baiting. Get an enemy mad enough and he may make mistakes—so Rigel had taught him.

"I'll tell them the truth, Rigel," Izar said. "He's too much a coward to order them to kill me. You're too 'fraid of the guilt curse, aren't you, Elegy? Brother Hadar?"

Hadar chuckled. "Yes, Brother Izar?"

The question was, how mad could Izar make Elgomaisa? Mad enough to strike him? Maaz was standing close by, still holding the helmet containing Izar's amulets. It was true that

Izar wasn't wearing his Lesath now, so it probably wouldn't respond to him, but he had primed it with two of the three needed words while he was still wearing it, so if he yelled out Edasich's name really loud a third time when he was being threatened, then she might come to the rescue. Worth trying . . . Of course, he might not be able to get rid of the dragon afterward, but they could burn that bridge when they came to it. The trick now was to make Elegy try to hit him.

"That character with the black fur isn't the queen's—"

"Shut up, brat!" Elgomaisa barked.

"Oh, can't I just tell them how Mom won't even let you kiss her? See, brothers, it's Rigel who cuddles her at—"

"Shut up!"

"That's shocking, Brother Izar!" Hadar said. "You're saying that Her Majesty Queen Talitha lets Halfling Rigel stick his thing in her at night? And Starborn Elgomaisa has to go and beat his meat in private somewhere?"

"Oh, no," Izar said, warming to his task. "He owns a sheep farm over in . . ."

Elgomaisa rushed at him, arm raised to deliver a backhand, but he didn't come close before Botein grabbed his arm and twisted it. Halted in his tracks, doubled over, the starborn yelped in pain.

"Archers, keep your eyes on the prisoner!" Hadar boomed.

Izar had his mouth open to scream for Edasich, but the threat had passed, so his trick wouldn't work. It probably wouldn't have worked anyway. So Hadar was still holding him, and Rigel was still about to die.

"It's no great secret," Rigel said. "The imps guessed, and then the news spread everywhere. If he thinks the queen will let him near her after I'm dead, he's even stupider than we all thought. Which was pretty stupid. Everyone hates traitors."

Released by Botein, Elgomaisa shouted, "I'll be a hero throughout the Starlands!"

Rigel laughed. "Don't get your hopes up too high. Talitha might cut it off."

Several of the Family chuckled.

How could he make jokes when he was so obviously about to die?

Elgomaisa looked ready to eat rocks. "Why don't you do it, Hadar? What are you waiting for?"

"Company," Hadar said. "Important company. I think it would be best if you didn't stay to watch, my lord. You might find yourself being questioned in court, shortly. On the Star, I would think."

The starborn went rigid, his lips curling back in terror. Had he truly never thought of that? He really must be as stupid as Rigel had said. Now he was too stupid even to see why Hadar wanted him to leave.

"Yes, go," Izar said. "Our daddy's coming to watch and he doesn't want any witnesses around who might say that he was here when the marshal of Canopus was murdered. I 'spect that's treason."

Elegy was actually turning pale! He hated Rigel so much that he hadn't worked out what he was getting himself into.

"'Course," Izar sighed, "it's too late to save you from the Dark Cells. You're helping Daddy, and that's treason, 'cos he's been outlawed." *Please, please, try to hit me!*

"Don't gloat, Izar!" Rigel said. "We're saving that up as a surprise for him."

"Shut up!" the starborn said. "You're right, Halfling Hadar. I'll go and tell my mother the good news." With a final sneer at Rigel, he stalked away from the archers and left the group.

Rigel put his left hand on his hip and leaned back against the great tree trunk that filled the corner. It was larger than the others. "I am in no hurry. Shall we talk about adults who make war on children?"

"Boss," Almaak said, "I'm worried the prisoner may escape. Shouldn't we sort of fix him there somehow? I mean, nail him in place with an arrow?"

"I don't think one arrow would be secure enough," Hadar said. "But we can start with one. Scheat, pin his left shoulder."

A bowstring cracked, Saiph blurred, and the arrow hit the wall about a pace away from Rigel. Rigel shrugged and leaned back against the tree again.

"Schemali," Hadar said. "And Sadalbari. On the count of three . . ."

He counted. The bows cracked as one. Again Rigel's right arm and sword blurred, and this time two arrows struck the wall.

Several of the Family members laughed at this new sport. Izar was trying to stay very still, hoping Hadar would forget he was there a little, so he might loosen his grip on Izar's arm, and then Izar might break free for just long enough to get to that helmet that Maaz was holding. All he needed to do was grab a handful of those amulets and shout one word.

"Clearly we need to try targets farther apart," Hadar said. "Scheat, the shoulder again. Sadachbia, you're a good shot, my dear. You try for his balls. On the count of three. Stop that, maggot!" This last was addressed to Izar, who had made his break for freedom. And failed. Hadar slapped a hand over the imp's face again and pinched his nose to cut off his air. "Prepare to fire when the brat turns blue." After a moment, when the audience had enjoyed a good laugh, "Going to behave yourself now? Very well, on the count of three."

That time Rigel did cry out. One arrow fell in two pieces, but the other pinned his left shoulder to the tree trunk behind him. Just one cry, then a hard swallow and silence. He went very pale and clearly could not move without hurting himself more.

"What's going on here?" said a new and horribly familiar voice.

Hadar turned to face the newcomers, angling Izar in the same direction. Tegmine had returned, bringing Naos Vildiar with him.

"Just softening him up a little, Your Highness," Hadar said. Even he had to look up to meet his father's eyes. "We got the brat, too."

"Good. Hang on to him." Vildiar looked over the group again. "Have you any last words, Rigel Halfling? I admit that you have caused me more trouble than I ever expected from a mongrel. But this is definitely the end."

"Let Izar go, please," Rigel said. "He shouldn't have to watch this." Blood from his shoulder had run all the way down to his foot now. His face was almost as white as the gravel.

"No, it is educational for him to view punishment and see the penalty for insubordination. His manhood training begins now. Carry on, Hadar."

"Yes, my lord. I'll call out names. Shoot at once. Try to avoid vital areas, so that we can all have a chance to do our bit for the great cause."

Izar, free to breathe but with Hadar's great paw circling his arm like a tourniquet, screamed, "No!"

"Quiet!" his father said. "Or I will have you gagged. Proceed, halfling."

Hadar shouted, "Diphda, Sadalbari, Schemali, Phact, Sadachbia, Rotanev!" Six bowstrings cracked.

Rigel screamed. Four arrows had missed or been knocked aside by Saiph, but two had hit their mark: one through his right elbow and another through his moon-cloth wrap. Now he was nailed to the wall in three places. He screamed again and again; the sound hurt Izar like hot iron.

Rigel's sword and gauntlet vanished, unable to help him further. Only the silver bracelet remained on his immobilized arm. He looked at Izar and his mouth moved as if he were trying to speak but couldn't. There was blood on his teeth.

Hadar said, "Now we'll hand the bows around so some of the rest of us can share in the fun. Maaz—"

"No!" Izar yelled. "Stop! Stop!"

"Izar?" Vildiar said. "If I tell them to stop torturing Rigel, will you promise to do what I tell you in future?"

"Yes, yes! Anything!"

"You promise?"

Again Rigel tried to say something and only blood came out of his mouth. He shook his head, but Izar couldn't stand it any longer.

"Yes, I promise! I'll do anything you say, Father."

"Good. Kill him."

"Rotanev," Hadar said, "Hold the brat for me, and give me your bow. This is my job." He took the bow and an arrow, and aimed.

He said, "Bye-bye, sucker!"

A fourth arrow sprouted in Rigel's body, low in his chest. For a moment he stared at Izar, speechless. Then his head fell forward while the rest of him stayed where it was, nailed to the wood behind him. Blood trickled down from his mouth.

The Family halflings all cheered, dancing and waving their arms overhead in triumph.

Clink! The silver bracelet fell off Rigel's dangling right arm. The amulet that could never be removed while he lived had deserted him now.

KNAVE OF IMPS

Chapter 1

Screaming, "Rigel! Rigel!" Izar broke free of Rotanev's grip and ran. The halflings were still yelling and cheering and thumping Hadar on the back. Izar was halfway there before anyone guessed what he was doing. Predictably, it was Hadar himself who realized first.

"No!" Hadar roared. "You leave that alone!" His jackboots went *crunch, crunch* on the gravel as he raced in pursuit.

The bracelet still lay at Rigel's feet. Izar grabbed for it as Hadar crashed down on top of him. For a moment the imp lay there, stunned by the halfling's monstrous weight. That gravel was sharp! It hurt!

"Where is it? What did you do with it, you little turd?" Hadar rolled him over and grabbed his arm, his hand completely closing around it like a twig. He peered at the empty wrist. "Where is it?"

"Other one, sucker." Izar drove the blade into Hadar's kidneys.

Hadar screamed louder than all the theme-park corpses together, his breath hot and foul. His eyes bulged in disbelief as he stared down at the weedy starling who had just stabbed him.

"Does this hurt more?" Izar asked, twisting the blade.

Judging by the noise, it did hurt more, so he kept on doing it. And then Saiph must have moved Izar's arm for him, because he didn't tell it to pull the blade out of the halfling and stick it in somewhere else, but that was *'zactly* what happened. Somewhere fatal, evidently, for by the time Tegmine and Botein grabbed Hadar and hauled him free, Hadar was a dead weight. Dead meat, red spittle trailing from his mouth.

Excellent!

Izar sprang to his feet, eager for blood. He wasn't normally left-handed, but from now on he was going to be fighting that way, and the shiny gauntlet that had been a perfect fit on Rigel's right hand was now just as snug on Izar's smaller left one. The sword was smaller, too, of course, because he lacked an adult's muscle, but even a short, narrow blade could kill, as he now proceeded to demonstrate.

Tegmine and Botein both grabbed for him. Saiph sliced off Botein's hand—the crooked one mutilated by Turais—and disemboweled Tegmine. The rest of the gang had crowded in, but now backed off, cursing. The object of all this violence had been to capture Saiph and now Starling Izar had it. Amulets flashed into swords.

"Put those blades away!" Vildiar shouted. "I'll deal with him. Dismiss your sword, Izar."

Botein and Tegmine continued to scream in their death throes.

"Killer!" Izar howled, mad with bloodlust now. *"Murderer!"* He charged at his father and drove his sword into . . . into nothing. It had gone. His bare fist struck muscular flesh.

Vildiar caught his wrist and held him. "You can't kill a starborn, son. If you killed me, you'd die of the guilt curse. Saiph is a defensive amulet, the very best there is, and it won't let you commit suicide. Now, will you behave yourself and do as you're told?" He let go.

"No!" Izar took aim at Almaak, whom he especially disliked. "Saiph!" The King of Swords returned, and immediately vanished as Vildiar grabbed its bearer again, this time swinging him up over his shoulder. Izar bellowed in fury and pounded on his father's back with both fists, but he was helpless in the giant's grip.

"I don't think Hadar and Tegmine are going to make it," Vildiar said. "Frankly, they don't deserve to, after that display of idiocy. Almaak, remove their amulets to make sure. Put Botein down too. She's useless now. Take their bodies to the compost pit. Leave that trash where it is—" He pointed at Rigel's corpse, which was still hanging on the wall. "And return to the current training center."

Vildiar walked away with Izar still over his shoulder and other chastened offspring trailed after him. He pushed aside the shield on the back of the throne and stooped low to go through the portal.

They emerged into sunlight and a pleasant, sea-scented breeze. Vildiar set Izar down on soft sand, close to where the breakers died away into hissing ripples. Then he put fists on hips and stared down at him from all his terrifying height.

"You promised me you would do as I said from now on."

"And you'd promised not to let them torture Rigel—and you . . . you had them kill him!" Izar fought back tears. Life without Rigel would be . . . was going to be . . . *unthinkable!*

"That stopped the torture. Is Hadar's name on your bracelet now?"

Izar looked, turning it. "Yes! And Tegmine." Well, that was good!

His father chuckled—a hollow, bassoon sort of noise. "I am both furious and amused that you grabbed that amulet. On one hand, you're going to be hard to control now. On the other, I'm proud of you for outwitting all those halfling clods, Izar, my son."

"I don' wanna be your son!"

"Well you are, no matter how much we both dislike the fact. If I appoint, say, Phact, as your governess, what will you do?"

"Kill her!"

"Scheat?"

"Kill him!"

"A true chip off the block, you are. I never tolerated discipline either. I shall have to appoint starborn babysitters. You can't kill them. Look around."

Izar did, and saw surf in the distance, friendly ripples close in, a silver beach and palm trees tossed by trade winds. Landward were flowering shrubs and the freestanding stone arch of the portal. There was no sign that anyone else existed in the world. Bright-colored parrots or toucans were flying above them. His view was blurred by tears as he thought about how much Rigel would have loved this place.

"My personal swimming hole," V said. "But I have also found it useful as a prison a few times. The portal works only for me. There is fresh water and the berries and fruits are all edible."

Izar did not comment.

"Again I congratulate you on the way you captured Saiph, Son. Nobody else remembered that the amulet would fall off his wrist when he died, and you outwitted Hadar brilliantly. The man had outlived his usefulness. Most of them have, now, but I shall keep a few around. Even kings need assassins once in a while. Meanwhile, I need time to think what to do with you, now that you have become dangerous to non-starborn."

Rigel was dead. Dead. Dead. Dead.

"It may take a day or so to arrange the handover of power," Vildiar continued. "You will be quite safe here."

By the third morning, Izar was wondering if he would go mad. He talked to the trees and the gulls, the turtles and fish. He ate until he was nauseated and then ate more, because there was nothing to do, no one to just *be* with.

The air boat that came floating in that morning was diamond shaped, with a seat at each corner, all facing inward. The driver sat at the rear; his seat was slightly higher than the others, although it didn't need to be in this case, because the current occupant could easily look over anyone's head. The two passengers at the sides were Sadalbari and Scheat. The boat settled down onto the sand, gently and quite steadily, being flat bottomed.

Vildiar regarded Izar disapprovingly.

"I should have thought to bring you a clean wrap. I am on my way to Canopus, where I will receive your mother's abdication and the Light of Naos."

"And then what?"

"What does that mean?"

"What happens to her. And me?" Hadar was gone but the Family still existed. Was he to be turned into a killing monster for his father? He bore the King of Swords; he was unbeatable.

Vildiar stared back at him under his heavy brows. "That will depend on your behavior." He bent and picked up a glittering chain. “Will you give me your solemn word that you will do exactly as I say and will not invoke Saiph without my express order?”

“Or?” Izar asked grumpily.

“Or I’ll put this collar on you and lead you around like a dog. It has certain occult powers that can be unpleasant at your end of it. I remind you that your amulet will not hurt me, and I am quite capable of breaking your arm if you annoy me.”

Izar wondered if Saiph would allow that. It might let his *other* arm be broken. Besides, he had no choice. He would really go crazy if he stayed here alone for much longer. “I promise,” he muttered.

“Louder. And politely.”

“I promise to behave, Father.”

“And obey!”

“And obey.”

“Then get in.”

Izar scrambled in and took his seat at the front. The two halflings scowled at him. They were frightened of him, but that was very small comfort.

Chapter 2

The boat came in over the palace from the east and landed in a small courtyard Izar had never seen before. Long rows of empty green and silver Naos thrones stood there, scores of them mourning a glory that Naos Vildiar had destroyed. They varied in shape and probably in age, too, and only one of them was ever needed now. It would be another twenty years before Izar was officially a prince and entitled to use one, and probably centuries before as many as a dozen of them were needed again. Even that assumption depended on whether his father would let possible rivals survive.

He couldn't help wondering again if both he and Mom would be sent off to the Dark Cells. They couldn't send the Saiph bearer to the Dark Cells without spilling a lot of blood, but when had blood bothered Naos Vildiar?

Two sphinxes and three halfling servants waited to attend the arriving prince, but Vildiar hardly glanced at them. He took his seat on the first throne in line and beckoned Izar to stand on the foot ledge. The throne rose gently and headed for the exit, just like an air car.

Izar could fly an air car now, somewhat erratically, but when would he ever be allowed to if he was a prisoner in the Unukalhai School for Monsters?

The Great Court was far from crowded. Izar had never seen a smaller attendance—perhaps not many people had been summoned, or perhaps not many approved of what was going to happen. What he had not expected was the bier standing in the center, and a snarl from his father suggested that he was surprised, too. The throne suddenly surged forward, so that Izar had to grab at the side to recover his balance. He continued to hang on as it sped the rest of the way to the eight-level dais, faster than he had ever seen a Naos enter the court.

For a moment he thought Vildiar was going to land dead center, right in front of the main throne, but at the last minute he banked and finally set it down with a jolt in just about the right place, one step down and on the right. Then he leapt to his feet and took two long strides toward the royal throne. His normally pale face was flushed with anger.

Commander Zozma came bounding out and blocked his path.

Confrontation.

"Her Majesty is still queen, Your Highness." Zozma had the sort of voice that rattled dishes on shelves.

"And you are still head of the Palace Guard," Vildiar retorted. He spoke quietly, but everyone in the court could hear him. "This, too, will pass." He spun around and stalked back to his proper place.

Zozma ascended the stairs to assume his position beside the royal throne. Sphinx Kalb appeared on the other side, and Chancellor Aspidiske followed her in and went to stand on the left, two steps down. He bowed to Vildiar. Then he bowed again, meaning he was also bowing to Izar. The crowd noticed and murmured approval.

Vildiar showed his teeth and said nothing.

Trumpets blared and Mom walked out with Elgomaisa at her side—hadn't she seen through that murdering traitor yet? Vildiar should have risen and bowed, but he didn't. The moment she sat down, though, he sprang to his feet and pointed a long arm at the distant bier.

"What is the meaning of this obscenity?"

Chancellor Aspidiske frowned at this breach of protocol. "The marshal of Canopus is entitled to a state funeral by tradition and an act of King—"

"Not for filthy halfling trash! State funerals are only for starborn."

Izar edged away. Normally his father remained ice-cold, always. He had never seen him rage like this, and he wondered what was provoking him so on his day of triumph. He had raped and plotted and murdered for two hundred years to win the throne and now it was to be his at last. Why so angry? Why wasn't he gloating?

Mom shrugged. The Light of Naos burned coldly blue-indigo on her neck and shoulders. "You seem to be under a misapprehension, Prince. Chancellor, summon the royal archivist."

Vildiar muttered something under his breath, so softly that not even the magical acoustics picked it up. Nasty Elegy was looking cross, so he obviously didn't know what was coming. Did Vildiar? Had he seen some possibility he had previously overlooked? Was it possible that a court officer, such as the marshal of Canopus, was legally a starborn, no matter what his breeding? Would the guilt curse apply in such a case? Izar recalled his legal lectures and magic classes and decided that race and rank didn't work together that way. But certainly something odd was going on, something that worried Vildiar and puzzled Elegy.

A tiny green shoot of hope sprouted in Izar's winter of dismay.

Aspidiske had hardly uttered Wasat's name before the ancient halfling came hobbling out from the side, wearing his collar of office of amber and onyx. He bowed to the throne and took his place on the Star of Truth, having trouble with stiff joints as he knelt. But he was smiling, so he knew exactly what was in the wind.

And the chancellor obviously knew what to ask him. "State your name and—"

"Stop wasting time!" Vildiar roared. "We all know him. What is he supposed to say?"

"Go ahead, Archivist," the chancellor said. "Tell us."

"Oh." The old man hesitated, having been expecting a prompt. "Well, when the late Queen Electra last appeared here, in court, before her people . . . she announced that Halfling Rigel, he who was later appointed marshal of Canopus, was actually her son."

"We all know that, too!" Vildiar said. This time he spoke more quietly, but his voice was hoarse with rage. "If that made the mongrel a starborn, then all halflings are starborn. Is that what you're saying?"

Wasat turned to face him. "Oh no, Your Highness. I am a halfling, my mother having been human and my father a starborn, although I do not know his name. The law clearly says that any child of such a union is a halfling, or tweenling, as the two terms are inter—"

"Just get on with it!"

"Yes, Your Highness. Her Majesty, the late queen, also gave Halfling Rigel a document at that time, which he brought straight to me for safekeeping. In fact he didn't even open it, because he already knew the name of his father." He produced a slim roll bound with a purple ribbon. "I testify that this is that self-same document, which has been kept secure in the royal archives ever since that day. With the permission of the court I will now read this affidavit, which I testify bears the late queen's private seal and her signature, both known to me."

He began to untie the ribbon. Vildiar went back to roaring.

"*Stop wasting my time!* Just tell us the name of the bastard's father, as if it matters a small splat of bird shit, so we can get on with the real business. We came here for an enthronement, not a half-breed's send-off."

Wasat seemed hurt and rather at a loss. He looked to Mom for guidance and she smiled and nodded. Izar had no idea what was coming, but he suspected that Vildiar now did and didn't like it, so it must be good news.

"Very well." Wasat turned to face him again. "The document named me. I am Marshal Rigel's father."

The audience gasped in unison, then growled in protest.

But Wasat was still kneeling on the Star and not screaming in agony.

"That is impossible!"

"Not quite, Your Highness. There have been other cases, although they are very rare. They seem to be rarer than they were in the distant past, too. But I was Queen Electra's secret lover for over a century. And twenty or so years ago, she stood right where I'm kneeling now, on the Star of Truth, and swore to me that there had been no others in that time and the child she carried was mine."

Vildiar leaned back in his throne and his bluster had all gone. For the first time in Izar's memory, he seemed uncertain.

"So he was a freak. He was still a halfling, wasn't he?"

The old man paused and chose his words carefully, as everyone did when located where he was. "As I said, Your Highness, although I am no lawyer, I have been told that the law is explicit in defining a halfling as the child of a starborn and a human, whether mudling or—"

"Wait!" Mom rose from the throne and walked down the seven long steps to the Star. Wasat hurriedly scrambled away on hands and knees to let her take his place, not taking the time he would need to rise.

"I am Talitha, Queen of the Starlands, and I testify that I have had my advisors search the laws high and low. Nowhere can they find any definition of a halfling other than the one Archivist Wasat just gave us. That definition does not fit Rigel. He could be a three-quarterling, but there is no such term under the law. The child of a starborn and a halfling can neither be a mudling nor a halfling, and must therefore be a starborn. A starborn with some mudling blood in him, perhaps, but still a starborn.

"Furthermore, *Vildiar Naos*, the earthlings classify a species as a group that can produce fertile crossbreeds. I testify to this court that I carry Starborn Rigel's child, a daughter, whose name appears to be either Altair or Altais, it being too early in my pregnancy for me to be completely certain either way. Starborn Rigel impregnated me a great deal faster than you did, monster. And he did so by being a wonderful lover, not a serial rapist."

The court was cheering as she walked back up to the throne. The crowd was thicker than it had been. Izar wondered if any of his friends were out there: Dschubba or Uk or Salm. Uk's parents brought him to court whenever one was held.

Vildiar was cowering back in his throne, his ugly face twisted in horror.

"Tell me again about the guilt curse, Father," Izar said, knowing that everyone would hear him. He jumped away and ran down to the Star. Both Vildiar and Mom shouted at him to stop, the first time he had ever heard them agree on anything. He ignored them both.

"I am Izar Starborn, and I testify that, when Rigel came to rescue me after I had been kidnapped, I saw him standing directly behind Naos Vildiar with his ancestral amulet Saiph on his wrist. So he could have killed him, and when I asked him later why he didn't, he said that he wasn't sure. Now I wear Saiph, and it won't let me kill a starborn either, because I tried to kill Vildiar with it, *and that proves that Rigel was a starborn*!"

The audience seemed to draw in one huge, communal breath and then roared in unison.

The queen said, "That must be right. Starborn Rigel didn't know why he hadn't killed Prince Vildiar that day. He came up with several theories, but I believe that Izar Starborn has found the real answer at last."

Izar Starborn! That sounded good. Izar Starborn swung around to point at his father on the green throne. "I saw you order Rigel's death. 'Kill him!' you said, very clearly."

He turned and walked up to the royal throne. Mom was still standing, waiting for him, so she could hug him. He hugged her back. She kissed him, which was all right under the circumstances and at least everyone would see that he was almost as tall as she was now.

Starborn Elgomaisa's face was as white as his hair was black.

"You, too," Izar said, more shrilly than he intended. "You used the same exact words. 'Kill him!' you said, meaning Rigel Starborn."

Elegy sobbed, "No!"

"Yes, you did! I was there; I heard you."

The nasty creature screamed, turned around as if to leave by the door behind the slab, and suddenly crumpled. He twitched and writhed on the floor.

Mom sat down. Izar stood alongside her and together they watched with interest as the guilt curse did its work. Izar had seen Queen Electra just fade away, but Elgomaisa was suffering more. He wept and retched and thrashed. Vildiar tried to raise his throne but it moved only a foot or so before crashing down again. He, too, slithered to the ground and began to wail in agony and terror.

Everyone could hear them and watch them die.

"Halfling!" Vildiar gasped, and the magic carried his voice to the farthest corners of the court. "He was halfling trash!" He seemed to be trying to crawl toward the Star of Truth, as if he could change an unpalatable fact by asserting its falsity there. He made it down one step before his strength failed him. He crumpled and just lay there wailing. The spectators had crowded forward to jeer and cheer his death throes. Gradually his noises became screams, too. Were Vildiar and Elgomaisa less brave than the old lady had been? Or was it because they were younger?

When it was all over, nothing remained of the two killers except their moon-cloth wraps and a scattering of amulets. It couldn't bring back Rigel, but it felt good all the same. The Starlands could finally live in peace again, as Izar had never known them.

The queen stood up. Now she would speak an elegy for Rigel and hold a proper funeral for him. She eventually had to raise her arms to get the cheering to stop.

"My people, this is a happy day, which has seen a great curse lifted from our land. The terror has ended. We now have no Naos other than me, although I have heard hints of several youngsters who have begun to display the mark but are being kept hidden by their families. In the meantime, we need to maintain our customs. My son is still a long way from legal adulthood, but over these last few months he has displayed courage and maturity far beyond his years. I therefore proclaim him Prince Izar Naos. Moreover, I need a designated heir, so I also declare him my regent-heir. Chancellor?"

What? Ship's biscuits! Izar turned—almost falling over his own feet in the process—and there was Aspidiske, holding a massive disk of gold links with a hole in the center.

All Izar could say was, "Huh?"

"We must now go down to the Star, Your Highness, so you can take the oath."

Highness? Him? He stumbled after the chancellor. *Salm, Uk, Dschubba, Uk, Salm—oh, please, please be here to see this!* He and the old man did the oath ceremony, although it was all a blur, like a very muddled dream. The damnable collar weighed as much as he did and almost made him trip over the steps again as he went back up. The court was cheering him! *Everyone except Mom would have to bow to him now!*

She didn't *have* to kiss him *again* in public! But she did and he put up with it. It felt quite good, actually. He waved to the nice people and they cheered all the louder. Vildiar was dead! Hadar was dead! Rigel . . . Now the funeral?

But Mom was smiling. "I give you leave to withdraw, Prince. You should go to the robing room right away."

"I want to stay for the funeral!"

Why was she still smiling?

"No funeral." She turned to face the court. "My people. There has been a slight misunderstanding, or perhaps I should say an exaggeration . . ."

Two-ton collar or not, Izar moved faster than a falling star—leaping right over Commander Zozma, around the end of the great black monolith, and up the steps in the back of it. Only once had he been inside the robing room. Like most of Canopus Palace, it had no roof, so it was another court, quite small and private, but with flower beds and palm trees and some comfortable divans.

On one of them sat a male starborn with sandy hair, and on the other a *three-quarterling* with white eyes and a bronze helmet.

"Rigel!"

Rigel just had time to jump up and spread his arms before Izar and his collar hit him like a runaway behemoth and they crashed down together on the divan. And then Turais joined the scrimmage, all wagging tail and slobber.

"Stars almighty, Prince! Are you trying to kill me all over again?"

"How did you do that? I saw you die! Saiph fell off your wrist. You had arrows in—"

"In just about everything, yes. Mage Achird keeps trying to explain it to me, but I doubt if he really understands it himself."

Mage Achird was bowing to Izar and giving him the salutation owed to a superior, so Izar had to get up and respond properly. Then he sat down and reached for the wine jug. Maybe wine would sober him up, and no one would tell a *prince* what he could or could not drink!

"Tell me too," he said. "That's a royal command."

"This is going to be hell," muttered either Tyl or Thabit, whom Izar had not noticed before, sitting in the corner, under the shade of a fig tree.

"You don't have to put up with it. I don't need a bodyguard anymore."

The halfling said, "You'll need a team of lifeguards if you try to go swimming in that collar."

Princes should not need to water their wine like starlings did. Izar Naos took a gulp of it straight, choked, coughed, spluttered, and lost the thread of the conversation.

". . . didn't know it myself," Rigel was saying. "But I should have figured it out when Saiph wouldn't kill Vildiar for me."

Izar had recovered enough to say, "Mage?" hoarsely. They all smirked at him, but he didn't mind. He couldn't mind anything on a day like today, with Vildiar dead, Hadar dead, Rigel alive, and him a prince! He had his adopted big brother back and was going to have a real baby sister. If he lived to be five thousand he could never top this day! "Tell me why this freak isn't dead."

"The key to it, Your Highness," Achird said, smiling, "is that Saiph is the strongest and most ancestral amulet around. Moreover, it's a defensive amulet, but Hadar and the Family were hunting Rigel and planning to kill him just so that they could get hold of Saiph! That's a paradox—a defense that itself puts its owner in danger. It did save his life when the arrows were loosed at him, and even when he could no longer move his arm, because even the shots through his chest and abdomen missed vital organs, where wounds would have killed him instantly. He must have somehow twisted out of their way to make that happen."

"You try involuntarily twisting when you've already got one arm and one shoulder nailed to the wall," Rigel said, and took a gulp of wine.

"Deception is one of the basic tactics in swordplay. When Rigel *fainted*, Saiph *feinted*. It abandoned him, because that was the only way it could save him from further harm. You all assumed that Saiph was leaving a corpse, but Rigel had just passed out from the pain. Vildiar carried you off. Almaak made sure Hadar and Tegmine were dead, as Vildiar had ordered. Botein wasn't about to stand still for that, but Sadalbari stabbed her in the back. Then they carted off their dead, leaving Rigel hanging there."

"You were spying on us?" Izar said angrily. "And you didn't help?"

Achird looked ashamed, as well he might. "Starborn Mizar and I had been seancing you for days. We saw Starborn Elgomaisa order Rigel to attend him at Vindemiatrix that morning, but we didn't know where you were going when you left Segin. So we lost you and could only watch the rainbow bridge, believing that there was no other way in."

"Hadar must have moved his troops in by portal," Rigel said.

"The one behind the throne was open," Izar told him. "Vildiar took me out that way."

"When you and Starborn Rigel arrived," Achird said, emphasizing Rigel's new title slightly, "we tracked you in with Elgomaisa. By the time we saw what was happening, it was too late to warn you or stop it. Fortunately Fornacis is another twig of the Phegda domain tree, as is Vindemiatrix. As soon as the last members of the Family left, I portaled in and cut Rigel down. His healing amulets had kept him alive, although barely, and I slapped some nova-strength reinforcements on them to pull him through."

Rigel said, "What I still don't understand is how Saiph could muddle up the Time of Life prophecy, or why."

Achird shrugged. "Prophecy's always tricky. How much of what you saw was right?"

"Maybe two-thirds. The people, and some of the dialogue. But I saw a forest with snow, not a log wall and gravel, and the fact that I didn't die was wrong! It was supposed to be prophesying my death."

"It did prophesy your death. If it hadn't been for Saiph, you would have died, and Saiph is stronger magic than the Time of Life. Two-thirds right is a spectacularly successful foretelling anyway. Fomalhaut wants you to come back and try again."

"Not likely!"

"He's babbling about a three-quarterling having a lifespan of at least a thousand years."

"Let him babble." Rigel refilled his glass. "Uh-oh!"

Commander Zozma had padded in, all menace, tail swishing.

"Marshal, the queen wants you."

Rigel laid down his glass with a sigh. "Where is she?"

"Still in court. The people refuse to disperse until they've given you a cheer or three."

"Me? Why me? What have I done?" Rigel looked so horrified that Izar almost burst out laughing.

"Well, it could be your courage," the sphinx rumbled. "Or your miraculous escape from certain death. Or your superlative service as marshal of Canopus. But I don't think it's any of those. Starfolk are just crazy about babies, and royal babies are special. They don't produce cubs easily, you know. Not like us sphinxes. I've lost count of mine." He purred seismically at his own joke. "So they want to cheer your virility. Royal command: Go out there and let them admire you, the Royal Stud. The females, I mean. The males are just jealous."

Zozma turned his dread eyes on Izar. "You, too, Your Highness. They seem to think you've done something worth cheering, too."

"I 'spect they just want a look at Saiph," Izar said, rising, staggering a little, and recovering his balance. *That wine was 'stremely powerful!*

"You're the First Family," the mage said and then spoiled the effect by laughing.

Rigel stood up also, looking glum. "They probably want to tear me apart as an imposter."

Izar clapped him on the shoulder, which was not so *very* much higher than his. "Don't worry, starborn. I'm Saiph-bearer now. I'll defend you."

About the Author

PHOTO BY LILA KLASSEN, 2008

Dave Duncan is a prolific writer of fantasy and science fiction, best known for his fantasy series, particularly *The Seventh Sword*, *A Man of His Word*, *The King's Blades*, and *Against the Light*. He and his wife, Janet, his in-house editor and partner for over fifty years, live in Victoria, British Columbia. They have three children and four grandchildren.